SUMMER
BY
SUMMER

Other books by Heather Burch

Halflings series

Halflings

Guardian

Avenger

SUMMER
BY
SUMMER

Heather Burch

BLINK

BLINK

Summer by Summer
Copyright © 2015 by Heather Burch

This title is also available as a Blink ebook. Visit www.zondervan.com/ebooks.

Requests for information should be addressed to:
Blink, 3900 *Sparks Dr. SE, Grand Rapids, Michigan 49546*

ISBN 978-0-310-72963-1

Any Internet addresses (websites, blogs, etc.) and telephone numbers in this book are offered as a resource. They are not intended in any way to be or imply an endorsement by the publisher, nor does the publisher vouch for the content of these sites and numbers for the life of this book.

BLINK™ is a trademark of The Zondervan Corporation

Cover design: Kris Nelson/Story Look Design
Cover photography: Veer, Shutterstock
Interior design: Denise Froehlich

Printed in the United States of America

15 16 17 18 19 20 21 /DCI/ 20 19 18 17 16 15 14 13 12 11 10 9 8 7 6 5 4 3 2 1

For my mom,
Mary Elisabeth McWilliams,
a woman who inspires me
to live life to the fullest.

PROLOGUE

I am in a hospital room.

To my right, the sun pours rays of heat through the window, but I can't feel its warmth. I reach toward the pane, only to have my arm tingle with goose flesh from the air-conditioned chill. My long hair is matted, a tattered splash against my shoulders, ends frayed from too many hours in the unforgiving sun.

I close my eyes and imagine him. Like me, his skin is sun-darkened against the sterile bed. I see him standing at a campfire, reaching down to take my hand. He has so much more right to live than I.

Yet I'm here. My throat closes, and the smallest of sounds escapes my lips because I've felt this pain before.

Can a person survive losing both boys she loves? If so, I don't see how. I squeeze my eyes tight and wish for the one thing I never believed possible.

I wish I was back on the island.

CHAPTER 1

Summer

"I said I'd like to offer you the job, Summer." Sandra Garrison blinked her long lashes, blue eyes sparkling as she leaned forward in the cushioned restaurant chair.

Stunned. My mouth opened but nothing came out. This was all wrong. I'd seen the other applicants for the position of nanny for her ten-year-old son, Joshie. The Garrison family spent summers in Belize, and their regular nanny wasn't able to go. After my interview, I'd sat in the hotel lobby and watched a parade of blond, gorgeous young women go into the restaurant and sit on the other side of Sandra, flipping their hair and laughing at all the right times. I'd been certain I wouldn't be considered. The Garrison's world of expensive cars and clothes was completely at odds with my practicality and my Walmart shoes. And then there were all those other applicants. Tan and beautiful, any one of them could have easily been Sandra's daughter. I didn't know Sandra was more interested in principles than labels.

"Did you hear me, Summer?" But that knowing smile on her face told me the truth. She knew I'd prepared for rejection.

"Yes, ma'am."

Her perfect brow winged up. "Please, it's just Sandra."

I forced out a breath. The job. I got the job. "I don't know what to say." It was my fresh start. The one I needed. The one I had to have or life and all its sorrow and craze was going to swallow me. I needed a change. And I needed someone to depend on me. As if reading my mind, Sandra withdrew a photograph from her purse and slid it across the table, her manicured fingertips catching the soft ambiance of the overhead light.

"This is Joshie."

I took the picture of the smiling ten-year-old and already my heart felt a little lighter. Off to the right of my line of vision, practically hiding behind a planted palm, my dad caught my attention. He was dressed in his hotel best and had driven me down from Sarasota to Naples for the interview. I think he'd been as nervous as me sitting in the lobby waiting. He raised his hands, shoulders, and brows in question.

I nodded furiously and didn't bother to hide my smile.

Sandra tossed a glance over her shoulder. "Your father?"

"I'm sorry. He was really excited for me. For this opportunity."

"Don't apologize, Summer." The server appeared and Sandra gently thanked him and signed for the check. I realized just how accustomed she was to this whole *living large* thing. I'd need to get accustomed too. So as not to standout like the sore thumb I was.

I started to hand the picture of Joshie back to Sandra, but she shook her head. "Keep it." I was surprised when she motioned for my dad to join us.

"Your father seems great. In fact, I watched you two in the lobby before I started the interviews."

"You did?"

"Mmm-hm. One of the reasons you shot right to the top of my list." She didn't elaborate on the other reasons. I couldn't fathom what they might be. "I noticed from your résumé you are involved in a church youth group?"

"Yes, ma'am."

"Well, I'll see that Sunday mornings are free for you if you'd like to attend in Belize."

My heart stuttered to a stop. "Oh, that's not necessary."

Her head tilted. "No?"

What could I say? That I've been doubting everything I'd thought I'd known since I was nine? That I wasn't dedicated anymore? Yeah, that would be great. Lose the job before ever starting it. "What I mean is I'm excited to have a complete change in my routine. I plan on being available 24/7 for your family. It's important to me that I do that."

Sandra seemed satisfied with that answer. "Okay, but if you change your mind, the offer is open."

My dad came over, inching his way closer as if his appearance at the table could cause Sandra to rescind her offer. I had the best dad in the world. Introductions were made and after discussing the plans, Sandra popped up out of the soft chair, shook both our hands, and left us standing there grinning like fools.

Dad leaned closer. "You're going to Belize for the summer."

My eyes widened, wind from the fans above instantly drying my eyeballs. "I know."

He mocked a frown. "Your mom's going to freak out."

My frown was genuine. "I know. She doesn't want me to go. Neither does Becky."

"You can't blame Becky. She doesn't want to lose her best friend for the summer. As far as your mom goes … She's worried about you. In her mind you'd be spending the summer getting ready for college, working, doing all the things young women do at this time of their lives." He pulled me into a hug. "You leave her to me. I want this for you, hon. I know you need to take some time before you decide what you want to do with the rest of your life. I'm hoping this experience will help you work that out."

I hugged him back and held on a little too tightly.

He tilted to look at me. "I want you to come back carrying less weight on your shoulders. Go find your happy. I want my girl back, my happy girl. It's going to be such an adventure for you to live in the tropics. Maybe when you come home, you can write about it."

Write about it? No, I couldn't. I hadn't been able to write anything for a year. Of course, I hadn't really felt anything either. Would I be this way forever? I glanced down at the picture of the grinning ten-year-old. No. I was on my way to healing, on my way to my fresh start. No doubt about it.

• • • • •

Four weeks into the trip, and close to my nineteenth birthday, that fresh start came to a screaming halt. Everything had been perfect for those first couple weeks. Then Bray showed up. The quintessential party boy I needed to avoid. I concentrated my time and effort on Joshie. He was a light in the dark place of my heart. And healing, though slow, was working its way through me. It was at the four-week mark that the world came crashing down.

It was one year after losing Michael.

Summers hadn't been my best season.

• • • • •

That day when Bray arrived had started like any other. I took Joshie down to the beach to collect shells. Around Belize, the water is murky—brackish, they call it, due to all the rivers that empty into the ocean. You have to get a fair distance from land to experience that gorgeous Caribbean crystal water shown on travel brochures. I was surprised when I first saw the real thing. And a little disappointed. I learned that my dream water surrounded the cays—tiny islands that dotted the coastline around Belize.

I also discovered a trip to the cays could be obtained for the right price. I made a good wage serving as Joshie's nanny. But before I could make my plans, Bray showed up.

He had just finished his freshman year in college at Florida State and hadn't made his parents any promises about coming to Belize, so Sandra was more than thrilled to get the call that he was on his way.

"Are you excited to meet my brother?" Joshie asked after he'd dumped a bucket of shells on my lap to sift.

I held a shimmering oyster shell to the sun and watched the rainbow dance across it. "Of course I am."

He squinted one eye. "My teacher said people begin sentences with 'of course' when they mean the opposite. Do you mean the opposite, Summer?"

I narrowed my gaze on him. "Of course I don't."

That elicited a smile. To drive my point home, I reached out and tickled his ribs. He squealed and ran a few steps away, slinging sand into my face.

I sputtered, then clamped my hand over my chest and feigned a heart attack. He laughed more. Joshie was a great kid. And way too perceptive. To tell the truth, I *wasn't* looking forward to meeting his older brother. Sandra, her husband Markus, Joshie, and I had settled into a nice rhythm. I really wasn't interested in shaking up our dynamic.

Joshie dropped beside me on the sand and tugged on my prone, heart-attack body, complete with tongue hanging out the side of my mouth. "Where do you live when you're not living with us?" He pulled my arm, wedging his feet into the sand for a solid grip. The sand had no concept of personal space. Neither did Joshie.

I sat up and began drawing a primitive map of Florida on the ground beside us. "Here's Naples."

"That's where we live," he said.

My finger trailed due north. "Here's Sarasota. That's where I live."

"Do you have other kids you watch in Sara—"

"Sarasota," I finished for him. "No. I just finished high school."

He stared at me hard for a few seconds. "I think you're worried Bray won't like you."

I couldn't care less if Bray did or didn't like me. I ruffled Joshie's hair. "I'm just scared he's going to try to take you away from me. Who will bring me seashells and make me wildflower necklaces if you're busy with your big brother?"

Joshie turned sullen, hands fumbling with the drawstring on his brightly colored Hawaiian print swim shorts. "You won't tell him I make flower necklaces, will you?"

"Not if you won't tell him I burp when no one else is around."

Joshie's laughter filled the air, his little boy cheeks rosy. "You do not."

"I'm thinking about starting."

"You're silly, Summer." Yep. That was me. One big ball of laughs. I had laughed a lot since arriving in Belize. Smart, precocious ten-year-olds could do that for you. Through Joshie, I experienced the whole world with brand-new eyes. And the world was a brighter place than I remembered.

Until Bray arrived.

Bray

Mom stood at the back door, yelling for Joshie to come in. I'd just arrived, and already she was changing everyone's routine. That was her. She spun from the door, her salon-lightened hair flying around her, face awash with excitement. Words bubbled from her mouth, but I just wanted to climb the stairs and get into bed. She paused long enough to ask me something. It was about dinner.

"No, I'm not hungry." Sleep. I needed sleep. Between Nick's party, the plane ride, and the killer headache that kept pounding my temple, I just wanted a bed.

She continued yammering about reservations at Monroe's—which was one of my favorite restaurants, something I'd normally jump at—but I'd run into Cory at the airport. "Can't tonight, Mom. Cory is having a party." Besides, I was committed to doing the whole *family* thing for the summer. I should get one night of real fun first.

Her head quirked to the side. "I didn't think the Wilsons were going to be here for a few more days."

I grinned, visions of island girls dancing in my head. "They aren't. Hence the party."

My dad slapped my shoulder. "We can manage dinner without you. Just glad you got here. If the Wilsons aren't going to be there, you boys make sure you stay out of trouble."

They both seemed happy. Dad, in his Tommy Bahama shirt and linen shorts, trying not to look like a businessman, and Mom trying not to seem disappointed that I was ditching on the first night there. They didn't think I knew what was going on, but I'd overheard a conversation between them during spring break. This would be our last trip as a family. For Joshie's sake, I knew I had to come—and make it the best family vacation ever. Even if there had been other offers to keep me busy for the summer. Like Katie VanBuren. Though I wouldn't have spent the summer with her family in the Hamptons. Katie was like one of those synthetic drugs wrapped in a colorful package, but instead of the promised fun, she was toxic. I'm not even sure why the two of us hit it off when we first met at a party on campus. She was a senior and I was just a freshman. We'd hung out a couple times, but after a party on a sailboat, I avoided Katie. I'd started calling her Katie Plague in my mind.

"Oh, here they come." Mom spun to the back door then back again. All that nervous energy, I half expected her to start bouncing up and down Tigger-style.

I glanced past her. Ugh. "I thought you hired a teenage girl to take care of Josh."

Mom cast a frown. "We did."

Clearly, they hadn't. Which ticked me off, because if I was going to make this a memorable family trip, I'd be spending a lot of time with the new nanny. The woman walking behind Josh was dusting sand from a long skirt. In that shapeless floral dress, she looked middle-aged, fresh from the grocery store or maybe teaching in a classroom. I'd be mad if someone put me in her care. Mousy brown hair flew in the wind and tangled in front of her face. Josh beamed and slid his hand into hers. Well, okay. Little Man actually liked the school teacher. Of course, Little Man liked school. She was probably the librarian. I'd expected a blond ball of teen hotness, and instead we got Suzy schoolteacher.

They stepped inside, and I realized the face didn't match the outfit once all that brown mess was gathered at the back of her neck. Her eyes were on me. Scared eyes. Okay, maybe not scared, but apprehensive. *Whoa.* She was actually young.

Why would anyone under the age of fifty dress like that? She probably lost a bet.

The question was still rolling around in my head when Josh jumped into my arms. We greeted each other, and it was great to feel him squeezing my neck and talking so fast that my ears burned.

Then, Mom introduced me to the girl.

Summer

It's not that I wanted Bray to give me any attention. But he looked right through me while Mrs. Garrison introduced us. His dad actually nudged Bray's shoulder to get him to stick a hand out in greeting. I shook it, mumbling how it was nice to meet him. His eyes darted to mine for less than half a second, and he almost quirked a smile before he looked away.

Less than half a second. Don't get me wrong; I was used to being invisible to this kind of guy. And though I loathed people who stereotyped, Bray was exactly what I'd expected. Spoiled little rich boy in his designer shirt, shorts, and deck shoes. Already tan, looking like a model, and obnoxiously stuck-up. His dark blue eyes matched his father's, but where Markus's were kind, Bray's seemed steel-hard. On top of everything, he had sandy-colored hair cut in a style just long enough to look perfect, probably even in a wind tunnel.

Sandra and Markus were so sweet it was difficult to see how they'd spawned such a jerk. When I say he looked at me for half a second, I mean that much at best. His eyes didn't even focus. They hadn't had time. It was like having to look at a train crash and knowing you didn't want to see the horrific carnage.

He turned completely away from me and started talking to his dad. "So, I'm gonna grab a shower and crash for a couple hours, then head over to Cory's."

Mrs. Garrison spoke up. "Oh, Bray! You should take Summer. She hasn't made any friends since we got here."

My face burned. She didn't *mean* anything by that, but word choice was everything. What really struck me was the horror that washed over Bray at the mention of taking me. I almost wanted to agree with Sandra just to torture him.

I cleared my throat. "I'd love to, Mrs. Garrison, but I can't tonight. I promised Joshie we would stay up late and map stars."

"Don't want to miss that, do you, munchkin?" Bray added, just to cement the prior commitment.

"Not tonight, Joshie." Mr. Garrison ruffled the boy's hair. "If you're playing golf with me in the morning, you need to be in bed by nine."

Panic set in. For both of us. I could practically feel Bray's plans of an island girl hook-up dissolving around him. He chewed the inside of his cheek. "Honestly, I don't really know how much of a party it will be. Cory just got here and ..." And what? He was scrambling.

"All the better," Mrs. Garrison said. "A more intimate gathering will be great for Summer to get to know some of the kids on the island."

My throat went dry. "Mrs. Garrison?"

"Sandra." She ran her hands through all that blond hair that had lightened since we arrived, making her even more beautiful. "I've told you a thousand times to call me Sandra." A perfect smile did its best to warm me, but frozen blood was difficult to thaw.

"Sandra," I started to explain, but what could I say? I glanced from her to Markus to Bray and back. They were the beautiful people. Even little Joshie. Mrs. Garrison had maintained her sweetness through the beauty, but not everyone was like her. "I'm sure Bray's friends are all very nice, but I just don't think I'd fit in there."

I said it. As delicately and gently as I could. She had to agree.

A diamond-studded hand waved through the air. "Nonsense. They're just young people. All barely graduated from high school or finished with their first year of college. It will be good for you to get out, Summer. You've been here for weeks and haven't done anything for yourself."

I'm here working, I wanted to remind her. *I didn't take the position to have fun and hang out with friends.* I looked to Joshie for help.

"No big deal, Summer. The stars aren't going anywhere. We can look at them tomorrow night."

Was the entire world against me? I had one ally: Bray. I met his gaze to find him staring at me, but I couldn't track his thoughts. Emotion carefully hidden. He worked the muscle in his jaw a few times, eyes scorching me. He sighed, and an instant later he flashed a charming smile.

"Sure. Yeah, it'll be good." But that smile didn't reach his eyes, and I knew he blamed me for ruining his first night on the island.

Stupid, *stupid* boys. He'd suffer one night. I'd suffer as long as my memory retained how I was treated by the pretty people at a party I didn't even want to attend. Again.

"Can't wait," I said, swallowing the lump in my throat.

Sandra beamed and clasped her manicured fingers together. "Great! You two will have so much fun."

Three hours later, I stared into my closet wondering why all my clothes looked the same. In celebration of my new job, I'd shopped for cotton dresses and skirts and, at the time, thought I'd gotten a great variety. But now they all looked like carbon copies. The blousy tops were pastel shades of soft cotton, and I really liked them until I thought about everyone going to this stupid party and all the girls dressed in too-short shorts and tight tops. I'd stick out like a sore thumb, which, by the way, is exactly how I felt.

I spun from the closet and headed to Bray's room to tell him I wasn't going. Public humiliation was not part of the job description. I stomped to the door and raised my hand to knock. Sandra's face — so alight with excitement — entered my mind, and though I tried to forcibly remove her, I couldn't. I dropped my hand and started to turn, but could hear Bray talking.

"Dude, it's not like I planned it."

A pause. He must be on the phone.

"She's not hot. Trust me. She's like the girl you get to tutor you through English lit." He laughed. "So, what about Vince's cousin, you know, that geek-dude who was here last year? They'd hit it off."

Anger began a slow simmer inside my stomach. He was planning to pass me off once we reached the party.

"Well, you gotta come up with someone to entertain her, 'cause I met this chick at the airport."

Heat flashed across my exposed skin.

"She won't just hang, because she doesn't know anyone here. She'll be following me around like that weird chick at my high school. What was her name?" He snapped his fingers. "Oh yeah, Bernice."

A pause. "No, I know she's not psycho, dude, or my parents wouldn't have hired her to take care of little man. She's just vanilla, you know? Blank. Not ugly, just nonexistent."

A sudden rush of fever across my forehead and nausea roiling my stomach took me captive. Slowly, I turned from his door. My nose tingled as I moved away, which was really annoying because I knew, I'd *always* known, what guys like Bray thought of girls like me. Nevertheless, something about hearing it — right from his mouth — hurt. It shouldn't have. But the shame manifested in the pseudo-flu racking my body.

Once I made it to my room, I closed the door behind me and blinked tears away as I stared up at the fan blades. My thumbnails found their way to one another in front of me and scraped together, a nervous habit I'd obtained last summer. It didn't help.

Whoosh, whoosh, whoosh. The blades of the ceiling fan continued to go 'round and 'round, drying the tracks of tears on my cheeks. No matter how long I watched, the blades would continue. No matter what I did, Bray was Bray. And I was Summer. And we wouldn't change from who we were. I looked at my closet, door swung open, inviting. There were thousands of Brays in the world. And thousands of Summers. I couldn't be afraid of him. If I was, I'd live my whole life in fear of the pretty people. What better place to conquer the beast? Here, where I knew no one and after this trip would never have to see any of them again. I pushed the Bray-flu aside.

I was going to the party.

CHAPTER 2

Bray

Mom loved the underdog. She was one of those people who still believed love could change the world and that if everyone recycled there'd be no war, famine, or death. Usually, I liked Mom's attitude—juvenile as it was—but not tonight.

I drove to the party in silence with Summer beside me. Dad sent us in his convertible Beamer—trust was not an issue for my dad. He believed the best of me. I glanced over and saw Summer was pencil straight, staring intently at the floorboard. Outside the car were palm trees trimmed in white lights, and the most interesting thing she could find was her feet?

I really hoped she'd change out of her librarian costume, but no such luck. Flat shoes, floral dress, and a white top. Boring. And it looked like you could make five outfits out of it if you were handy with a sewing machine. Seriously, we could park the car in the folds of that skirt. Her hair was combed down in meticulous, straight lines, and a ribbon of all things held it off her face. Very *Little House on the Prairie*.

I should say something. "You smell good."

I felt her head snap toward me followed by a loooooong pause. "Thanks." The word was small and almost sounded like a question. She really did smell good.

"What scent is that?"

Her hands folded over a giant flower on her skirt. "Vanilla," she said, then let out a long and—if I wasn't mistaken—embarrassed sigh. Her eyes returned to the floorboards.

I didn't know what that was all about, but I had to chuckle that she *wore* vanilla when I'd told Cory on the phone she *was* vanilla. Guess I didn't know how accurate I could be.

"We're here. You bring a suit?"

Her eyes met mine in the dim light of the dashboard.

"They have a pool."

"Oh." She shook her head. "No."

Of course not. That would be too easy. "Come on, I'll introduce you to everyone." I stepped around the car and opened her door, which seemed to surprise her. When she stood, the wind threw the vanilla scent to me again as if marking me. Most of the girls here on the island smelled like coconut. And I'd hoped to carry a little of that home on my clothes . . . but unless Summer found someone to entertain her, I was on babysitting duty. My night was already over.

Summer

Vanilla. My face flushed each time I thought of it. It didn't matter what Bray said about me. Vanilla was my signature scent, and if he didn't like it, too bad.

But he did like it.

And I hated the fact that his recognition gave me the faintest hint of triumph. I didn't want there to be triumph. That would suggest a battle. There was no battle here, simply a group of people who were everything I wasn't. And it was okay for me to step into their world, just like it would be okay for them to step into my world. That was why I'd come. I could peacefully coexist.

The house was a gargantuan island thing filled with golden, glowing light seeping from every window. We walked in without knocking and headed for the back. A breeze blew through the house as we rounded a corner, and my breath caught.

Bray stopped, and I felt his eyes on me but I didn't care.

It was like being inside and outside at the same time. The arched wall of slider doors was open, exposing the yard and everything beyond. The moon hung low over the water, which looked like it was sneaking up on the house. A torch-lit lanai waited beyond the arched open doorways. A sparkling pool with a built-in rock waterfall anchored one corner of the landscaped yard. People were scattered around, but I barely saw them. It was the most beautiful place I'd ever seen. And I was instantly glad I'd come.

A low and velvety voice drifted over from beside me. "Nice, huh?"

I smiled, trying to take it all in. Then, I closed my eyes and inhaled deep. Capturing it. In case I never saw it again.

"Why'd you do that?" His words were a whisper, and in them I heard the intrigue.

"I'm stealing it," was all I said.

I'd expected him to mumble some stupid remark, but he didn't. He just stood there beside me, probably trying to see what was invisible to him.

Bray's breathing was in rhythm with the water, and I hated to admit it was nice. Deep inhales, the faintest rumble in his throat on the exhale. I glanced over. He closed his eyes and mimicked me, drawing a cavernous, full breath.

His face was smooth and he looked like less of a jerk with his eyes closed, his strong jawline close enough I could reach over and run a finger along the taut skin. But then his eyes popped open, and the moment was gone. He shrugged. "Now what?"

My gaze dropped to the tile floor. "Now nothing." I wouldn't explain it to him. He wouldn't get it.

"*Braaay!*" A girl with dark hair and slick, shiny lips came running at him and fell into his arms. "You *made* it."

And that was my cue. I slinked past the drink station and an outdoor kitchen and meandered down to the water's edge. That's where I'd spend the evening. Staring up at the stars and wondering how the pretty people can do this night after night and never even notice the sky. It was a perfect black-velvet blanket with pinhole lights puncturing it. Sometimes at night, I liked to stand at the ocean and listen to the sea. And even though the Garrison's house wasn't far, it somehow felt different here. Sounds and music from the party drifted down to me, buffered by the expanse of soft sand. Tiki torch light flickered behind me, casting an occasional shimmer on the approaching waves. I smelled salt and sea and torch fuel, the combination euphoric. I could probably sit here all night. But my mind began to drift to last summer, and I had to shut down the momentum or I'd end up curled in a ball crying. So I did what I always did and mapped the constellations one by one. It kept me busy the entire evening, giving me false hope that this night would end okay.

"Hey, you looked lonely down here." The guy's words were a little slurred, causing a thread of panic to trickle down my spine.

"No, I'm good."

Instead of turning and going back, he stepped closer and extended a hand. "I'm Morris."

"Summer." I shook his hand and shot a look up to the house where Bray stood at the drink station with that girl draped on his arm.

"Summerrrrr," he repeated. "I'll go get you a drink."

Panic turned to annoyance. "No. Thanks. I don't drink." Even I could hear the finality in my words.

He shrugged. "Not even water?"

He grinned, eyes glossy and nose red. Of course, eighteen was the legal drinking age in Belize, but that didn't make it okay in my book. I'd seen what alcohol could do to an otherwise intelligent young man. And for a hot instant, I wanted to reach out and punch this guy in the face and tell him just how stupid he was. My hands fisted at my sides. "Not even water."

His brows rose as he stared at me. "Lighten up. I know, let's forget about the party going on behind us and take a walk down the beach."

When his arm came around me, I ducked, twisted, and headed back up to the house, pausing only to grab my shoes, and then scurried toward the lights and music at the back patio. My night was ruined. Over. I didn't even want to look at the stars anymore. I headed straight for Bray. He'd moved to a lawn chair and the girl was on his lap.

I stopped at his table where island girl was chattering about something they all seemed intently interested in.

"I want to go home. Now." I crossed my arms over my chest.

Bray sighed, lifted the girl from his lap, and pulled me a few steps away. He glanced behind me to Morris who was making his way to the table. "He'll leave you alone now."

My voice lowered, anger stirring in my stomach. "I want to leave now. I'm done being hit on by juvenile drunks."

But Bray wasn't listening. His attention had gone to the table where Morris had his arms draped around Bray's island girl. And that's when the fight began.

Bray took two steps away from me and threw a fist at Morris's face. Island girl ducked out of the way and Morris hit the ground. "Come on, we're leaving."

Bray took me by the arm, but I wriggled free. We were nearly to the front door when I stopped. "I'm not going with you if you've been drinking."

His eyes burned into me as he stared, still a little out of breath from the exertion a moment ago. "I didn't drink anything."

My gaze narrowed on him, but the words were final. Forceful. And if I wasn't wrong, completely honest, so when he continued to the convertible, I followed.

He didn't bother to open the car door for me when we got outside, but he slammed his with such force, the whole car shook. I sat in silence. The cool night air as he turned out of their driveway did nothing to soothe the tension between us.

"Sorry I brought you here."

My anger boiled. *Sorry he brought me here?* Not sorry the guy hit on me or was a jerk, but sorry he brought me here? "It's not like you wanted to." My acerbic tone must have shocked him a little, because his eyes left the road.

"It's not like you wanted to come," he countered.

I angled to face him. "No, I love watching a bunch of childish idiots act like they're God's gift to the world."

His eyes narrowed on me. "And what makes you so far above all of us?"

I sucked in air. Was he kidding? Was he actually accusing me of being the stuck-up one? "I don't think I'm above you. I think people like you — the *pretty* people, the rich people — think the world revolves around them. And the really awful thing is, it kind of does."

"So, this is about money. You don't like me because I have money." He kept a tight grip on the steering wheel, both hands white-knuckled. But his gaze would dart to me now and then, his eyes an eerie glow in the green dashboard light.

"I don't like you because all you see is what's in front of your eyes."

His face clouded for an instant.

I threw my hands up in surrender. "Just forget it, okay? I'm not like you and you're not like me and we don't *like* each other."

That muscle in his jaw twitched. "If you have such a problem with people who have money, why did you take this job?"

"You are so full of yourself; you just can't get past it, can you? I adore your family. Your mom and dad are awesome. And I already love Joshie like he's my own brother. It's *you*, Bray. You're a jerk. You and all your rich kid friends are more concerned with what car you're driving than with anything that really matters." I knew this speech could cost me my job, but right now, it didn't matter. I was invested. I wanted him to know it. "Do you know how hard your mom worked to get the dinner reservation at Monroe's? After she found out you were coming, she went down there three times when she couldn't get it over the phone. She waited for an hour the last time, hoping they would have a cancellation, and they did."

He swallowed.

"And you blew it off for friends and a party that will be just like your next party and your next and your next. Because that's what you care about."

A little of the fire left his eyes. "I didn't know. She should have told me."

"She shouldn't have to, Bray." He stopped at the big stucco entrance to their posh island neighborhood — tonight, even the entrance made me feel like I didn't belong.

I got out of the car and slammed the door.

"What are you doing?"

"Walking the rest of the way." A block or so down the street, I could see the Garrison's house. I was only a few steps away when he spoke, raising his voice above the soft engine of the car.

"Get in. I'm sorry." The condescension in his voice caused fire to shoot down my back.

"No." I stopped and turned to look at him. "You don't get to have everything you want. People aren't your servants to order around. And, honestly, I can't stand to spend one more minute with you."

"Fine." His hands left the steering wheel and he threw the car into park.

I turned and kept walking. Half a block away, I spun back around and stared into the bright headlights. "What are you doing?"

"I'm waiting on you," he yelled. "I'm not going to leave you out here alone in the dark."

Now he wanted to be chivalrous? He was just being stubborn. The house was only a few dozen yards away. I pointed to it. He answered by slipping the car into drive and coming up slowly behind me. Just a few feet back, Bray motioned me on by brushing his hand through the air. That went down like acid. I stood my ground.

"Well, we can sit here all night," he said. "Or you can storm into the house. But my mom's going to wonder why we didn't come in together."

Sandra. I hadn't thought of her.

"Miss Always-Thinking-of-Others, how you gonna handle that?"

After a moment of victory, he pulled up alongside me.

I drew a calming breath as the car stopped and Bray reached over the seat to open the passenger door.

I gathered my skirt around me and got in.

"Look, it's very clear we don't like each other. But we're both stuck here. Truce? For mom's sake? And for Joshie's?" He thrust his hand out toward me.

The last thing I wanted to do was shake it. But I had to. If the family was called on to pick sides, they'd stick with their son. "Truce," I echoed and slid my hand into his. *I just wish you weren't such a jerk.*

My thoughts must have been easy to read, because before he drove the rest of the way to the house, I'm pretty sure he answered them. It was under his breath, but I heard the words. "You never gave me a chance not to be."

· · · · ·

Sandra had a weird look in her eye. She had all morning. I kept catching her staring at me when she thought I wouldn't notice. Though I was kind of doing the same thing to her. She wore a red silk tank and a short silk skirt that hugged her perfect figure. I glanced over my long dress. Yards of material and an elastic waist. I could weigh three hundred pounds and it would still fit. I'd found a roadside clothing store in town and had purchased a couple more long skirts, but when a cruise ship full of senior citizens swarmed the place, I realized maybe I did dress a bit ... old. From a distance, Sandra—old enough to be my mom—looked younger than I.

I usually didn't compare myself to Sandra. She was all elegance and beauty, I was all level-headedness, and I was fine with that. But come on, I was eighteen, almost nineteen. Not seventy-four. Sandra had never made a big deal out of what I wore or how I looked, but this morning something had shifted, and I didn't like it at all. I felt like a lamb in preparation for shearing.

Sandra came to rest at the small kitchen table where I was drinking orange juice and picking at a bagel. There was a grand table in the formal dining area, but I liked the cozy warmth of the kitchen and the glass table that overlooked the tropical backyard and sea beyond. Sandra hovered over me, and I could practically feel her buzzing with excitement. My gaze trailed up to her and held.

"What are your plans for the morning, since Joshie will be at the golf course with his dad until noon?" There was a look—calculating, sweet, almost saccharine—in her blue eyes. Sandra was scheming. It was good-natured scheming, most likely, but still.

Think fast, Summer. You have plans. Make something up. "I'm ..."

But nothing manifested. No words, no ideas. I was helplessly trapped in that blue prison. "I'm not busy," I blurted.

"Great!" She clasped her hands together, slender arms making an inverted V in front of her. "We're going to the spa."

I cringed. Did she mean *we* as in her and me, or was she just letting me know she and Bray would be gone? "Uh."

"Bray will sleep till noon, and then we can all have lunch together."

We. Meaning her and me. *Oh dear.*

"I really should write some letters home." I was scrambling here. I didn't want to go to a spa. "I promised friends I'd write and I've been so busy."

And that's when it happened. Her blue eyes paled and her mouth tipped into a sad frown, and I wanted to shoot myself with a whale harpoon for being so insensitive. Sandra had taken me into her home, given me the care of her child, and treated me like family. My face was hot. I needed to get out of this.

"I understand," she mumbled, blinking those giant sapphire marbles. "It's just that I don't normally have a girl to dote on."

Ach! Stab me again and get it over with. Seriously, I was lower than slug spit. "Sandra." I had to think fast. "I would love to go to the spa, but I . . ."

She leaned forward.

I dropped my head in true embarrassed fashion. "I can't afford it." I knew she didn't plan on me paying my own way. She hadn't let me pay for anything since I'd been here, but to let her think I really didn't *want* to go would be like stealing milk from a kitten. I wasn't a horrible person. What could I say? I didn't want to go because I didn't fit in?

Her eyes lit up. "Oh, no, no, no. That's not what I meant. I mean, I wouldn't expect *you* to pay for your spa services. It's my treat." She reached out and plucked my hand. Very BFF style.

I nodded. Tried to share her enthusiasm.

She squeezed my fingers. "It's just so much fun for me to have a girl around."

That's when I saw it. The hope of a woman who could spend a small fortune on a daughter, but never had the chance. I saw it and I watched it slowly slip from her gaze and disappear with each blink of her long lashes. She had boys. Boys and golf and basketball and skinned knees, not girls and dresses and ribbons and flowers. With a long sigh, I conceded myself to today's job description. For the next few hours I wasn't Summer Mathers, nanny. I was Summer Mathers, dress-up doll.

Bray

I'd tossed and turned all night with horrible nightmares of an evil librarian. In my dream, she'd slap me every time I spoke. When I stood to leave, she started throwing books at me, and all my friends were laughing because I didn't know what to do.

When Mom woke me and said she'd be back at noon so we could all have lunch together, through the haze I said, "Is the librarian going?"

She laughed and told me to go back to sleep. Summer Mathers was unlike any girl I'd met. She was mean. But not the kind of mean girl I'd known, those who were constantly trying to one-up their friends. I was starting to think maybe Summer was mean to the bone. Except not to Joshie. They adored each other. The last thing I'd wanted was to call a truce with her, but I had a mission this summer and it was to get my family together. If it was for the last time, so be it. But in the back of my mind I hoped maybe Mom and Dad might reconsider their decision. If they could spend one really amazing summer with me and Joshie and remember how things used to be, maybe there was some hope. If not, I guessed we'd all have a lot of good memories to hold onto while we navigated the rocky road ahead.

The clock read 12:15. When I heard the door downstairs open and close, I mustered my strength, intent on not letting Summer throw me off my game. She was good at that, and I needed to be at top performance to pull off this whole family thing.

Mom faced me as I came down the stairs, but Summer wasn't with her. I wanted to ask where the nanny had run off to, but Mom didn't notice me because her head was tucked into a shopping bag. "Here they are," she mumbled to a woman with her back to me. Mom was in the zone, holding something to the lady's ears. Must be earrings. The woman tossed her hair to accommodate the earring selection.

That's when my gaze drifted over her. The first thing I noticed was that her waist was tiny. Above that, long, full hair was streaked with lines of blond and landed halfway down her back. From behind, she was gorgeous. Her feet were tucked into wedge sandals that highlighted the muscles in her calf. When she bent at the knee to adjust one of the straps, a perfect set of legs tilted. I stopped on the stairs, feeling a little guilty for thinking one of my mom's friends was so hot, but hey, who could blame me?

I managed to get to the bottom of the stairs when I heard a familiar voice. One that sent a cold chill down my spine. My eyes darted around the room looking for Summer, and that's when I realized.

My knees went weak and I felt like I might vomit. My fingers closed on the stair railing. The hottie with my mom was Summer.

She turned around.

Her green eyes grew troubled for an instant. It must have occurred to her what was happening because she became all coy and smiled like she meant it. "Hello, Bray."

I shut my mouth. I don't know how long it had been open, but it was dry inside.

My mom's voice came from somewhere. "Don't be rude, son. Say hello."

"Hello," I parroted. Summer pivoted to face me fully and just stood there until my mom took her by the arm and led her to me.

She stopped face-to-face with me and stared up into my eyes with those strange green ... wait. She didn't have green eyes. Not like that. They were a soft sea foam shade—like a mermaid might have. "Are you wearing contacts?" I hadn't really meant to ask that, just think it.

Those green eyes sparkled and seemed to laugh at me. "No."

My mom brushed her hand over my arm. "Doesn't Summer have the most unusual eye color? It really pops now with the blond in her hair. Also the makeup."

It didn't look like she was wearing much, just a hint of color here and there, and soft glossed lips that looked like they needed to be kissed. *Whoa.* I took a step back, tripping on the stair behind me. That mouth was full of toxin. Poison, and as soon as she opened it to say something, I'd be slapped right back into reality. But she didn't say anything. She just stood there and let me inspect her.

Mom was buzzing like a downed electric wire, and the intensity started to get to me. Summer pulled her bottom lip into her mouth and bit down. When she did, something shot from my gut outward. It was too hot in the house. No one had turned on the ceiling fans.

"Bray." My mom used her tone reserved for her children. "Aren't you going to tell Summer how pretty she looks?"

And that's when the events of last night rushed into my head. The librarian informing me about how shallow I was, her utter hatred of me, my friends. "You look just like one of the pretty people." My words were flat. And had the exact effect I'd hoped. Her tiny nostrils flared for an instant, chin tilting back a degree. Satisfaction was sweet.

Soft pink lips hardened into a straight line. She cast a quick glance to my mom, who was busy adjusting the bracelets on her wrist. Then her eyes narrowed on me for an instant, and I had to bite back a smile.

While my mom looked back and forth between the two of us, I offered Summer my arm. "Shall we go to lunch?"

She looked at my limb like it was covered in leprosy. "Love to," she said, taking it.

Against me, her body was stiff as a board. Mom hummed as she led us out the front door.

· · · · ·

We ate at an outdoor restaurant that overlooked the water. Other places were usually crowded with tourists and their endless supply of shopping bags, but this was a local favorite and kept a secret from the brightly dressed island visitors. Summer looked incredible. I found my eyes trailing to her as we ate, wondering how such a pretty girl could be hiding inside such a nasty personality. Whatever. It didn't matter. I had bigger concerns. "So, Mom, I was thinking maybe we could all take a tour of Xunantunich."

Mom's fork stopped in midair. "But you've never wanted to go there."

I shrugged, trying to act interested in my fish tacos. "I know, but we should, right? You've wanted me to go with you forever."

Mom directed her attention to Summer. "Xunantunich is a Mayan ceremonial center. It's just incredible, Summer. You'll love it."

Whoa there. I didn't mean her. "Mom, I know you're all into the whole 'it feels like a spiritual place' kind of thing, but Summer might appreciate a day off."

I felt Summer stiffen across the table, probably not wanting to get caught again in a struggle between Mom and me about what was best for her. The party had proven Mom's inability to tame the teenage clique stereotype.

Mom placed her fork down with intent. "I'm constantly trying to give her a day off, and she constantly refuses. Now that we're going to do something fun, I wouldn't hear of her wasting the day alone at home while we're at Xunantunich." She placed a hand to her heart. "It's one of my favorite places of all the Mayan ruins I've visited."

Summer offered a tight smile.

Mom looked at me. "For your information, Summer is a spiritual being herself. Deeply involved in a church youth group back home."

"What a surprise," I mumbled.

Summer used a fingertip to angle her hair behind an ear. I hated that I found the motion hot.

"I wouldn't say deeply involved." Was that a red stain across her cheeks? Had Summer lied about it or something? I should have just left it alone, but it was too intriguing.

"What *would* you say?" I leaned forward in my seat.

Those strange green eyes met mine across the table. And something, something real and almost ... painful flashed in them.

She pulled a breath, and I was pretty sure her gaze had gone misty. "I um, used to be." She offered my mom a nervous smile. "Everything on my résumé was true, I just ..."

But Mom had picked up on the sudden change in Summer as well. "Of course it was. I'd never doubt that."

Summer blinked, nodded again as if the motion would pull her strength from the ground where it had melted into the concrete and place it back on her shoulders. "I've been away from my youth group for the last year."

I continued to listen, but my heart almost ached for her. She shrugged. "Just got busy I guess."

Mom placed a hand over Summer's. I'd itched to do the same — which completely took me by surprise. "You miss it though, don't you?" Mom's ever-understanding eyes stayed on her.

"Yes," she whispered. It was one word, and in it, the sorrow of the world.

Summer

Xunantunich was everything Sandra had promised. The ruins were set atop the Mopan River and jutted into the sky surrounded by trees and vegetation at the base. The lowest level was a wide section of stairs, the upper a rocky pyramid. I stood on the top of the steps while the Garrisons climbed higher.

Bray's voice surprised me. "Aren't you coming on up?"

I angled to face him, gathering my hair behind me. It hadn't been windy at the bottom, but up here, the breeze tossed it around. "No. Thanks."

He slipped his hands into his pockets and followed my gaze out to the landscape of green tropics around us. "The view is ten times better up there."

"I'm ... good here."

"You can see Guatemala from the top. How often can you stand in one country and look at another?"

"I suppose you could in Canada." I didn't want Bray's inquisitions, though he seemed genuine enough. In fact, since the lunch at the taco place, he'd seemed fairly civil.

"Where else?"

"Lots of places in Europe. I've seen pictures of a castle in Germany where you're overlooking the French countryside."

Bray shifted his weight. "You're scared of heights, aren't you?"

He wasn't being mean ... at least, I didn't think so. He was just asking a logical question. "A little."

The wind shifted, and Bray's scent, a mix of spiciness and sweat from the climb, entered my nose. I didn't hate it. "It's okay, Summer. We're all scared of something. Those who say they aren't are lying."

I couldn't help but smile. I didn't bother to tell him my worst fear was claustrophobia. "Go on up with your folks and Joshie. I'll wait here for you guys."

Before he left, he touched my arm. "You sure?" His dark blue eyes were soft now. I didn't want to like that they were filled with concern.

"Positive." I smiled. He smiled back. What do you know; we could be civil after all.

CHAPTER 3

Summer

"He's shallow, Bec. One nice gesture doesn't erase all that." I lay on my bed, staring at my pink-painted toes. I'd rested them on a pillow for good viewing while Becky, my best friend, yammered on the other end of the phone line about summer in Sarasota. I hated to admit it, but the makeover had been fun. Almost as fun as Xunantunich, even if I didn't climb to the top.

And I liked my sparkly pink toes. They were like tiny little peek-a-boo surprises every time I uncovered my feet.

"I bought some new clothes. It's really too hot for the long skirts I've been wearing." *And I don't want to look like a senior citizen tourist anymore.* I wiggled my toes so they would sparkle. "Shorts mostly, a few shorter skirts. We found a sale and Sandra insisted. I paid for most of the clothes—I refused to try them on otherwise. She'd already spent a fortune at the spa. But I think she ended up enjoying the day more than I did; wow did she have fun! You know, fixing the ugly duckling and all. I think the entire place decided it was their duty to bring me out."

"Do you like how you look?" Becky asked.

I leaned up and took in my reflection in the closet mirror. "I feel pretty, Bec. It's nice to feel like that sometimes."

"You've always been pretty, Summer. You just hide it."

I ran a hand through my hair and admired the shades. "I'm not trying to hide anything. I just never gave it too much thought." Becky didn't understand. She grew up in a house full of girls, older sisters who'd taught her how to wear makeup, how to dress in clothes that were flattering. My mom was a work-from-home CPA. She never wore makeup and usually was still in her pajamas when I got home from school. Not that she was too lazy to change, she was just too busy. Work came first. Appearances second ... or maybe last after everything else. I cast a glance to my closet and had to smile. It didn't look all the same anymore. There were cute tops, tanks, shorts, and sandals alongside my ballet slippers and floral dresses. Variety. Oh, and two new swimsuits. One, a ridiculous hot pink bikini Sandra picked out and insisted on buying, complete with a bright cover-up and a yellow floppy hat. Very island chic.

"So ..." I could hear the question in Becky's voice. "You're not going to have some weird identity crisis now that the world sees how beautiful you are, are you?"

I chuckled. "No, I'm still the same. It's not about clothing, any-way. It's about attitude. People acting a certain way because they think they can, hurting others."

"You're pretty jaded, Summer."

Silence. I was. Jade was the new shade of me since last summer. Some things that happen to a person make them stronger, and some things shatter them into bits. If you are strong enough, determined enough, one day those bits meld back into a whole being. I was mid-meld and wondering if I'd ever fully recover.

Outside, the wind whistled through the palm trees. We'd stayed quiet on the phone for a while. "Are things good back home?"

"Yes. I'm doing a summer stint at a daycare for children

recovering from the burn unit at the hospital. It should help me land a spot in the nursing program at Sarasota Memorial."

"That's great, Becky."

"They wanted applicants with patient care experience. It's all about strategy getting into the programs. But I'm loving working with the kids. They're so strong and amazing. They don't let anything get to them. It's an experience I'll never forget."

Becky. Always quick with compassion and always the girl with the future plans. We'd been friends since middle school, and I think she'd wanted to be a nurse that long.

"Summer." Her voice softened. "Just so you know, I've been leaving fresh flowers at the graveside each week. Just like you asked me to."

I closed my eyes. I could picture it so clearly in my head. Becky walking the winding path, pausing beneath the massive oak tree. Removing the old flowers and placing fresh, new ones there. Before my mind could read the headstone, I closed out the image. "I knew you would."

After our good-byes, I hung up and listened to the soft sound of waves rolling onto the sand. Pretty jaded. That was pretty much an understatement.

· · · · ·

"Mom tells me you'd like to try diving." Bray had stepped outside onto the back patio and was now blocking my perfect view of the ocean.

"Uh . . ." Yes, I was a great conversationalist.

"Cory and I are taking some people out on a charter dive trip. You could go. It wouldn't cost you anything. Free trip." He grinned down at me.

In the last few days, Bray had made plans for the family—including me—to hike the rainforest, visit the unusual animal sanctuary where the jaguars lived, and take a boat trip to the Great

Blue Hole. It wasn't that I didn't appreciate being included, I just sometimes felt like a third wheel. I wasn't part of the family, but there I was, smack in the middle of family photos — which Bray insisted on taking everywhere we went. Sometimes he'd ask me to take pictures of the four of them, but half the time he was behind the camera. It almost felt like he was trying — a little too hard — to make me comfortable. I had no idea how to take that.

"I don't know how to dive."

"No problem. Cory, the guy with the awesome house, is a dive master. They do a one-day class. It won't give you a full dive certification, but will cover you for the dive on the cays."

The cays. Ooooooh. That made it tempting.

"Why is it free?"

"Cory's dad owns a dive shop here on the island. He has to go back to the States for a week and Cory asked if I'd go and help him out. I told him you were coming with me. The group of tourists already paid for the boats, so it's all good. Room for one more."

Perfect. Though my desire to see the cays was great, there just seemed to be something disingenuous about this offer, the smile that accompanied it, the charming voice.

"It's really sweet of you, but I don't think I want to go."

He shrugged. "Yes you do." Bray dropped onto the swing beside me. I could feel those blue eyes penetrating right through the lie I was getting ready to tell him.

I huffed. He was right. I did want to go. Especially since it wasn't going to be him and a bunch of friends — if that had been the case, no way. He and Cory were taking tourists. I'd be just another sightseer along for the ride. And I would finally get to experience the cays and all that magical clear-blue water. I must have been smiling.

I felt him lean closer. "You're gonna love it." The words vibrated close to my ear. Warm breath feathered my arm, floating down to my hands and disappearing into the coastal breeze.

"Diving. It's ... it's a little scary." I glanced over at him because I needed him to know, really know, that the whole idea frightened me because I'd be putting my life in his and Cory's hands. Sure, I knew people went diving every day, and I was pretty sure Cory had never killed anyone. But diving was dangerous. And I didn't turn over my life to people easily. Trust was an issue for me. I'd trusted Michael and look what that got me.

I'd trusted God. I didn't understand why good things happened to bad people and bad things happened to good people. But the fact was, they did. All the time. Again, trust threw me a curve ball. I searched Bray, the planes of his face cutting a strong profile beside me. He was motionless for a few moments, as if he understood the battle going on inside. But then he pivoted to face me, his deep-water blue eyes filled with a mix of certainty and strength. Bray's tongue slipped out to moisten his lips. "I'll keep you safe, Summer. I swear."

My heart fluttered. I wanted to believe Bray was using his alpha-male skills on me like he'd probably done on a thousand other girls in high school and college. But there was something honest in the depths of his eyes. My mind begged to trust it. My heart assured me trusting him was a one way ticket to nowhere good.

That night, I opened my Bible for the first time in almost a year. I read for a while and my gaze seemed to stall on one line. *I wish above all things that you would prosper and be in health.*

I thought on that for a while. What was it saying to me? Was it God's message to me that good things—like prospering and being in health—were His plan for me? It didn't say *above all else I wish you sickness and poverty.* There had been a time when I read this book with fervor. But when the crisis came, I felt like God had given up on me. But what if I had it backward? What if I gave up on him?

I'd agreed to go on the dive trip. But I couldn't quite as quickly open my heart to a God I felt had left me when I needed Him most.

• • • • •

It was a two-dive day, and by the end of the second dive, I was exhausted. And amazed. The ocean floor was alive with its own city of fish and coral. The underwater world was so quiet, I felt like I could have left a thousand cares there and they would have floated to the bottom and waited, trapped in the endless shifting and swaying of the seafloor. Scuba diving could easily hook me. It was possible it already had.

I was also amazed at how professional Bray had been. He'd assisted Cory in getting gear ready, had helped pull sandwiches from the coolers on the tiny island where we stopped to eat lunch, and had been, in a word, charming.

And I wasn't the only one to notice. The group of tourists was there for a family reunion, complete with one colossal-attitude teen girl who rolled her eyes so often I thought they would stick. She was also incredibly distracting. Her bikini top had about as much material as two cotton balls held together with silly string, and the bottoms were a miniscule triangle that resembled a sticky note cut on the diagonal.

She'd flirted with Bray all day. By the end of lunch, he was flirting back, which was kind of sickening because she couldn't have been older than fifteen. And that made me think that those little glimpses I'd seen of something deeper in him might've all been part of his game. Or maybe he really was a dive master on a trip with tourists and it was his job to make sure they had a good time, even the obnoxious teenager. I didn't really have a good read on Bray. And that bothered me because I liked to feel like I had a handle on the world. Probably why I preferred to keep my feet on solid ground. I wasn't a fan of surprises.

I was in Bray's group. He'd kept me close throughout both dives, likely because he didn't want a drowned nanny on his conscience.

At that moment, however, he was lost in preparing for departure now that our island lunch was done. From the cays, the two boats would head back to mainland Belize. I hated for the day to be over. I'd miss the clear water, the jumping fish. I had to admit, it was freeing, floating beneath the surface, seeing another world, one so much bigger than my own. Since Michael died, my world had gotten smaller and smaller. Maybe fear had turned me inward. If so, I needed something, something monumental to shake me out of that. If I stayed on this track, I'd end up spending my whole life alone and bitter. In many ways, I was already there.

As I got onto the boat ahead of the group, intending to soak up a few last memories by myself, I noticed the teen girl's mom.

Cory was putting the gear into his boat when I approached. "Is she okay?"

He followed my gaze to the woman. She was still trembling and had been for the last half hour. "I told her to wear a wetsuit, at least a shorty like the one Bray had you wear. People don't realize the water zaps your body heat even though it feels warm. Looks like she got too cold and now she can't get warmed up."

"What should we do?" The woman's lips were a strange bluish-purple. Not blue like little kids who spend too long in a chilly swimming pool. Dead blue. Like Michael's had been.

"She'll be okay. I'd build a fire if we had time." He pointed overhead to a group of dark gray clouds bubbling on the horizon. "But that's headed this way. Best to get back as quickly as possible."

I started helping him by placing dive gear into the boat.

Bray waded through the water from the second boat over to us. "I've been watching her for the last few minutes. You need to get her back now, Cory." I could see the worry in his eyes. That was a new thing, and it caused me to worry too, but I kept working.

Bray nodded toward the shivering woman. "Go ahead and take her back. I can finish gathering stuff up here."

I looked behind me at all the gear that remained. "I'll stay and help."

Bray's face creaked into a smile.

I pointed to the storm clouds. "You'll get caught in that if I abandon you, and what would your mother say?" Nothing like bringing up a guy's mom to knock the wind out of him.

"Oh, I can stay and help too," Little Miss Bikini chirped, skipping over from the other boat.

Oh, please no. Dear Lord, if you love me, please no.

Bray shrugged. "Sure."

And that fast, my prayer died.

We got Cory and everyone else loaded, and Bray was pushing their boat off the beach when bikini girl's dad insisted she come with them. I breathed a sigh of relief. Maybe my prayer for deliverance had made it to heaven. Now, Bray and I would be alone. I kicked at the sand. Oh, that wasn't much better.

We took turns glancing at the approaching storm, watching Cory's boat disappear from view, and concentrating on loading the rest of the gear. By the time we were done, the mud-colored clouds, complete with flashes of angry lightning, were nearly upon us.

"We're going to have to book it to get back," Bray said.

Bray started the engine and pushed us off the beach. He'd just put the boat on full throttle when he paused and looked back. "Where's the other cooler?"

I searched the boat, and then remembered. "Cory rinsed it out and left it to dry against a rock."

Bray pressed the throttle. "He'll have to go back for it tomorrow."

I put my hand over his. "It's right at the edge of the water. If we leave it, there's no way it'll be there. We have to go back."

"It's just a cooler."

"I told him I would make sure we got it. But—" I looked up at the clouds pressing down on us. "Maybe I could buy him a new one."

"Yeah, if you have a few hundred dollars lying around."

My eyes rounded.

"They're specially made for the dive boat. He'll just have to turn it in on his insurance."

That made me angry. "I gave my word, Bray. That may not mean anything to you, but it matters to me. Unless—" my eyes darted across the sky. "Unless we're putting ourselves in danger."

"Nah, I think we can make it." And he turned the boat back to the island and ran her full out until we were practically on top of the beach.

Bray grabbed the cooler and backed the boat off the shore just as the first fat drops of rain began, and the storm got worse than we expected faster than we anticipated. I held a towel around my shoulders as the howling wind slammed against me. The boat was like a cork in a bathtub, bobbing, and rocking with every blast of air that seemed conflicted on which way to blow. Waves became swells, and we rolled up one only to crash down the other side.

Bray's face was a mask of attention, devoted solely to navigating the storm. Lightning struck the water, something I'd never seen before. Right after, everything on the boat got bright. I clamped my hands over my face as a crash louder than thunder rocked my whole being. It shook me from the inside out, and I wondered if the lightning had struck me.

Bray had released the helm and it spun unguarded, the boat following the chaotic rotation. He righted us just as a huge swell crested on the side of the boat. Water flooded the boat deck. I felt my body being hurled forward and scrambled to grab something, but there was nothing there but air, rain, and sea spray. I landed against the rock-hard wall of Bray's body.

His arm came around me as he fought the helm with his other hand. "It's gonna be okay. We've just got to power through it."

I was locked under his arm, the only place that felt safe, and he was willing to keep me right there, but he needed both hands on the wheel. Reluctantly, I pushed from him. "I'm okay," I assured him, then grabbed the railing.

He gave me a weak smile. At the front of the boat, a compartment popped open on the next wave. Orange peeked from inside. "Summer, put on a life jacket."

I hadn't even thought of one until he said it. And he hadn't said it until he saw it. How stupid could we be? I worked my way to the front of the boat and grabbed a jacket. They smelled musty, even in the wind, the scent so strong it took my breath. When I went to snap it closed around my midsection, I noticed the trembling in my hands. I finally got it shut and carried one back to Bray. He shook his head.

"Put it on," I yelled over the storm.

He huffed and slipped his arm through the opening. He wasn't trembling like me. He seemed solid, except for the tension around his mouth and eyes. I took it as a good sign. He was an accomplished boater. Maybe he was used to navigating weather like this.

But when his warm eyes turned to look at mine, I knew this was new territory. "I've lost power," he said. Something in my heart died right there. I knew we weren't getting out.

CHAPTER 4

Summer

We bobbed in the water for what felt like hours. I'd curled into a ball and tried to keep the soaking wet towel tucked around me to hold in what little body heat I had. I was wearing only my swimsuit, a T-shirt, and shorts, and I wished I'd brought a pair of sweats. Or a fur coat. Or a slicker. Rain pelted the side of my face, and I lay there like a helpless baby watching Bray try to steer a boat that was impossible to guide. I didn't know what happened between the helm and the rudder, but whatever it was, he had little, if any, control. The motor had long since stopped, and we were being dragged through the ocean by wind carrying us farther and farther away from the mainland.

Bray's white T-shirt was soaked and clung to his arms where muscles bulged from fighting the waves and movement. I stared at a spot on his shoulder where the shirt was see-through. His collarbone rose and fell with each breath. When he caught me staring, he winked.

I tried to smile, but when I did, my eyes filled with tears. I held my breath, trying not to make the whole thing worse, but the pressure in my head finally broke the dam and tears sprung. I reached from under the towel to wipe my eyes, which was stupid, really, as my face was slick with the mix of rain and seawater, but tears just seemed so desperately weak when Bray was putting up such a strong front. My hand shook so hard, it was like a drum against my cheek. My fingers were cold and dead already.

Then he was there. Crowded around me and placing his hands over mine. His face was inches from me and I fought to lean up, but he held me still. "I won't let anything happen to you, Summer."

And then he was gone as quickly as he came. I swiped my eyes and looked down at my hand, no longer shaking. Maybe we were going to get out of this after all. He'd sounded so sure. So certain. Maybe our rescue was just seconds away.

"I see something up ahead," he said. "Looks like we might have found land."

Bray

It wasn't mainland Belize—that much I knew. The wind had whipped us in multiple directions, but if my sense of direction was right, the mainland was far away. What I hadn't told Summer was I didn't really like what I'd seen when the lightning lit the sky. Yes, something was out there, and yes, we were headed right for it. The problem was it looked like a mountain jutting up from the water and touching the sky. If it had been a nice sandy shoreline—even in these swells—I could get us there, even if we had to swim. But a rocky cliff? No, we were goners for sure.

As the lightning and thunder argued above us, I wiped my eyes to make out the shape ahead. One edge seemed to stair-step down, which meant there might be a spot we could swim to, but I couldn't see clearly enough to know what lay beyond. Was it shoreline? Or just miles of more water?

With each great flash of white light in the sky, the rocks came closer. I glanced over at Summer, who was curled up on the seat with her knees drawn to her chest. She was shivering, but had a smile for me when I looked down at her. I should have sent her back with Cory in the other boat. But when she volunteered to stay behind—stay with me—something swelled inside my heart. Summer was unique, and I knew there were layers and layers to her. And knowing that made me feel really bad about asking Mom and Dad to send her back home to Florida. It had been that day after our visit to the ruins. I had wanted to convince them that family time—just our family—was important if this was our last summer together.

The lightning lit up the world again, and I realized we were getting closer, moving faster as the wind picked up and chose a single direction—straight for the cliffs. Could we survive the impact? I wasn't sure. If the boat sank, would we have the energy to fight the mighty current until we could find a safe place to get onto the shore? If, of course, there even was a shore. Summer already looked worn out. I was also tired from the day, from the stress and fighting a boat I couldn't steer. If we didn't slow, at least a little, we'd be like a car hitting a brick wall.

"Brace yourself," I told her. "We're going to hit the rocks."

Just before impact, a wind grabbed the side of the boat and thrust us hard to the right of the rocks. There! I saw shoreline. "Summer, I see—" But I didn't get to finish, because the wind knocked us back. We were going to hit the rocks. There was no way to stop it.

Summer

I heard the scraping and punching just before we felt the impact. Bray dove on top of me and I was surrounded by him, long legs and arms, chest against my side. I sucked a huge breath when water whooshed up over the side of the boat, sending our bodies helplessly out to sea. Instantly there was a tug, pulling me under. I fought, trying to stay topside, but every breath in held more water and less oxygen. My legs lashed out, kicking, and I felt Bray groan against me. He was holding me. Trying to help me. The water was so cold. I needed to be still and let him help me. Through eyes that burned, I looked behind me for the boat, but it was already moving away from us so fast, we'd never catch it. We were helpless, bobbing in the water.

As I tried to relax, something hit Bray in the back, and I felt the impact through both our life jackets. The cascading water pulled us away from it; flashes of whitecaps tumbled then slammed him back into the dark line before us. The rocks. He was being pounded by the rocks.

"Swim," I yelled through my sea-scalded throat.

He unwound his legs from mine and we both swam hard and fast away from the rocks, but it was no use. Each wave dragged us right back. Exhaustion worked my muscles into Jell-O, and I think we both realized swimming was futile. On the next wave, Bray lunged, one arm hanging on to my life vest. He pulled himself onto the jagged ledge while keeping me from slamming into it. The rain had slowed, and a stream of moonlight hit the rocks so that they looked like dark ice picks jutting out of the water. We'd be shredded if we stayed there.

He got to his feet but stayed bent at the waist, dragging me along the edge just out of reach of the rock shards. I could hear his muffled groans as the sharp stones were no doubt cutting into his flesh. The storm wound down as the rocks became less jagged. When Bray pulled me from the water, I sank into mud. Fear of being dragged back into the water took hold of me and I screamed and jerked free of the muddy sand. A wave hit me and almost buckled my knees. It was hard to walk in the mud. I clung to Bray who snatched me up completely out of the water. I dangled there in his arms for a moment, hanging on and breathing short, tiny gasps of air. His eyes rolled and his body went limp. But we were on solid ground. Mostly. He dropped and I tried to catch his weight as he fell, but there was no strength to call on. I fell beside him. Waves washed up onto his cheek and I feared the ocean would open its angry mouth and swallow him, so I pulled myself up, grabbed the corner of his life jacket, and began to tug. When he wouldn't budge, I screamed, got a better grip, and tugged again. Adrenaline must have surged because I was able to drag him, my feet digging into the muddy, sandy ground. The texture made it difficult to get any sort of leverage, but what I lacked in ability, I made up for in sheer determination. Bray had saved my life. Maybe multiple times. No way would I let the sea win this tug of war. And I told it so.

"You can't have him." My teeth were gritted so tightly, I thought the back ones might break off. In answer, a huge wave hit us, knocking me off my feet and pulling Bray a few yards back into the abyss. "No," I screamed, scrambling up again. "You. Can't. Have. Him."

He was twenty yards from the waves before I stopped pulling. Exhausted and with water running down my face and neck, I dropped to my knees. And right there, I cried. Because I'd said those words once before in my lifetime and they'd done me no good at all.

Bray

I jerked awake to the sensation of the sun burning my eyelids. The sharp rays caused me to attempt to turn onto my side. Every muscle in my body ached. It was hard to move. I tilted my head up to see why and found Summer half lying on me, her hands clutching my life jacket in a death grip. I moved her hair to see her face, but she groaned. *She's hurt.* That single thought snapped me into action. My eyes scanned the immediate area. Rocks on one side, beach on the other. I shook her, hoping she wouldn't hear the panic in my voice. "Wake up!"

Sand caked the thick brown lashes that hooded her eyes. Her head moved slightly. She blinked several times, frowned, and then there they were, those green seas of calm. "We're alive?" she croaked through a throat that sounded about like mine felt.

When she leaned up to move from me, a sharp pain hit my side. I winced. She took this as an invitation to throw herself off.

"Did you break something?" she said, and before I could answer, her hands were unbuckling the life jacket and throwing it open. She stared down at my chest, a frown on her face and her green eyes darting across my midsection. The hand she put to her face was caked with dirt and sand. "I don't know what to do."

It would be comical, if it wasn't so bad. I pulled in a breath, poked around until my finger found the exact spot of the pain. "I've had cracked ribs before. I'll survive." When I went to sit up, she tried to help. I shook my head and did it myself, moving at my own pace. Which was slow.

Once in a seated position, I examined her. Her hair lay in clumps around her face; it was either still wet or so full of sand it couldn't dry properly. No cuts or bruises on her face. Jacket intact. Legs also caked with mud and dirt, but she had great legs, and let's face it, nothing could change that.

She smiled. "You're getting a little color back into your cheeks."

All over, I wanted to correct her, but didn't. We both removed our life vests. "Are you hurt?"

She raised her hands. "Guess not. That was horrifying."

I nodded, not wanting to burst her bubble, but I didn't really think the nightmare was over yet. This island was too quiet.

"Do you know where we are?" she asked. She knew I didn't. I

could see it in her eyes, but she was searching for something, anything to give her a little hope.

"No."

Her green eyes dropped. "Surely there are people here," she barely whispered.

"I hope so. Let's look around."

Summer

We both took our time standing. Bray had cracked ribs—so he said—but I had to wonder if they were completely broken, from the way he moved with one hand pressed against his ribcage and wincing with every breath. But each time I made eye contact, he painted on a smile or winked. He didn't want me scared. But I was scared. We'd crashed, the boat had sunk beneath us or drifted off into the abyss somewhere, and now we were lost, standing on a deserted beach, staring into the foliage of an island he didn't know.

"Hey." He captured my chin between his thumb and forefinger and raised my head to look at him. "It's okay. We're alive."

His blue eyes had lightened from the dark, intense shade they'd been last night, and his sandy colored hair lay in tiny spikes on his forehead. Like mine, the strands were full of real sand which made his hair look thicker.

"We're alive," I echoed. It's funny how we take life for granted when there's no threat to it. Since last summer, there'd been plenty of times I'd wished I was dead, just to stop hurting, just to quiet the pain. But I realized it's easy to think that way until death actually tries to take you. My mind, my flesh, and my spirit didn't want to die, no matter what my heart said. I wanted to live. And apparently, my body was willing to fight, violently if necessary, to accomplish it. Blood worked its way through my chest, limbs, and head. Everything hurt, but I was breathing. For the first time in a long time, I thanked God I was alive, and if I was going to live through something like this, I was glad I wasn't alone.

"Do you think the other boat made it back to the mainland?" I asked Bray.

He stared at the horizon for a few seconds. "Yes. I should have insisted you go with them. It's my fault you're here."

"It's my fault we went back for the cooler."

"No, the responsibility to get you back safely was mine. I'm sorry, Summer."

I shrugged. "No worries. Like you said, we're alive." I pivoted and searched the area inland of the beach. Before us, a wall of trees and brush waited. "Looks ominous."

Bray turned and followed my gaze beyond the sand, beyond the layer of shrubs and bushes to the deeper part of the island. He cupped one hand around his mouth, the other pressed against his ribcage as he yelled, "Hello?"

We waited. Trees and a forested area closed off the view. Who knew what was inside there. He did a 360° turn, examining the lay of the land, and hollered again. I mimicked him, though my voice didn't carry far. Off to our left were the rocks he'd walked across. Seeing their rough edges made me think of the night before and what he'd done to protect me. I looked down. There were cuts and scrapes between his ankles and knees, but his feet were still in the tennis shoes he'd worn.

My feet were in sneakers too, though the side of one was ripped wide open. "You saved me from the rocks last night."

"It was a team effort."

"Thank you, Bray."

"You're welcome, Summer."

I'd noticed him taking deeper breaths, testing the cracked ribs. "How are they?"

"Actually feeling better. Maybe they're just bruised."

I wasn't sure that was the truth, but I wouldn't call him on it right now. "So, where to first?" We'd sort of already given up on the "yell and be rescued" scenario. By this time, I'd done all the standing on the beach and looking around I could. The sky was hazy gray, otherwise I'd recommend sitting in the shade and waiting.

He pointed to the rocks. "We need to see if the boat is still there. We may be able to salvage some things from it if it didn't float away. Also, if it's visible, a search party will be able to see it from the air." He turned away from me. "Just in case the island is uninhabited."

I didn't like the way he said that. It sounded very final—like he'd already determined we were the only people here. But he couldn't know that.

We climbed onto the slippery rocks as softer waves pelted the land. Where the sea dribbled over the stones, it sounded like a faucet, a lovely stream of running water. My mouth was cotton, throat still scalded from swallowing seawater and screaming the night before. Thirst for water caused me to lick my dry, cracked lips. I slipped on a rock. "How can these things be so slick, yet so jagged?"

Bray led the way. "Be careful—they'll cut your ankles to pieces if you don't pay attention to where you're stepping."

I inspected his ankles. Yes, that was for sure. After a while, we reached a rock big enough for both of us to stand on. I squinted in the bright sun that had decided to poke through the clouds. The searing reflection bounced off the water and stung my eyes. It took a bit for them to adjust; when they did, I took in the expanse of open water before us. Miles and miles of ocean. The sound of waves lapping against the rocky terrain kept rhythm as we watched the waves roll and ripple. For several minutes, we didn't speak. Maybe we couldn't. I felt very small beside the big sea and had to look behind me at the island to remind myself I stood on solid ground. After a while, the muscles in my legs began to shake and I dropped to a seated position.

Bray walked a few yards away. "Summer, look." He pointed to a spot at the water's edge. I couldn't see it from my vantage point, so I stood and moved toward him.

There, below the water, were the remains of the boat. Just beyond it, dark, dark blue. My heart beat a little faster, as if rescue was only minutes away, but that was silly. The boat was down there and we were up here and it wasn't seaworthy anyway. "How far down is that?"

"Maybe thirty feet." Bray was busy examining the area around us, so I tore my gaze from the boat. Not far away I saw a cooler, upside down and caught between two rocks. Bray offered me a hand and together we made our way to it. "Good thing we went back for it, huh?" He grinned.

I nodded and refused the voice in my head that reminded me a cooler was of little good with nothing to put in it. "Bray, over there." A few feet beyond the cooler, something bright green caught my attention. Bray got to it quickly, sailing over the rocks like a pro. He held up the mask and snorkel.

I nodded, enthusiastic because it felt like we were making progress.

Bray sat down and unlaced his tennis shoes.

"What are you doing?"

He folded the strap back and held the mask to his face to see if it fit him. He'd done the same thing with me when I was doing my dive lesson. Breathing in a bit of air caused the mask to remain attached when he removed his hands. No leaks. The first threads of panic started weaving through my system. I grabbed his arm. It was warm and strong beneath my fingers. "Bray, what are you doing?"

He nodded toward the boat. "I need to go down and see if I can salvage anything from it."

That's what I was afraid of. "You said it's thirty feet down."

"Maybe. Maybe less."

The thought of him entering the water and leaving me alone caused my chest to squeeze. My head shook from side to side. "I don't think it's a good idea. We need to stay together."

"Summer, there's an emergency kit on the boat, there may be water. My throat's raw from being thirsty. Yours has to be too. We can't survive without water. And my dive knife is inside one of the compartments. We may need those things if we aren't rescued right away."

Not rescued? That was inconceivable. We had an entire island to check out. Surely someone lived here and there would be people searching for us. "Let's put you in the water as a last resort, 'kay? I mean, the boat's not going anywhere."

He stopped. "See that dark water?"

Of course I did; the back of the boat disappeared into it.

"The boat is on a sandbar. The waves could drag it right off the edge at any time. This may be our only chance to salvage anything from it."

I bit my cracked lip, knowing he had to go. And I knew that his leaving meant I'd be alone. That thought terrified me. "Okay."

"I promise I'll be right back."

And I believed him.

Bray glanced up at the sky. "I'd say I've got a good two or three hours before dusk. We must have been asleep half the day. Be back in a sec."

It was eerily quiet with Bray beneath the surface. I counted the seconds as I watched his strong body, now blurred by the water, dive deeper and deeper. Going farther and farther away from me. I was no stranger to fear, but I couldn't seem to stop my racing heart as the image of Bray disappeared as he reached the back of the boat. I jumped to my feet, hands covering my mouth as if the scream was right there, just waiting to come out. Unable to see him, I squeezed my eyes shut and did the only thing with the power to hold me together. I prayed. When I opened my eyes, I could see him again, now at the edge of the boat. He came back up quickly, using the railing as a springboard. When he breached the surface, I released the breath I'd been holding. That was the first *real* prayer I'd prayed in a year. Where anger had once caused me to run away from God, desperation was drawing me to Him.

Bray swam to me. "Okay, I may have to make several trips down, but it's not beyond my reach." He was already out of breath. I didn't think he could do it several more times. His mask had fogged over a bit. He spit in it and smeared the spit around. I'd seen Cory do the same thing. Cheaper than No-Fog, Cory had told me. At the time I'd thought it was really disgusting. Now, I appreciated the fact we were equipped with a natural form of anti-fog for occasions like this.

"Be careful," I hollered as he dove again. A couple minutes later, he brought up the first survival items. I used the cooler as a treasure box, filling it with the things Bray carried to the surface. I'd wait at the edge of the rock, and when he rose I'd take each item from him. He retrieved his dive knife first, but kept it with him on the following trips, strapped to his leg. The waves were gentle against the rocks, so he was able to rest at the edge between trips down. Before diving, he'd take a couple minutes to sip the air. "Does that make it easier to hold your breath?"

"It fills your blood with oxygen."

Oh. I guess oxygen-filled blood was better for wreck diving.

The cooler was filling up. We had a section of rope, a first aid kit, and two small buoys. I refused to let my excitement at our newly acquired items wane. But really, with this mix of things, there was little we could do. Possibly build a very small floating first aid station.

"There's not much else on board that wasn't washed away. I'm going after the anchor next."

"What?" I dropped the first aid kit I'd been inspecting from the outside. "What do you mean you're going after the anchor?"

He moved the mask to the top of his head, snorkel dangling by his mouth. His shoulders hovered in the water line. "We could use it."

"Why would we need an anchor?"

He shrugged. "I don't know."

I stood from the rock and put my hands on my hips. "*I don't know* isn't a good enough reason. It's an *anchor*, Bray. Used to hold things *under* the water."

He chuckled. "I won't take any chances. I already cut it loose. I'll just wind some of the rope around my ankle . . ."

I dropped onto my knees and grabbed his shoulders. "Don't you dare!"

He started laughing.

The urge to smack him almost overtook me.

"I'm kidding." He took the mask off his head and flung water from his hair, then rubbed an open hand down his face.

"Thank God. Get out of the water, because it's making me nervous." The late afternoon sun was still hot, but less so than before. The breeze had cooled and the island was preparing to settle in for the evening. With no rescue plane all day, we'd need to settle down as well.

"I was kidding about wrapping the rope around me. I really am going after the anchor though. It's heavy. We could use it to break open coconuts or use it to hammer a stake into the ground. It could be a valuable resource for us, Summer." The mask went back on his head and slid over his eyes. Before I could argue, he winked with one goggled eye and dove.

It took him three tries to get the anchor to the surface. On the second try, I noticed a group of fish jumping out of the water a couple hundred yards from where he dove. On the last try and just as he breached the surface, fighting to swim with the anchor in one hand, I saw the reason why the fish were so active.

Horror sucked the air from my lungs. "Bray!" I screamed, the sound burning my throat as the gray, triangle-shaped fin punctured the surface of the water.

Bray glanced behind him then swam toward me, arms and hands slashing the sea, legs and feet pumping, throwing arcs of water as he moved. The fin drew closer but Bray kept up the pace, his body chewing up the distance to me and safety. The pounding of my heart grew louder and louder in my ears, stealing the oxygen from my body for each pulse until I thought I'd pass out. Every muscle in my body tightened as if I could help propel him. The distance between him and me was closing, but the space between him and the shark closed faster. Then the fin went under water, and having watched Shark Week on the Discovery Channel, I knew what that meant. "Bray!" It was a scream and a release of all the fear that had built inside me. I was still screaming his name when he reached the rocks.

My hands plunged into the water, closed around flesh and yanked. Bray was slick and breathing hard, but just as he made it out of the water, the shark broke the surface, turned, and headed back to the dark blue. I clung to Bray, my hands fisting at his back, my face pressed against his heaving chest. Fatigued arms came around me and held me. Tension slowly released, my muscles melting into a rubbery mass. For a few minutes, neither of us spoke. The sun was riding lower in the sky now, casting an orangey glow across the ocean.

I listened as Bray's breathing slowed and closed my eyes. "Don't ever do that again," I said in a small voice.

"I dropped the anchor." His words rumbled against my ear.

I pressed closer to him, clasping my hands together at the small of his back. Bray was strong, solid. More so than I would have given him credit for. I was preparing to squeeze, but remembered his cracked ribs. "It must have been awful, carrying that stupid anchor."

"Not so bad." One of his hands, flat against my back, moved slightly—a twinge—but the sensation caused me to tighten more, cracked ribs or not.

"Well, you're not going back after it," I assured him.

We unwound from each other slowly. Bray flicked the wet hair from his eyes. "Come on. Let's carry the cooler to the sand and see what all we've got."

CHAPTER 5

Bray

I hadn't really allowed myself to get scared. I needed to protect Summer, and that emotion overrode all others. Until the shark. I'd seen the absolute terror on Summer's face and knew what must be behind me. Like an idiot, I'd wasted precious seconds turning to confirm. But, hey, seeing is believing, and maybe *that's* what saved my life. A gray fin coming at you can really put you into high gear.

It was getting late and bugs were out. Their buzzing songs filled the early evening with more racket than we'd heard all day. It pressed on us, a noisy reminder that we didn't belong here. This was their territory. That's when I noticed the giant palm. "Summer!"

She rushed over and drew a quick breath as I tilted the edge of the palm leaf toward her. There in the center of each leaf was a small reservoir of water.

"Go ahead," I told her, and she bent at the waist, holding her hair from her face. She sipped the first water we'd had. I held several more leaves open for her.

"You next," she said and held the leaves for me until we'd drained every single one. They tasted a bit earthy, but it was water, and we needed it desperately.

"Do you think there are more of these?"

"I don't see any others. Any plant could hold some water after a rainstorm like we had, but the sun has dried most of it." I gathered some brush from the edge of woods while Summer wound the rope around her arm. The bugs were loud at the edge of the forest. I smacked my neck, obliterating a mosquito. They didn't seem to be bad on the beach, so I dropped the brush near the water's edge and hoped there would be a lighter in the first aid kit.

We'd only had a little water in nearly twenty-four hours, and this was becoming my main concern. Summer's lips were cracked and bleeding in one spot. Her skin was burned, and with all that moisture cooked out of her, she had to be thirsty, though she didn't complain.

"I never heard a boat or a rescue plane all day."

"They may be searching other areas. We'll have to assume that we'll be here for the night."

She closed her arms over her body, wrapping in as tight of a ball as she could. We sat on either side of the cooler. I pulled the first aid kit from it, moved the cooler aside, and sat the kit gently where the cooler had mashed the sand into a tabletop. "Here goes."

Inside we found basic first aid. "We've got bandages, Neosporin. Oh, and lip balm." I held it out to Summer.

She dusted off her index finger and used it to smear balm across her chapped mouth. "Aaahhh." She rubbed her lips together and closed her eyes. "You next." She reached to hand it back to me, but paused when she noticed my sand-caked fingers.

I shrugged. "Don't worry. I'll get some later."

She started to put the lid back on then paused. Her green eyes met mine, tentative, but also determined. She swallowed, swiped her finger into the lip balm again, and leaned toward me. Summer had to scoot closer to reach my mouth, but did so, her hand steady and moving in. She didn't look at me, just concentrated on her finger. A half-moon nail was visible above the fingertip that came closer and closer to my lips. Something in me wanted to lean too, and close the distance faster, but I stayed still. Her fingertip finally made contact and slid with a gentle stroke from the center of my bottom lip outward. Velvet smooth skin pressed a little harder as she neared the edge. In the closeness, her eyes were flecked with tiny bits of gold. I couldn't look away. When she encountered a rough patch on my lip, she flashed a frown and rubbed back and forth over it, pressing harder as she went. Then she dove into the lip balm again. This time she started on the outside corner of my top lip and brushed the smooth, waxy balm over me. Her finger was cool, and her fingernail scraped against the skin just above my lip, causing my neck to break out with goose bumps and my mouth to feel like it had been hit with a mini electric current. My eyes drifted closed for half a second because nothing had ever felt so good.

Summer replaced the lid to the balm, but didn't move away. "I'm sorry you lost your anchor." Soft words came from her mouth, complete with hot breath that feathered over me.

"It was probably stupid to go after it." And it was stupid for me to react to Summer's finger against my lips, but a little part of me had. Just like that little part of me loved sharing the underwater world with her. Summer was nothing like the girls I usually went for and that made her ... a bit intriguing.

"You couldn't have known about the shark." Again, she tilted close so she could see every crack in my lips, her words warm across my skin, eyes scanning as if making sure she hadn't missed any spots. My chest squeezed at the nearness of her mouth to mine. She smelled like the sea and life and promise. It was a mistake to be this close to her. Because something primal stirred in me, shooting through my system and wrapping tightly around the lowest part of my stomach. Suddenly, my senses hit high alert. A few moments ago, Summer had been my ally. The person I was shipwrecked with. We were equal. Both committed to helping one another. But now, with her gaze scraping across my lips, Summer was a woman. Even her scent had changed.

Rather than continue to think about what this new awareness meant, I concentrated on the words she'd spoken. "I should have known about the shark, Summer. I know not to swim at dusk, because that's when sharks are feeding. Dusk and sunrise. Also, my leg was cut, and I would have been bleeding all that time in the water. It was a stupid mistake. I'm sorry."

The sun was setting, but in the dim light remaining, her eyes smiled. "It's okay. We're alive."

I had to chuckle. I wasn't much of a partner or protector. All I'd accomplished was getting her lip balm. Great; when they find us dead, our lips will be moist and strawberry flavored. From now on, I'd be more careful. What if the shark had gotten to me? That would have left Summer on this island alone until rescue. "In the morning, we have to find water."

She swallowed, and her eyes drifted inland where the canopy of trees overhung vegetation as dark as the water behind us. We were face-to-face, two tiny specs on an unforgiving island. Alone.

I dropped my gaze. My fingers fumbled through the kit because suddenly there was a wash of red across Summer's cheeks, visible enough to notice even in the failing light. I chanced a glance at her. She stared at her fingertip as if it had had a mind of its own and had tracked the path to my lip without her consent. Summer was embarrassed. She replaced the lid and dropped the balm into the kit, then quickly clasped her hands in her lap. I hid my grin and forced the emotions that were flickering in me aside. It would take all my energy to keep us alive until help came. Why hadn't they come already? The entire day I kept expecting to hear a rescue plane. But nothing. I didn't want to scare Summer, but our situation was quickly becoming dire.

"Why didn't we see a rescue plane all day?" Summer asked. Had she read my mind?

"I'm not sure. Tomorrow we'll get some kind of signal set up. Honestly, I figured they'd have come by now. I know my dad. He isn't a man who waits around. But I guess it could take time to secure a plane or helicopter." I shrugged and focused on the kit. "Look, needle and thread. In the morning, we'll stitch up that rip on your sneakers."

She nodded and examined the small pair of scissors. She pointed. "Tweezers too. We can perform a very tiny operation."

"I was hoping for a lighter."

She dove into the kit until her fingers closed around a little plastic square. "Matches!" Her elation quickly dwindled when she held up the closed package and water dripped out of it. She tossed it on the sand.

"Still worth trying." I opened the pack and inspected the contents. It was soaking wet except for one corner. One match head was lighter in color than the others. I carefully removed the match. We gathered the brush, knowing the match may only stay lit a second. Before I could strike it, Summer grabbed my hand and closed her eyes.

"*Please*, God. We need this to work." Her eyes popped back open and she nodded.

A tiny flame burst, then fizzled out. But an ember dropped and lay glowing on the bits of brush we'd collected. It felt like an eternity before it took, both of us staring down and scared to breathe. Thin lines of smoke curled up, and soon a nice tear-shaped flame emerged.

One small obstacle conquered. But I knew I'd lie awake beside the fire smelling Summer and her fresh scent and wondering what to do to maintain my sanity.

These islands were unforgiving.

Being stuck on one with someone like Summer? Impossible.

Summer

It was still dark when I woke up the first time. I had curled up as close to the fire as I dared. Bray slept on the other side of the flames. He must've stoked up the fire because it burned brightly and with more flames than I remembered it having at twilight.

I leaned up on one elbow to look out over the water. It was a shadowy, empty abyss, with waves moving toward us then retreating back into the dark loneliness. I'd always enjoyed the sound of the ocean. But not now. Not here. It was a bitter reminder of where I was. Shipwrecked on an island.

I tried to not question why a search plane hadn't come. But with the ocean on one side of me forcing cool air up over my body and with the firelight on the other side of me, the question rolled over and over in my head. Where was the rescue plane? Wasn't it standard to send out a search party when people disappeared on the water? Surely they hadn't given up on us.

Watching Bray throughout the day, something had become clear. Like me, Bray had expected a rescue team. But as the day wore on, his attitude had shifted from waiting mode to action mode. He'd said tomorrow we'd have to find water. If he was expecting a plane or boat, he would be staying visible on the beach, not venturing deeper into the island. The weight of our situation caused my limbs to tremble. What if … what if …

I closed off the sob that swelled in my throat. But another followed. Tears sprung to my eyes. I was so thirsty, I wouldn't have thought tears possible, yet there they were, blurring the golden flame before me, causing the dancing flames to swell. I lay back down and pulled myself into a ball, drawing my knees up to my chest. The ground moved beneath me, gritty sandpaper sticking to my sunburned skin. And this made me cry more. Silent sobs escaped as I lay there, curled in the fetal position, staring at the fire, and listening to the waves.

Bray's voice interrupted me. "Hey. Summer, what's wrong?" Groggy words accompanied the sound of him moving. In an instant he was beside me. He stretched out behind me and gently slid his hand down my exposed arm.

But I couldn't stop the tears. In fact, they increased as if I'd been holding back, and now a great dam burst, allowing my entire body to react. I wasn't one to cry. I hadn't cried like this since last summer.

Bray's hand against me was warm, littered with flecks of sand, but I didn't mind. There was body heat. I felt as though I had none of my own, and this realization caused more tears.

He whispered against my ear. I sniffed, wishing I could hold it together. "Summer," he said. "It's okay." One of his arms slid very slowly beneath my shoulder. He turned me toward him. Most of his body wasn't touching mine, just close.

"I'm sorry, Bray." It was all I could say. All I could manage.

He tucked my head into the hollow of his throat and stroked my hair. "Don't apologize. You don't have anything to apologize for." His words were little more than vibration against my cheek where it rested at his throat. There was strength in his voice.

I sniffed again and tilted to look up at him. In the darkness of only flickering light, his eyes looked black. "I'm stronger than this. I swear."

Something flashed in his eyes. Pity, maybe? I wasn't sure. "You don't have to be strong right now."

But I did. He didn't understand. I always had to be strong, because every time I thought I didn't, the universe proved me wrong. I hated crying. I hated being weak. But that's exactly how I felt: weak and lost. And all alone, except for a guy who mistakenly thought weakness was somehow okay.

I started to push away from him, but needed my bearings first. I pulled in a deep breath, causing my body to arch. When I did, Bray settled me deeper into his arms. Now, we were touching, and though every warning signal in my mind should have been going off, all I could do was stay there and accept the body heat he offered while exhaustion and hopelessness took turns on my psyche and my eyelids. Soon I found myself drifting off to sleep, tucked between Bray and the crackling fire.

• • • • •

Bray was already up and on the move when I woke. I rubbed the sleep from my eyes and tried to focus on him as he hovered over me like some strange, long-legged bird.

"What would you like for breakfast?" Smiling. He actually had a smile on his face.

"Umm." No mention of last night when I'd had my little crying fit. For that, I was thankful. I pressed my fingertips beneath my eyes to see if they were puffy.

"You can have coconut or coconut. Either one." He was proud of himself. I could hear it in his voice.

I stretched and tried to wrestle my hair into some kind of order, but it was useless. "Mmm. Coconut's my favorite."

"Good choice!" He passed me and bent to tend the fire. "I was afraid you'd already ordered room service."

I blinked the sand from my eyelids. "Oh, I did. Eggs, bacon, toast, and hot coffee. You'll have to cancel the order, though. I'd much rather have coconut." But my mouth watered at the mention of a real breakfast.

He glanced back at me over his shoulder. A half smile tilted his face, and the wind caught and lifted the hair from his forehead. I'd mustered and he was glad. It wouldn't do for him to be stranded on an island with a crybaby. He turned back to the fire, and I watched him build it up. Knees bent, hunched over the embers, breaking sticks and laying them just so across the flame.

He really was a great-looking guy. But off the island, we were people from different worlds, and his included a steady supply of parties. I knew firsthand what kind of havoc that created. What kind of carnage it left in its wake. No matter how well Bray and I got along on the island, nothing changed who he was. And who he was could be lethal to girls like me. I'd lived that once. With Michael. For Michael, I'd put on a smile and gone to the parties with him until I watched him sink bit by bit. At first, Michael didn't drink at all, then he'd have a couple beers—by the end, he was getting drunk on a regular basis. And I had no power to stop him. But I did stop going with him.

I walked away from Bray to give myself a little space.

"By the way," he said.

I turned to face him and noticed the tinge of color on his cheeks.

Bray pointed to a spot that had been cleared, a narrow path through the edge of woods. "I made a sort of makeshift bathroom through there."

"Oh. Thanks." We really were stranded. No water, little food, no bathroom.

Thankfully, Bray returned to his task, and I dipped my hand into the ocean, drawing up some water to pour over my sand-sticky legs and arms. My throat was raw from being so dry, and all that water was right there in front of me. I scooped a little more into my hand and drew it to my mouth.

His voice stopped me. Deep, rich, as close as it'd been last night when he'd held me while I cried. "I wouldn't," he said.

And I knew exactly what he meant. Saltwater would only make me thirstier. I squeezed my lips closed and splashed the water over my face.

"Good girl," he whispered. "Besides, I have something for you to drink."

I turned to face him. "Water? You found water?" The idea of drinking my fill and letting it roll over my tongue and down my throat caused my heart to pick up beats.

But the smile Bray had been wearing dissipated, and I knew there was no water. He motioned for me to follow him. We passed the fire to a makeshift table and chairs. He'd dragged a couple of large pieces of driftwood to the cooler. On the ground beside lay a pile of fresh coconut husks. Bray held out the coconut to me.

"All that for one coconut?" I pointed to the pile.

"Yeah, it was the size of a beach ball. I cut away layers and layers until I got to this." He held up the brown, furry ball.

I sat down on my driftwood.

"Careful, it's open at the top." I angled the coconut, and sure enough, there was a crack in the center of one of the three indentions. "Tip it up to your mouth. There's milk inside. It might not be Perrier, but it will help hydrate you."

Nothing had ever tasted so good. The smooth milk coated my throat and instantly helped with the thirst. Even though some shreds of the husk got into my mouth, I drank the slow droplets and sucked on the coconut to give me more. After drinking most of it, I held it out to him.

"Keep going. You need to drink it all so I can crack it open to get to the meat." His dive knife was in his hand.

My gaze narrowed on him. "What about you?"

"I already had some. You get the rest." He concentrated his attention on the knife's blade.

When I didn't move, he looked up at me. I pressed it toward him again. "I don't believe you. Your turn."

A dimple appeared then disappeared on his cheek. "Fine." Strong hands tilted it up and he sucked hungrily at the shell. A dribble of milk ran down his face. When he finished, Bray used a large rock to whack the shell until it broke into five pieces. His muscles bulged beneath his T-shirt. Breathless, he handed me a chunk still bearing moisture from the milk. I caught the drip with my lips, and then used my front teeth, chipmunk style, to gnaw at the sweet fruit. My stomach growled at the first bite. Bray worked his dive knife against his chunk, and when a fat piece fell off in his hand, he held it out to me. I bit in and sighed. "Food," I said around the white meat. "Actually a mouthful of food."

He cut another chunk and popped it into his mouth. "I'll never again complain about eating."

"You used to complain about eating?"

He shrugged. "No more than anyone else. Just griped about not knowing what I wanted or wishing I was at McDonald's when I was at Taco Bell."

My mouth watered. "I love Taco Bell."

"Yeah. Me too."

Clouds obscured the sun, giving us a few moments of shade. I welcomed it. "What's our game plan?"

"Water. Shelter. Food. In that order." He dropped his breakfast on the cooler and used his dive knife to point inland.

A cold chill swept over me. Giant vegetation loomed like guardians of the fortress woods.

"Intimidated?" Bray asked me.

"That would be an understatement." We'd survived the beach. There was the tiniest measure of confidence here at the water's edge.

"We have to, Summer. There's no water—"

"I know, I know." I dragged a breath and let it hiss from my lips. "I just . . . don't like bugs and things."

"No problem. It's not the bugs you need to worry about. It's all the animals that eat the bugs."

My eyes widened.

"I'm kidding. Listen, my dad and I have been hiking in Belize since I was Joshie's age. It's not as bad as you think."

But my heart pounded. "What about the rainforest?"

"There are some pretty big bugs in the rainforest, but there's no rainforest on this island. At least, I don't think there is." He stood and pulled me to my feet. "See that?"

I squinted above the tree line. With the sun shaded, the interior of the island was easier to see. Bray pointed to a spot where a cropping of small green mountains met the sky. I nodded.

"Looks lush there, so I'm thinking there may be fresh water. This is a good-sized island. I have no idea where this island is, exactly, but there's enough variety of terrain with the rocky section along the ocean, the beach area we're at now, and the lush interior that I don't think we'll have a problem finding more food. Shelter, we'll have to build unless there's a cave."

He must have read the horror on my face, because he instantly redirected.

"We'll want a shelter close to the beach. So no cave, okay?"

I nodded, trying to wrap my mind around cave dwelling on a deserted island. "But the number-one priority is water, right?"

"Right." I saw the concern as it crawled into Bray's eyes. He was wondering if he'd given me too much information all at once. But I could take it. I was strong.

To prove it, I said, "We can only go three days without water. And what was in the coconut is only a smidgen of what we need to replace all we've lost roasting in the sun. Plus, the merciless wind from off the water is drying us out externally. Add sweating to that and ..."

"And we need to find water, pronto."

I nodded. "Then let's go." I sounded brave.

Bray wiped his knife off on his shorts and tucked it into the sheath. He strapped the knife to his thigh. "Not just for diving anymore."

I smiled and tugged on my tennis shoes. "Hey, you stitched this."

He nodded. "Knew we'd be going inland. At least, I'd hoped you'd want to go with me."

"Did you think I'd just sit here while you go do all the work?" My arms crossed over my chest.

"No, I didn't."

"I'm not a baby, Bray. Even if I did act like one last night."

"You didn't, Summer."

He was just being nice. I watched him stoke up the fire. "Good thinking. No more matches."

"Actually, I'm hoping the other matches in the box have dried out. But the fire is also good for signaling a rescue plane or boat." He moved to the edge of woods and grabbed both life jackets.

"Are we taking those?"

"No. I want them visible from water and the sky." He stretched one out on top of the cooler and placed the other at an angle against it.

Bray was smart. I wouldn't even have thought of doing that. The fire, maybe. But the life jackets? No. I was in good hands. Maybe we were actually going to survive this.

Bray

Summer seemed a whole lot better than she had been the night before. I couldn't say I hated holding her while she slept, but the circumstances could have been better. I'd kept her in my arms all night and hadn't moved for fear of waking her. Today, my joints screamed because of it, and my side was aching.

I'd listened to her breathe with the sounds of the waves and crackling of the fire closing us in a cocoon. Being on the beach pretty much alone didn't scare me; I'd slept near the shore plenty of times in Belize while camping with Dad or after beach parties. The only annoying thing was the crabs. I woke once last night to find a small one crawling onto Summer's arm. I removed it without her knowing. From now on, I'd watch for crabs. There wasn't much more than that on the beach that could hurt us.

What I wasn't as sure about was the island interior. This wasn't the swamps of southern Florida. This was the jungle. Florida swamp, I could navigate. Jungle, well, I didn't feel quite as confident. But we had no choice. I just hoped there'd be water.

One small puncture in an otherwise solid wall of foliage would be our entry point. I knew how to look for animal trails. There should be at least some inland animals on the island.

The sun-dried bushes cracked and popped as we stepped beyond the safety of our makeshift camp. Here, the sand was darker, mixed with dirt that would help me pick up any kind of tracks. Right away, I saw the telltale sign of rat tracks. I peeked back at Summer. Best to keep that find to myself.

The cloud cover was nice while we were on the beach, but, as we dove deeper into the jungle, I wished the sun would come out. With the dappled light and the dense foliage overhead, it felt like we could be missing things. Like a creek. Or a snake. Or a café. Maybe a Starbucks.

"What?" Summer said, and I had to retrace my thoughts to see what I'd mumbled.

"White chocolate mocha at Starbucks." That was all I had to say.

A long sigh. "My favorite is mocha raspberry."

"With whip?"

"Of course. If I go in on a Saturday and they ask if I want whip, I say, 'Yes, it's whipped cream Saturday.'"

"And if you go on a Tuesday?"

"It's whipped cream Tuesday."

"I get it." I took Summer's hand and helped her over a log.

"Bray?"

Something in her voice made me stop. I turned to her.

"Do you think they've let my parents know I'm missing?"

A splash of cold snaked down my spine at the thought of our parents thinking we might be dead. "I don't know, Summer."

"My mom didn't want me to come here." Summer had stopped

on one side of a log. She stared down at it. "We have to promise to take care of each other while we're here, okay? For our families. For Joshie. We have to be strong."

She was strong. "Okay." I reached out and took her hand, partly to help her over, partly for reassurance that I wouldn't let her down.

Her denim shorts hugged her thighs as she straddled the felled tree and then threw her other leg over so that she could pause in a seated position. There, she rested until I gave her hand a gentle squeeze. She squeezed back, letting me know she understood. We had to keep moving. Had to keep our minds on the task at hand, not on what was happening with our folks.

"Sssshh." *Slap*. Her hand clamped over my mouth, eyes wide and staring into me with such fierceness, I thought daggers might fly from them.

The rustling came from beyond us. Crunching dry leaves. Summer's hand, still pressed against my lips, trembled.

Silently, I slid the dive knife from the sheath. Something moved just beyond the patch of brush beside us. It leapt into the clearing and Summer jolted.

The fat gray squirrel inspected us for a moment, then his bushy tail quirked in warning. A tiny nose twitched, and he scampered up the tree.

Summer let out a laugh. "He sounded like a giant coming through the dead leaves."

I dropped to my knees and started scraping away the brush.

"Bray, what are you doing?"

"Where there are squirrels, there are nuts." Summer landed beside me, and the two of us foraged.

She found the first one, and you would have thought it was the Hope Diamond the way she grinned. Our search took us to the bottom of a hollow tree. Inside, we found a handful more. "What kind of nuts are these?" she asked.

"Not sure, but I don't think we can pass up anything since we don't know what we will or won't find."

"Right." Summer bobbed her head, and sandy locks of her hair fell in front of her face.

"We can take them back to camp and eat them later. Are you okay with that?"

"Sure."

She was resilient, I'd give her that. I continued to dust the ground, but Summer had stopped. Sitting back on her haunches, she brushed her hair behind her ear, and her eyes darted back and forth. "Do you hear that?"

All I heard was her breathing.

Summer cupped her hand around her ear and I did the same. Off to the right, a steady whooshing sound. "That's not the beach — it's too constant, no waves."

We rose at the same time and broke out into a run. The forest cleared enough for us to zero in on the sound. I paid attention to the turns so I could find our way back to the beach. As we neared, we knew it had to be water, though we still couldn't see it. Maybe we'd come to the edge of the island, but I doubted it. Unless my sense of direction was completely off, I knew we should be somewhere central. Plus, no mountains yet. If we'd traversed the island, we should have at least seen a difference in the terrain. No, we hadn't made it across. That meant somewhere here in the middle of the island was water. From the increasing sound, I'd guess it to be lots and lots of water.

Lots was an understatement, I realized as we stepped into a clearing. Summer had gone before me and was standing still, breathing hard from the run through trees and brush, and when she turned to look at me, her face was alive. She stepped aside, giving me full view of the clearing. A waterfall anchored the lake and poured from a rocky mountainside. The glistening white water splashed into a

crystal-clear pool. It was the best thing I'd ever seen. I glanced back
to make sure I had a fix on which way the beach would be. We'd
hiked for over an hour, and I needed to know I could retrace our
steps so we wouldn't get lost navigating our way out. We had a bit
of a path now, which would make the trip back easier, but still. One
wrong turn and we could be spinning through the foliage for hours.

Summer grabbed my hand. "Come on!" A hundred feet away,
she abandoned her tennis shoes. She was in ankle-high water before
I could stop her.

"Summer, you should probably keep your outer clothes dry."

Her face fell into an instant frown and her mouth tilted into a
bow.

I knew she was shy. Her hand flattened over her shirt as if unsure
what to do.

"Just dive in. We can dry your clothes out at the fire."

Her bottom lip slid between her teeth and she kneaded it. Something in my stomach flopped. "No," she said in a small voice, stepping from the water. "You're right. My clothes need to stay dry."

I angled to face the water, giving her what privacy I could.

From my periphery, I could see Summer stripping from her pale
gray T-shirt. Everything in my gut seized into one ball.

"Your mom picked out this swimsuit." When I started to turn
toward her to answer, she yelled. "Turn around!" But it was too late;
I'd seen how the bright pink bikini top clung to her. It fit perfectly,
and I had to force myself to look away. I knew behind me she was
shimmying from her jean shorts.

I turned away from her and entered the water. She was mumbling something about wishing she'd worn her one-piece. Why had
she worn the bikini? My mind played with that question while I lowered my body into the cool lake. Moments later, she was beside me.
We reached down and pulled handfuls of water into our mouths. It
wasn't enough. I drank until I couldn't stand the thought of more.

Summer's lips skimmed the waterline. "This feels so much better than the saltwater."

"Right?" I filled my mouth and shot the water out in a stream, just 'cause I could.

"Saltwater is sticky." Her hands reached up and scrubbed at her scalp as she ducked under the water over and over, leaving a trail of dirty sand with each douse. She inhaled a deep breath, causing her chest to rise, and she leaned back, floating on the surface, her arms outstretched, hot pink swimsuit bobbing like a buoy. Suddenly, I was thirsty again.

I mimicked her—though floating on my back had never been my specialty. Above, a canopy of trees hung over the lake, closing it off from much of the sun's glare. I stayed there, beside her, thinking how things were finally looking up.

That's when I heard the plane.

CHAPTER 6

Summer

I don't remember swimming to the edge of the lake, but there I was, grabbing my shirt and shorts and pulling on my shoes. The buzzing of the rescue plane grew louder. They'd never see us here in the deeper part of the island. Without talking, we ran, Bray in front of me. Longer legs and wider strides caused him to easily pull ahead. When he reached the large tree trunk he'd helped me over, Bray turned and looked at me. "No," I said. "Keep going."

I could climb over the tree myself. In sections where the path was clear, I looked overhead, trying to catch a glimpse of the plane, but couldn't. I could still hear it, though. Buzzing like a fly by my ear, first along one side of the island, now moving toward our beach. I kept hoping it would get louder, but it didn't. Just seemed to stay an even distance away. But a plane was *there* and it had come for *us*, I was certain. That was really all that mattered. They'd see the campfire. Thanks to Bray, they'd see the life jackets. We were going to be safe.

When I reached the beach and burst through the foliage to the smooth sand, Bray was yelling and waving his arms like crazy. My heart almost burst; the plane was moving away.

I yelled and ran all the way to the ocean, where water splashed into my tennis shoes. "Hey! Come back." I turned to Bray. "They're coming back, right? Just circling around for a better view?"

But I could see in his face they weren't. His dark blue gaze met mine.

I pointed beside him. "But the fire. The jackets."

He stared over at them. Shook his head.

"How could they not see those?"

I spun around to stare at the sky where the plane grew smaller and smaller. The whine of the engine was getting more and more faint. It was the loneliest sound I'd ever heard. Helplessness cut into my stomach, causing me to drop to my knees. The plane was just a tiny speck now. Almost completely gone from view. "Maybe they're sending word that we're here," I whispered.

Bray met me in the water and reached a hand down toward me. "Maybe."

I gazed up at him, searching for hope. "I mean, maybe they couldn't land here. So, they're sending a boat back for us, right?"

I saw the war in his eyes. Agree and give me false hope, or just tell me the truth. Bray ran a hand through his hair. He drew in a long breath and watched the horizon. It was cruel to make him choose whether to lie to me or not. I slipped my hand in his and let him pull me up from the water.

"It's okay. I already know."

Bray squeezed my hand.

"They didn't tip their wings or anything, did they?" My fingers instinctively intertwined with his, clinging to him because he was all I had.

His head shook slowly. "If they'd seen us or the camp, they would have let us know they were coming back."

Bray released my fingers and wrapped his arm around me. "I'm sorry, Summer. It's my fault we weren't here."

I threw a hand in the air. "If they didn't see bright orange life jackets and a blazing fire, odds are they wouldn't have seen us, either." Anger unfurled inside me. "No, Bray. It's not your fault. But I think we can only count on ourselves. No more waiting for a plane. When it comes, great. But until then, it's up to you and me." Nervous energy flew off my body in palpable waves. We had water. We had a stash of nuts and coconut. We could sleep on the beach. We could survive. For a while at least. "Right now, surviving and making our situation the best it can be is the most important thing."

Bray watched me with a wary eye while I stoked up the fire and chattered about finding shelter. "Those giant palm fronds could make a decent roof. Not that they would keep us completely dry in a rainstorm, but I don't really see *another* rainstorm hitting in the middle of summer." I'd done my research on Belize before taking the job. It didn't rain much this time of year. Good thing there was water on the island. If we had to depend on rainwater for hydration, we'd die.

I sat on my driftwood and pulled my soggy shoes from my feet. I wiggled my raisin toes and propped my shoes against a log where the flame could dry them out. "We *could* split up to search the rest of the island—you search in one direction and me in another—but I think it's wise to stay together."

Bray remained silent, but whenever I stopped what I was doing to look at him, he'd nod. He was watching me a little too closely. Didn't he understand what was happening? The plane came. And left. It was all up to us now. I sucked a lungful of air, trying not to get frustrated at him. "We can haul the cooler to the lake and fill it. But it'll be heavy coming back, so we should maybe do that at dusk." I snagged some of the medium-sized sticks Bray had collected and tried to break one over my thigh. It bent, but wouldn't give. "You know what? Those mammoth mosquitoes will be out at dusk. We need to get the water in the daytime. And we'll have to keep the cooler closed so bugs don't get into it."

I focused my attention on Bray and blinked when he didn't answer. The cloud cover was gone, so the sun beat down in merciless waves on us. I shot a look up to the relentless burning ball. "Probably smart to stay in the shelter as much as possible during the heat of the day. We should collect more coconuts and—"

Gazing above, I hadn't heard him moving toward me. But there he was, hands finding my shoulders and sliding down my arms. His hands were always so warm against my wind-cooled skin. A small part of me wanted to melt into that touch, just slouch there, letting him hold my weight. But we had work to do. Didn't he realize that? Work. And lots of it. I opened my mouth to speak, but he slid his index finger to my lips. I swallowed.

For the longest time, he stared at me. His gaze drifting from my eyes down to my mouth, across my hairline, around my jaw and down to my throat. Suddenly, I was very aware of the strong young man holding me by the shoulders. His dusky blue eyes had darkened, causing my skin to prickle. I didn't know what Bray was doing. Couldn't read his thoughts. He just stood there, trapping me, eyes dissecting me. Maybe he thought I was going crazy. All the talk of shelter and water when our hope of rescue just flew away. The intensity of his inspection deepened. His eyes narrowed to slits. But he didn't look angry, just inquisitive. His cheek quirked, and I could feel his breath fanning over my skin.

Bray licked his lips. "What happened to you?" It was a whisper. Not accusatory, just filled with curiosity. "What have you lived through that made you so strong?"

My eyes dropped to his throat. I couldn't hold his gaze any longer. All I could focus on was the tiny pulse in his neck below a barely visible five o'clock shadow. What had happened to me? He'd never believe it. And I'd never share it because I promised myself that if I lived through it, I'd never *ever* relive it.

But I didn't know how to answer Bray. I wouldn't lie to him. Yet I couldn't tell him the truth. I opened my mouth to speak, and when I looked up at his eyes, I saw Michael's looking back at me. My blood stopped moving, ice chips in my veins. I tried to inhale, but I couldn't breathe deeply enough to satisfy my lungs.

Bits and pieces of last summer swirled uninvited through my head. Scattered snapshots of a still-blurry few weeks. Michael. Strong; he'd grown tall over our sophomore year and stood about the same height as Bray. And that's not where the resemblance ended. Michael had grown into everything I thought Bray was, a reckless partier. No longer the sweet boy who'd given me my very first Valentine in second grade, complete with little hearts he'd cut out and folded together accordion style. I still had it, tucked into the chest of Michael's things I hid in my closet. Each item had a special meaning. First, there was his mom's wedding announcement, with its embossed satin letters. I liked it so much, I'd made the mistake of telling Michael, and he'd bought me a bridal magazine and told me to start picking out all the things I'd want for our dream wedding. And that invite had a deeper meaning as well. His mom married a wealthy businessman our freshman year. By junior year, Michael was driving a BMW, had become popular, grown tall, and dropped his baby fat, making him, well, one of the pretty people. He went to parties while I went to youth group. But he'd never stopped caring for me. We'd been best friends since first grade when I beat up the class bully for picking on Michael, the new kid.

In the bottom of the cedar chest, a plastic trash bag held the shirt he died in. I guess it was morbid to keep it, but they'd cut it off him at the hospital and just discarded it by his bed. Just like they'd eventually discarded his lifeless body. But even at the hospital, I knew it was too late. I knew he'd never wear the shirt again. Any, for that matter. I was with him when life left. He wasn't coming back.

Arms closed around me. Safe. Warming the sudden cold. I blinked. It was Bray. With his hand, he guided my head to his chest. He held me there. Not speaking, just breathing. His hand stayed against my hair, radiating heat into me from my head down. "Let's not talk about it, okay?" Bray said.

Good. Because I couldn't. And somehow, he knew that. The slightest nod of my head answered him.

"One day," he whispered. "When you're ready."

How many people had said that to me? More than a few, and each time it made me angry—like they had a right to demand my story—but strangely, Bray spoke those same words and it made me feel understood. He hadn't pressed. And he didn't seem to want to hear the story out of morbid curiosity.

I squeezed my eyes shut and said the one thing I'd never said. "Okay, one day." I hoped I'd be forgiven for the lie. Where this subject was concerned, *one day* would never come.

Bray

It took all my strength to not press Summer. Some horrible tragedy had taken place in her life, and if I wasn't mistaken, the wounds were still raw. She'd completely shut down at one point, but before that, tiny glimpses of pain manifested in her gaze as she relived ... whatever it was that caused her to be so fiercely tough, yet so shockingly delicate. I had to know more. There were layers to Summer. Layers as intriguing as they were alluring. And I had to be careful with her—on a lot of levels. She was a little bit like the wild cats at my grandpa's ranch. You could feed them, maybe even touch them, but move too quickly and *zip*. They were gone. And you were bleeding.

Of course, there weren't many places to hide here. We were together. And alone. But there were more ways than one to check out, if not physically then mentally. The last thing we needed right now was for Summer to check out on any level. So, I didn't press. But one day would come. If I wasn't wrong, she needed to talk. Right now, I'd give her space. I needed space myself after watching her earlier as she dove into the clear lake, and all that fresh water running over her body and disappearing into the seams of her swimsuit ... Yeah. I needed to watch myself. Summer had no idea how hot she was. And that made it even worse.

I glanced over my shoulder to find her situating the nuts we'd gathered on the cooler top. Her hair was wet and lay in strings over her shoulders and back. The wind was in it, drying the ends and causing her to angrily brush through it. A little laugh escaped my lips. Her hair was everywhere in this forever breeze and, apparently, it was driving her nuts. I forced my thoughts away from Summer and concentrated on my plan. Tomorrow, I'd explore the east side of the island. Something about this place was becoming vaguely familiar. Like I'd seen pictures of it. Maybe it was known as Cannibal Island, and the east side was where all the tribes lived. No. Probably not. In fact, in the deepest reaches of my mind, I suspected maybe ... just maybe ...

And that's all I'd allow myself to think, because if I was right, there might actually be some provisions for us. But if I was wrong—I was probably wrong—there'd just be more of what we already had. A whole lot of deserted island.

Right now, all I really wanted to do was relive swimming at the lake with Summer. Her clothes were wet where she'd pulled them over the bright pink swimsuit, and the moisture created a perfect replica of her bikini. I figured Mom had picked out the swimwear. It was too flashy for Summer. She was a one-piece kind of girl.

Without realizing it, I'd moved to where she sat counting nuts. "Why'd you wear the bikini on the dive trip instead of your one-piece?"

She stopped counting and looked up at me with her soft, green eyes. "I don't know." Red tinged her cheeks, and I knew she was lying.

"Why, Summer?"

She huffed and anchored her palms on her thighs. "I ... it was sort of a last-minute decision."

"But why?"

Her head dropped. "I thought you'd like it."

Something solid hit my chest.

She angled away from me to look out over the water. "I'd treated you so badly when we first met, and you've been so nice to me, teaching me how to dive and all." She shook her head. "It was a stupid, snap decision, like I said."

"I have a confession to make."

She turned to face me. "First, I love the bikini. But that's not the confession." My heart pounded, telling me to stop, but I had to be honest with her.

Summer blinked, waiting.

"I asked my mom to send you back to Florida."

Summer's mouth dropped open as a frown creased her forehead. "What?" she whispered.

I ran a hand through my hair in an attempt to remove the yuck I felt. "I'm so sorry, Summer. But I felt like we needed time together as a family. I asked her to send you home after the dive trip. I told her I could take care of Josh."

A short puff left her mouth, and Summer dropped from her knees to her butt. A mix of emotions splashed across her face. Anger was there, then confusion, then something like determination.

"Why are you telling me this?" The warmth was gone from her voice, and I hated that I was the cause.

"We're here. We're together. And I think we need to be honest with each other. I'd do anything to be able to take it back."

"Did your mom agree?"

"No. She flipped. Got really mad at me."

Her eyes narrowed. "Then I wouldn't have ever known if you hadn't told me."

"No. Probably not."

She pulled a deep breath and let it out slowly. Chin tilted back, she extended a hand for me to shake. "Okay. I can live with that."

What? She should have been throwing fists at me. I'd tried to get her fired.

Her eyes widened. "Are you going to shake my hand or not? We're in this together, Bray. You were honest with me. I appreciate that. Kind of pricks my pride, but you were honest."

"You're a really unique girl, Summer." I shook her hand, and we continued counting the nuts.

After a while, she glanced over. Her lips weren't smiling, but her eyes were, her long hair flying like a cyclone around her head. She'd forgiven me, just like that. And now there was something I could do for her.

"Turn around," I ordered, my voice coming out in a low growl.

Without even flinching or arguing, Summer pivoted so that she sat looking out over the water. I slipped behind her and rested my back against the cooler.

My fingers dug into her scalp and tugged gently until strands of hair slid over my knuckles and through my hands. Over and over, my fingertips dug in at her scalp and slid down, down until they emerged at the ends where the palm of my cupped hand brushed her shoulders and arms. The golden and brown strands began to dry as I moved. One hand had become the comb while the other moved sections of hair from her shoulder to her back. After a couple of minutes, Summer settled against me. I continued working the hair, holding it out for the wind to dry, then combing through another section. I moved slowly. There was no reason to hurry. In fact, I was already dreading when the hair would be dry and I'd have no excuse to run my hands through it. I felt the exact moment when tension left her body. Her shoulders dropped by a tiny margin. I pressed my lips together hard and tried to concentrate on the task.

When I hit a snag, I worked my fingers to loosen the strands, and then gently tugged until it was free. The sun rode low on the horizon. Another snag. I pulled. Summer groaned.

It almost undid me. My lips had gone dry again, but I didn't mind. It was the best kind of torture I'd ever experienced.

Summer's head lolled against my collarbone. Her chest rose and fell in long, deep measures. She was asleep. I moved just enough to reposition her so that I could see her face. I wondered what she would think if she knew I spent so much time watching her as she slept. Her full lips, eyes shaded by thick half-moon lashes, a small nose that flared when she got angry. She was beautiful.

With her head tilted back in the crook of my arm, the wind threw her freshly dried hair into her face. I frowned and used my hand against her cheek to force it off her and stop it from blocking my view. Her cheek was soft and smooth against my calloused hand. Even though she was sunburned, her skin was fresh and dewy. I ran my hand over her cheek again, using the same slow strokes I'd used on her hair.

Her lips parted and a tiny moan escaped her mouth. Oh man. What was I doing to myself? I rubbed my hand over my own face, but my fingers smelled like her. Feminine. Woman.

I cleared my throat.

Her eyes fluttered, and then opened. It took her a moment to focus. When she did, she stared up at me. And I stared into her. "I fell asleep," she mumbled.

One side of my face slipped into a smile. That was all I could manage. "It's okay."

The self-consciousness tried to take hold of her. I saw it, creeping into her eyes, crawling over her body, fitted so perfectly against mine. She squirmed.

"Don't move, please."

Summer's body tensed for only a heartbeat, and then relaxed against me. But her eyes stayed focused. She forced the barrier of her shyness away and looked right into me. And there we stayed for a long time. Her eyes on me, mine on her. Neither of us speaking, neither of us moving. Just ... looking.

I'd had my fair share of girlfriends. I'd spent a good bit of time lip-locked with one party girl or another. I wasn't a virgin. But I'd never ever experienced anything as intimate as this. Maybe it was the island, the fact we were all alone and our survival depended upon each other. Maybe it was Summer. Her fierce desire to be resilient and her ability to do it in the face of such monumental odds.

I'd spent plenty of time looking at girls. But I can't say I ever really *looked* at a girl. At least, not like this. Everything about her was incredible. From the way she walked to the freckle on her ankle. It was all genuine. It was all Summer. No pretense, no games. No trying to be someone else. It was just her. And that caused a new kind of hunger. Deep. But willing to wait for her. Summer wasn't the kind of girl who would rush into anything. This I knew.

But I could control that part of me that wanted to claim her. Of course I could. I wasn't a beast.

Summer

I'd almost thought Bray would kiss me. But a part of me was thankful when he didn't. There'd been a long sigh, a sad-ish smile, then he'd moved, and that was my cue to stand. My hair was dry and felt like it had after I'd spent the day at the spa. Every nerve ending was alive and prickly, and when the wind blew I thought my head would combust. I reached with both hands and scrubbed my scalp. There. Nerve endings tamed, at least for now.

"I think I got out most of the tangles."

I nodded, pulling the hair over my shoulder and examining the ends. "If college doesn't work out for you, you could become a stylist."

He folded his arms over his chest. "Nah. My skills are for you only."

Something hot shot right down to my gut. I swallowed and tried to ignore the sensation, but it lingered, little sparks shooting from a frayed wire. I needed to change the subject. "I'm hungry."

"Me too." But there seemed a bit of irony in his tone. I ignored it.

Fact was, Bray was a really cute guy who probably could get any girl he wanted just by batting those dark blue eyes and flexing those biceps. And . . .

We were on an island together. Alone. Him and me. Problem was, I wasn't emotionally available, and maybe easy hook-ups were okay with him. They weren't okay with me. Ever. But Bray wasn't pushing for that. He was just being . . . nice. And though the honesty about trying to get his folks to send me home cut at my heart and certainly my pride, I understood. Now, more than ever, I understood the importance of family. I had a great one myself, even though they didn't have all the details about Michael and everything that happened that night or after. They tried to support me. As much as I'd let them.

Bray didn't have to tell me. He chose to, and that warranted respect. Even if he'd called me vanilla before he knew me, even if he'd come to defend the honor of a party girl and not me, Bray and I were here. And maybe we were even both growing a bit. Changing a bit.

But I needed to be careful, because this Bray I could really like. I needed to remember that it was only the island that brought us together. And one day we'd leave the island and return to who we each were. Which meant I couldn't let this — any of this — happen. Because, with Bray acting so sweet, so concerned, and so much like my hero, if I wasn't careful, he could ruin me. I wouldn't spend the rest of my life scarred by Bray Garrison. No matter how convincing he may seem at the moment.

We could be friends — nothing more. It was then I remembered another promise I'd made. A purity promise. I hadn't thought about it for almost a year. But now, here it was, reminding me. Like there was any need. I'd never go there with Bray.

"I'm going to roast these before we eat them." Bray made a little pocket over the fire with a few rocks from the jagged section of beach off to our left.

I smoothed a section of sand by the fire using several dry palm fronds as a broom. Makeshift bed. When I finished on my side, I'd do Bray's. "Why roast them?"

"Honestly, I'm not sure what kind of nuts they are, and some are poisonous raw."

I stopped what I was doing.

Bray's mouth slid into a smile. He really had the most intriguing smile. It lit his whole face and made the deep blue of his eyes dance.

"You must be a dentist's dream." Oops. Hadn't meant to say that out loud.

One brow rose. "What's that supposed to mean?"

"You have perfect teeth." I busied myself with the broom. "I'd think you would be good advertising." I was instantly aware of Bray blocking the sun, hovering over me.

"Is that all I am to you?" His tone was teasing. "A piece of meat?"

I gazed up at him. "Of course not. You're also good for fetching water." I pointed to the cooler. "Go get some water, piece of meat."

"No respect," he mumbled, shaking his head.

I hollered after him. "And when you get back, bake those nuts and fan me with a palm frond."

He stopped at the edge of the forest. "This isn't a dictatorship, you know."

"Of course it is," I teased. "I already voted."

He shook his head. "You don't vote in a dictatorship."

"Thank you. Glad you know that. Now get to work before I have you replaced."

He bowed, turned, and walked away, and I giggled. It was the only sound other than the waves. The noise from my own throat sounded foreign. The teasing of Bray sounded foreign, as did the lightness it caused inside me. I used to be a happy girl. But that was before Michael died. I used to hum when I got ready in the morning; I used to dance when I helped Mom clean the house. Music blaring, feet moving, hips rocking, shoulders bouncing. I used to be fun. But that was before that horrible summer and everything that followed. I missed those things. But now, it was like my body was just too heavy to move to music. My throat was too full of pain and unspoken words to sing. And my heart was too heavy to write. I used to write all the time. About everything and nothing. I missed writing most of all.

The sun was low, softer; soon it would be dusk. I sat at the edge of the ocean and watched as tiny fish jumped out of the water. The fire crackled behind me. I heard the crunching of leaves and knew Bray was making his way back to the campsite. I'd created a nice bed for him. After giving him a hard time, I owed him that.

"I hope you didn't get too bored while I was gone." He grunted, and I knew he must be carrying the cooler closer.

Why hadn't he just dropped it by the fire? I snapped my fingers. "You will address me as Princess or not at all."

Another grunt and I looked up to find the full cooler hovering near my head. "I think I will address you as Drowned Rat."

"No!" I squealed and tried to get up, but it was too late. The water missed my head, but caught my shoulders, and its icy coldness slapped me from the neck down.

Without thinking about it, I dove for his legs and he landed in the ocean. Somehow, his hand had grabbed my arm and pulled me along. We fought there, both trying to douse the other, both trying to gain the advantage, both laughing too hard to really care who was winning. Off to our left, the waves splashed against the jagged rocks, but here, the ground was sand—not great for getting a grip, especially if you're a 105-pound weakling struggling against a rock-solid body. Bray had pulled me deeper and deeper into the water and I was helpless to resist. Years ago I'd learned how to snag someone's leg and dunk them. Time to sink Bray into the ocean. My leg entwined around his. For a moment, he stopped moving. My ankle hooked his calf and I felt the muscle there tense. His shoulders tensed too, even his eyes. Suddenly, they were fierce and dancing. He was breathing heavily, as was I, and when my chest rose, it brushed against his.

Bray swallowed. It almost seemed he was fighting something inside. Some invisible force that materialized in his eyes then sparked outward, reaching to me. His hand against my spine softened and slid down to the small of my back where all my nerve endings came alive.

Oh. *Oooooh.* This, this wasn't good. Well, it felt good. Instantly, I was aware of our two bodies riding the movement of each wave. In tune with each of our deep breaths. Eye to eye, chest to chest, my leg twined around his. I needed to move away, but couldn't. I was frozen. Bray's face was splashed with water droplets. I watched one slide down his cheek and disappear into the corner of his mouth. I wanted to taste that drop of water. I wanted to touch my lips to Bray's and see if they were as soft as they looked. His hand on my lower back pressed into me, drawing me closer. My ankle was still hooked around his leg.

I did the only thing I could. I jerked my ankle and knocked him off his feet. He went under. So did I. We both came up sputtering and laughing.

With my two feet planted firmly on the sandy ocean floor, I ran my hands though my hair. Bray shook his head, sending arcs of water in all directions. "I guess I deserved that," he said.

"I guess I deserved the cooler of water on my head."

"Have you learned your lesson, Princess?" He reached for me. I reached for him and our fingers twined together.

"I suppose. Really, you only made more work for yourself."

"What? Having to get more water? It was worth it."

"Not just that. Look at my hair." I pulled my hand though it to show him the mess. "I'd offer to pay you to dry it again, but unfortunately, I don't have any money."

"I'll still do it. You can owe me." His fingers tightened and he drew me closer.

Water rushed up over our shoulders and down our backs. Mine broke out in goose bumps. I could owe him. He'd saved my life after all. It was just a little more added to that debt.

Summer

I gasped in a startled breath, and immediately coughed sand back out as my shoulder was wrenched from my body ... at least, that's how it felt.

"Summer! Come on! Wake up!" Through tiny slits for eyes I watched his shadowy body run to the fire and stoke it up.

"Leave me alone," I muttered, because my body felt like I'd been hit by a truck—which was pretty unlikely given our current address.

"Okay." There was a playfulness to his tone. "But you're gonna miss out."

I stretched. Fact was, I was curious as a cat. "Miss out on what?"

"What I found this morning."

My mind tried to catch up to the conversation. Coffee. I needed coffee. "Let me guess. You found a mermaid."

The fire rose, blazing and crackling with the fresh wood. Snakes of flame ran over the bark, devouring it. "Better than a mermaid."

"Atlantis." The wind carried the campfire smell to me.

Bray turned and looked down at me. "Better than Atlantis."

"Oh, I know. You found a *mirror*!" I leaned up on one elbow.

"Very funny, Miss Snark. Maybe I won't tell you."

"Pleeeeease tell me." I'd give in to his ridiculous game if he'd stop being so morning cheery. He reached down and scooped my arm. Before I knew it I was on my feet and finding my balance.

"I'll show you." Bray dragged me through what felt like a hundred miles of island jungle. Actually, it couldn't have been more than a quarter to a half mile, but some sections were so dense, he had to clear and cut as we went.

"You're lost." I told him.

"No. I came this way earlier."

I looked ahead of us at the thick jungle. "Doesn't look like it."

"I was excited. I didn't take time to cut back the trees." He pivoted to face me and raised his arms. That's when I saw the crisscrossed red welts.

"Oh my gosh, Bray." I grabbed his shoulders. "Are you okay?"

"Yeah." But he didn't move away from my examination.

With a gentle touch, I trailed a finger over one of the bumpy red lines. "Are you sure?"

"I'm sure." But his voice had deepened, like it had in the water yesterday. He *liked* the fact that I was worried about him.

"Okay then." I *didn't* like the warm pool in my stomach. "Show me."

He led me through one last clump of trees and brush. "Look."

I noticed a path cutting off to the right. A trail. Overgrown, but definitely cut back and large enough for a small car to navigate. "Is it a road?"

"Hasn't been used for a long time, but something like that." He pulled me onto the path where the hiking was much easier. "Wait until you see what's around the bend."

We picked up the pace and rounded the corner edged by jungle woods. My feet froze in place as I stared straight ahead, unable to move, unable to speak. The large building looked so foreign out here. Overgrown on every side, roof caved in, as if the jungle was angry and trying to swallow it. Behind this building lay another, equally flooded with greenery and equally out of place. Both utterly deserted. The doorway was zigzagged with vines, and several windows were busted where branches and leaves filled the holes.

It looked like something from a tropical zombie apocalypse movie.

"What is this place?"

"It was going to be an eco-resort. Beach, hiking in the jungle, rock climbing. We're on Sovereign Island."

My eyes flittered to Bray for a moment, then back to the stucco structures. "You know this place?"

I followed as he moved closer to the building. "I'd started thinking some of the island looked familiar. I remember my dad showing me the brochures for this place. Thought about bringing me and Joshie when the little man got a few years older. But Hurricane Shelly hit and wiped it out."

There was no fighting the smile that grew on my face.

"Summer, I don't want you to get your hopes up. I don't know if the place was gutted or not. The buildings aren't safe enough to stay in, and I don't know what, if anything, is inside."

"Party wrecker," I teased. Of course the structures weren't livable. Not with the roofs caved, but still. "So, you haven't looked inside?"

He shook his head. "I thought it would be better to get you first."

"Well, let's dive in."

A felled tree blocked the entrance to the main building. We opted for a large window alongside and worked our way through the internal rubble: a mix of scattered ceiling tiles, palm fronds, bricks, and molded electrical wiring, all covered with jungle greenery.

The entire back of the building was crushed, and as we worked to clear a path, we realized the attempt was unlikely without a chainsaw. I stood in the center atop a mass of wood and junk, surveying the prospects—or lack thereof. Bray found a half-buried leg of a plastic beach chair. After fifteen minutes of digging, he pulled it from the rubble. It was broken down the center.

Hope of provision faded, though neither of us spoke. We poked around for a while longer, but lost our initial enthusiasm with each new disappointment. Sweat ran down my spine. "How can there be *nothing* good here? It was a hurricane, right? It's not like they had weeks to clean everything out."

Bray stopped tugging on a board and turned to face me. "There may be some decent stuff below all the brush, but we can't get to it without a saw." His face was red from exertion and sweat ran off his brow. "Or maybe there's nothing. After the hurricane, they probably returned. For a while it was up in the air whether they'd rebuild. The resort was really close to opening when the hurricane hit, but Dad told me they decided on a total loss. And after they cleared what they could salvage and the insurance adjuster came, it was probably looted. Everyone knew about it."

"Well, that's just rude."

Bray used the back of his dirty hand to brush the sweat from his forehead. "No different than us taking what we need."

I crossed my arms. "Helloooo. Survival."

"It looks like everything is pretty picked over. Let's get out of here." He took my arms and drew me off my jungle mountain.

"What about the other building?"

"Are you up for more disappointment?"

I squared my shoulders. "Always." I started to turn to the doorway, but his grip tightened on me.

"I'm sorry, Summer. I really thought ..." His brows furrowed, framing his eyes. Eyes that wanted to protect me. Had wanted to offer me some hope to cling to. What he didn't know was he, with his morning coconuts and forever disposition of optimal cheer, was hope. And as long as I was with him, I felt like I'd be okay. I'd also made another hope discovery. Sometimes, I'd wake up praying. I hadn't gone to sleep praying, but sometimes, in the middle of the night with the wind at my back and the fire warming my face, I'd awaken with words and prayers on my lips. I hadn't done much to reach out to God while I was here . . . , but I had to wonder if He wasn't reaching out to me.

When I didn't answer, Bray repeated his words. "I'm sorry."

"Don't be sorry, Bray. Look. We have extra firewood now. The roof is made of metal, so maybe if we can find something to cut it, we could use it to help wall up a shelter. And it will be a great wind bank." But his frown was still there, so, I slowly reached up. First, my fingertip scrubbed at the lines drawing his brows together, the motion making the tiniest of smiles appear on his face and the lines disappear. My hand opened to cup his grimy face. "Even if we don't find anything else, you've improved our situation."

Bray pressed into my hand. "Okay. Let's go check out the other building."

Bray

When we first entered the second building, all I saw was more of the same. Same overgrown rubble, same junk. Summer climbed over the trash and disappeared.

"Bray."

First I thought maybe she'd found a snake or something. I catapulted myself over the piles of debris and found her working feverishly to push away climbing vines. A seven-foot-high iron shelving unit covered one wall, and Summer was reaching to the top shelf where a folded tarp enclosed in plastic waited. From toe to fingertip, she reached, the muscles in her legs and arms taut and lengthening as she stretched. She was only inches away from claiming it when the wood beneath her shifted. She stopped, waited for things to settle, and then stepped onto the bottom shelf. I rushed to help her, but a few more feet of rubble stood in my way.

Summer stretched up, grabbing the edge of the tarp with her fingers.

"Careful," I said. But it was too late. The shelving unit shifted, the metal groaned, and Summer screamed as both tarp and unit came down on her.

I lurched forward, hoping to stop some of the momentum, but landed prone with my fingers inches from the downed shelves. "Summer!"

Dust rose, coating everything in a hazy cloud. I curled my fingers beneath the heavy metal unit and tried to drag it off of her. It wouldn't budge. My throat closed and my eyes tingled with the onset of tears. Fear, real and deep, rushed through my system. "Summer!"

She didn't answer, but I heard a cough.

"I'm okay." The words were faint and laced with the same fear gripping my chest.

I dug my fingers beneath the cool iron and grunted as I pulled again, this time moving the unit a few inches.

"Wait." I could hear her wiggling beneath the thing. "My leg is trapped." Her breaths were growing shorter, faster. "Bray!" She was starting to panic.

"I'm here. Don't worry. I'll get you out. I swear." My eyes scanned the area, looking for something, anything to use to pry her out. Beneath the unit I could hear her pounding on something.

"I got my leg free." Some of the fear in her voice left. Some, not all. "Hey, I can see light on my right side. Maybe I can ... can ..."

I dove over the unit and began digging on the side of the shelves. I pulled and jerked until a trembling hand reached out from beneath. I grabbed it. And for a couple seconds we stayed there, breathing hard and thankful to be touching again. I continued to dig until I could pull first her shoulders, then her torso, out. She wiggled and pushed against the prison until she finally scrambled out, and we both collapsed, her on top of me. Exhausted, we lay there for several minutes clinging to each other.

"Did I rescue the tarp?" she finally said.

I leaned up to look behind her where the tarp lay. "Yeah."

Her face broke into a smile. I started laughing, and for a couple minutes I couldn't stop. Summer rolled off me and laughed too, her head still on my chest, her hair splayed across my upper body. My free hand cupped her face the same way she'd touched mine. The motion tilted her chin so that we could look at each other. "Thank God you're okay."

It wasn't until we stood to leave that I noticed a door. "Summer, look." It had been blocked by the shelving unit and now stood there like one last beacon of hope and possibility.

"Can we get it open?" She stepped closer to it and turned the knob. "It's unlocked."

"I don't know. The hinges are on the other side, so maybe." I cleared what I could from the floor and gave her a nod to open the door. It slid a couple feet then stopped. It was enough to slip through and certainly enough to peer inside. She took one look, and then grabbed my shoulders. "It's beautiful, Bray! It's a kitchen!"

I stopped trying to clear the floor and followed Summer inside. With no windows and the roof undamaged, the place was almost pristine, with barely dusty stainless steel counters. Holes marked where appliances once rested, but other than the missing appliances, there were things in every direction. Things that could help us stay alive. A long metal wall housed a variety of knives, from simple paring knives to butcher knives to meat cleavers. The one big problem with this space, it was hot. Hot like a sauna. Hot like a stove when the oven is on.

"Why do you think they left this stuff here?" she asked.

"I don't know. Maybe someone was trying to hide it all."

Summer turned to face me. She stopped in the middle of the

room, hands stretching across the stainless steel island in the center of the kitchen. "You mean, hide it and come back and get it after the insurance was settled?"

I shrugged, scouring each wall and finding hope in every corner. "Maybe."

"But they didn't come back for it?"

"I guess not. Best-laid plans." Off to the left was another door. Smaller than the entryway. It must have occurred to Summer at the same moment it occurred to me. We both headed toward it. She waited. I motioned for her. "You opened the last one and had pretty good luck. Open this one."

She pulled a deep breath, took my hand, closed her eyes, and I thought she might be saying a little prayer or wishing like you do before blowing out your birthday candles. Then she reached with her free hand and shoved the door open. We both gasped.

Shelves and shelves of canned food.

I'm not sure if Summer's laughter or crying started first. They were both in there, inside her, fighting for dominance, slipping out of her mouth in a groan and then a giggle. We entered the pantry like one might enter a holy place. Though for us, it was a holy place. It meant assured survival.

Her fingers reached out to stroke a large can of peaches. But she couldn't contain her elation so she gripped one of the shelves and dropped her head forward. And cried.

I started to step away, give her space, but something in me pushed closer to her. I reached out and rested my hand at the small of her back. Through her shirt I could feel the muscles tighten and release with each sob. I didn't move. Didn't interrupt. Just stayed there with her. I had the feeling Summer usually held everything in, until now. Until the island. That couldn't be healthy. Her narrow shoulders rose and fell, arms bent into a V, fingers intertwined in the bars of the metal shelving unit. Hair shrouded her face, and I had to fight the desire to move it away so I could see her. So she'd let me in. It was a special place, and I wanted to be part of it. I swallowed, not really sure why something as elemental as crying could do such a number on my head. Fact was, Summer—everything about her from her laughter to her tears—was getting to me.

Finally, the tears stopped, and she lifted her head and stared at the ceiling, wiping her cheeks. "I'm not supposed to do that," she said.

I frowned. "What? Cry?"

"Yeah." She angled to look at me. Her lips were red and swollen, eyes still wet. "I promised myself a long time ago that I wouldn't cry. Ever again." Slowly, she unlaced her fingers from the shelf.

All around us food waited to be examined, but I couldn't rip my gaze from her. "How's that working out for you?" I didn't mean to sound callous, but seriously?

"Not so good."

"You might as well promise yourself to stop breathing. It's an emotion, Summer. There's no controlling it."

She crossed her arms, one brow raised in a peak. "You haven't cried."

I put my hands up in surrender. "Not fair."

The brow rose higher. "Why?"

"Because I'm the big, strong ape man with a very delicate ego. I can't cry in front of you. You might laugh at me."

Aaahhh. There it was. Her smile. And even the barely lit room got a little brighter. "Ape man, huh?"

My hands found their way to her shoulders, because I had to touch her. "Summer, it might be chauvinistic, but I want to be strong for you. I've gotten close to tears a few times, you just haven't seen me."

Her head tilted slightly and her green irises became a strange shade of wonder. "You have?"

"Yes. About ten minutes ago when the shelf fell on you."

A series of emotions skated across her face before she looked away. I wished I knew all the things that went on in her head. Like why she'd stopped going to her youth group, but sometimes at night I awoke to the sound of her prayers. I wished I could peel back the layers and find out what was inside.

Her attention returned to me so fast, it took me by surprise. "I'll never make fun of you, Bray. Not for ... feeling."

"I don't know. I'm really just a big marshmallow. Give me a good TV commercial and the waterworks start."

"You cry at commercials?"

"Well, only the really poignant ones," I teased.

She raised her hands between us. "Okay, you're right. I like Ape Man better. Delicate ego and all. Real men don't use words like *poignant*."

"You're safe from emotional guy. We don't have a TV. But you know what we do have?" I reached behind her and snagged the can from the shelf. She hadn't seen it yet, that was certain.

"What?" Her face beamed.

"Coffee."

I've heard Hollywood pays young girls to scream and that the playback is used in horror movies. Summer could get a full-time job. I wasn't sure if my eardrums would recover.

Summer

We downed a can of peaches and a restaurant-sized can of tuna. Some of the food was out of date, but not by much, as the island had only been struck by the hurricane a year ago. We inventoried food for what Bray figured to be two hours — according to the movement of the sun, which was the only clock we had — and gloried in the idea that we didn't have to live on coconuts any longer. The kitchen was well stocked with pots and pans but no actual plates or glassware. We ate food right out of the can, and by the time we'd finished, I felt like my shrunken belly had been inflated with a tire pump. I was exhausted and ready for a nap.

"You know the best part?" I said to Bray. He'd gotten quiet over the last several minutes.

"What?"

"We can use the coconuts on our skin. It will cut down on the chances of cuts, infections, and sunburn if we keep our skin moist."

"Would that work?"

"It already has. I've been scraping the last little bits of coconut out and using it on my face. For a while there, I felt like if I smiled my cheeks would crack." I was surprised at how quickly Bray made his way to me. Suddenly, he was right there, right in front of me.

His hands came up to slide along my cheeks, over my forehead, down my throat. "You are soft." His voice was a gravely whisper. The sound dove into my stomach and curled around my insides.

"Are you just looking for an excuse to touch me?" We stood by the stainless steel counter in the hot, dusty kitchen, so I clamped a hand around the edge, letting the solid surface equalize me. Bray could throw me off ... or shore me up with just one touch of his hand.

"Do I need an excuse?" There was no pretense in his tone. No humor, no wit. Just honesty. And that scared me a little. My grip on the counter tightened as I thought of how it felt earlier to have Bray pressing his hand to the small of my back as I'd cried. He hadn't tried to calm me down. Hadn't told me to stop. He was simply there. There for me.

I didn't know what to do with that. My whole life, I had always been the strong one. Well, until I shattered and broke into a thousand pieces last year. And that shattering was okay, because no one knew. Not my mom or dad. Not Michael's mom. Not my youth pastor. Not even Becky, my best friend. I'd walked the earth as a corpse, helping Michael's mother with funeral arrangements, and only later, in the safety of my room after it was all over, did I allow myself to shatter. People say a heart can be broken. But they forget the rest of the organs. How your mind spins trying to undo what was done. How the lungs ache with each new breath. No, it's not just a heart that breaks.

I died that day right along with Michael.

I blinked, suddenly aware of something going on around me but unable to access what. Bray leaned toward me, hands still cupping my soft cheeks. His tongue darted out and licked his lips. He was going to kiss me.

What would his mouth feel like against mine? It would be a tender kiss. He would brush his lips against mine and possibly taste the faint hint of coconut that lingered around my mouth. Then, he'd step closer, closing me in the one place I felt safe on the island, his arms.

Millimeters from my mouth, he stopped. His focus lifted from my lips to my eyes. He was waiting. For me.

"I'm sorry, Bray." I pulled away. Sorrow and anger at myself whooshed into my system because I wouldn't let Bray kiss me. Couldn't let him. I swallowed, and the pain from disappointing him burned all the way down my throat.

He pressed his lips together in a tight line. The muscle in his jaw worked out the frustration he didn't want me to see, but it pulsed from him in waves so powerful, they could knock me over if I wasn't careful. For a few seconds, he just hung there, hands still raised to the spot where I'd moved away from him. Then his lips quirked, and I saw a tiny dimple in the left side appear then disappear. He dropped his hands with a clop. "I'm going outside for a while. You'll be okay?"

I frowned. It wasn't like him to leave me. "I ... I'm okay." Was

I? Guess I had to be. When he got to the door, I hollered for him. "Bray? Are you all right?"

He froze for a second, half through the doorway. His hand gripped the trim work. "Yeah. I just want to check on something."

He wasn't convincing. I pulled a deep breath and tried to concentrate on the provisions around me rather than the person I'd just rejected. I'd made an art of pushing people away in the last year. But when you're stranded on an island, self-reliance can only take you so far. Bray needed me. And whether or not I wanted to admit it, I needed him.

CHAPTER 8

Summer

I packed some utensils, a can opener, food, and other essentials into a large stew pot. It was getting heavy, but Bray and I could carry it between us, each holding one of the handles. He'd been gone for quite a while. I began to wonder if he was coming back at all when I heard his voice. "Summer, come out for a sec."

I tried to lift the pot myself. No way. "Okay," I called.

I worked my way to the door, avoiding the newly piled sections of food. He was standing at the main door, and I was glad to see he had a smile on his face. "Come on out, you need to see this."

I brushed the sweat-sticky hair from my face.

"You need me to come in and help you?"

"No. Well, maybe. I packed us a pot of food and stuff for the beach. I can't lift it. Need an ape man."

He rushed inside, sailing over the debris like an athlete. Before I could even get to the door on my own, he'd rushed past, grabbed the pot and carried it outside.

"Wow. Ape man good."

He gave me one of those half grins that made my stomach hurt and snagged me by the hand. "Come on."

"Uh ... aren't we taking the pot?" I had to readjust my feet to keep from tripping. It was as hot outside as it had been inside.

"No. We can come back for it." He dragged me along an over-grown path leading to what I assumed was the east side of the island. We hadn't explored this section yet, but something had tripped his excitement button. I tried to rally, the muscles in my calves and thighs screaming and shaking with each new step. Exhausted, I let him drag me. I felt the breeze and knew we were near the water.

He stopped. "Okay, close your eyes."

My hands instantly went to my hips.

"I'm serious. I'll navigate you through the last tree line. But you gotta get the full effect when you see this."

I closed my eyes and let him lead me through the trees. The breeze was strong now and I could hear waves, but gentle ones, not like our beach.

"Open your eyes." He'd said it against my ear, confirming how close he actually stood.

Soft blue sky, blue-green water, and a half-moon of white sand around the most beautiful lagoon I'd ever seen. Scattered palm trees anchored the crescent-shaped cove, giving shade and swaying in the soft current of air. The breeze was gentle here, as were the waves. It was paradise. The water beckoned. Low swells reaching toward us, climbing the white sand then retreating back into the sea. "It's beautiful."

"That's not the best part." I could hear Joshie in Bray's voice. Little boy, excited, energized with a secret, thrilled to be the bearer, eager to spill the knowledge. "Turn around."

I did and what I saw almost made my knees give out. There, nestled just before the tree line, was a hut.

Bray motioned beyond it. "There are several. Or were — most of them were wiped out by the hurricane. But this one is livable. I already checked it out."

I couldn't breathe. We had food. We now had shelter. We weren't going to die. When I swayed toward him, he caught me. I fell into his waiting arms. "Thank you, Bray."

"No more sleeping on the beach. Not that you've been sleeping much."

"I didn't want to tell you, but one night I woke up with a crab crawling over me. I haven't slept very well since then."

"I know. I'm sorry."

He'd been hugging me, but when he said this, I tilted to look up at him. "What do you mean, you're sorry?"

"I fell asleep. That's why it was crawling on you."

I pushed a little farther away because I needed to see his face. We'd spent three nights on the island. "Are you saying you've stayed awake to keep the crabs off of me?"

He chewed the inside of his cheek. "Maybe."

That moment I lost a little piece of my heart to Bray Garrison. I could feel my eyes welling, but swallowed the emotion until I had it under control. "Thank you, Bray." It was all I could manage. And seemed to be all he needed to hear.

One of his hands came up to touch the side of my head. "You're welcome, Summer. Go on in and check out your new condo. I'll go back and get the food. We can get some dinner started soon."

Rather than stare at my new home away from home, I watched Bray as he disappeared beyond the trees. He'd stayed awake to keep crabs off of me. Who does that? I owed him my life ... and maybe even more. This Bray made me want to believe again. *This* Bray was a far different person than the one I met in Belize.

But the Bray in Belize was the real one, and I needed to remember that. I needed to remember what we'd been like at the house— *that* was real life, before we came to the island.

Wait. Before we were *stranded* on the island. We didn't come here. This wasn't a vacation. Wasn't a choice. This was life or death.

Even with food and shelter, it was still life or death. I also needed to remember that. A giant wad of despair worked to swallow my new joy.

Which oddly made me feel just a bit more stable, a bit more on solid ground. I took in the hut. It was probably the size of a one-car garage, with a bamboo-trimmed porch running the width of the front. Three stairs led up to the porch, and I was thrilled I'd no longer be on the ground. The bottom step was partially covered in white sand that danced across it in the breeze like an invitation. I was glad the hut sat on sand rather than in the woods, otherwise the aggressive foliage would have claimed the whole thing by now. Instead, there were several feet behind the hut before the tree line bulged toward it. Hand on the rail, I stepped onto the second step and bounced a little. Solid as a rock.

The porch was shrouded by an overhanging roofline covered with palm fronds, but the underside was wood or maybe painted metal. I couldn't tell which and didn't really care as long as it kept the bugs out and the sun off. Two large hooks hung from the porch ceiling, which seemed odd, but I was sure we'd figure out some way to use them.

The door hung open, and it too was wood. But not like the lumber I'd seen in log homes. This was different, rich in color and barely scarred by the weather. Probably some exotic kind of wood. It practically glowed.

Inside, more of the same warm-honey timber. Walls, ceiling, all lined with the stuff. There was a front room and a door on the left that led into what I assumed was a bedroom. Windows were on every wall I could see from my vantage point. They opened outward from the center like miniature French doors. One window was broken, but the rest were intact. The stuffy hut smelled like wet wood, though the inside seemed dry enough. After propping the door open fully, I went to the window in the front room. I tried to open it, but it wouldn't budge. I headed across the empty space to the bedroom and pushed that door open a little farther, introducing myself to the room. Something fluttered in the corner, causing my heart to stop. I waited, released a breath, just as a bird emerged from the corner and flew directly at my head. Hands flailing, I ducked just in time to get out of its way. He disappeared through the open door. A hand fell against my heart, which I could feel pounding through my T-shirt.

Though most of the cabin was bare, a bamboo-anchored cot rested against one wall, holding a thick, plastic-covered, marine-blue mattress. I nearly sank on it right then, but couldn't be sure what was living in, on, or under it, so I decided to wait for Bray. Maybe we could drag it out to the beach and remove any unwanted squatters.

He returned just as I'd started gathering wood for a fire outside. "So, what all is in this pot? Feels like everything but the kitchen sink."

"Actually, I thought we'd use the pot *as* the kitchen sink. Sorry it was so heavy. I just kept piling food and utensils in there."

"In a few minutes, I'll need to run back to the beach and bring some of the coals over to start the fire here."

I nodded. And continued listing the pot contents. "I grabbed a can opener too. Also, a couple knives. I didn't bring them all, just a couple. Oh, and a little gadget in a carrying case."

"What gadget?" He dropped the pot on the sand a few yards from the hut.

I dug around inside, excited all over again that we had food. Actual food. "This." I held it up to him.

His mouth dropped open, and he slid it from my grasp.

"Honestly, I didn't figure it would be much help, but I was just sort of intrigued by it."

"Summer, do you know what this is?" His eyes were so wide, I wanted to step away.

"No."

"It's a magnesium fire starter. Just one of these will light hundreds of fires."

Suddenly, my discovery went from intriguing to downright awe inspiring. My hand fell against my chest. "I almost tossed it into the rubble."

Bray set it gently in my hands, then grabbed both sides of my head and kissed my forehead. "Good job."

"I almost threw it *away.*"

"But you didn't." He nodded toward the hut. "How do you like it?"

"Amazing." My bottom lip slid into my mouth and I bit down.

"Summer."

I fingered the fire starter, focusing on the tight stitching that held the case together.

"*Summer,*" Bray said, a little louder, though he wasn't more than six inches away.

There was a problem with the hut. One he may not have noticed, but one I certainly noticed and ... and ...

"Summer!" This time his tone sharpened.

Slowly, I looked up and met his gaze. "Well, um, I ..."

There was a whimsical glint in his eyes. "Don't worry, I'm going to sleep on the front porch."

Relief flooded me. "You ... you are?"

He nodded. "I know you're pretty shy, and I don't want to make you uncomfortable."

Guilt raced over my skin and down my jelly spine, but sleeping in the same room ... on the same bed ... No, I just couldn't. It had been different on the beach by the fire. This was way too intimate. "Maybe we could take turns. One night I could have the bed, the next night you could."

He cocked a brow. "And leave you outside? Uh, no. That's not going to happen."

He'd never let me do that. After all, he was the guy who didn't sleep so I could and he'd stayed awake for the sole purpose of keeping the crabs off me. "Well, we can work something out."

"We already did." In every muscle of his face I saw resolve. There'd be no more discussion of who slept in the cabin and who slept outside.

My elation at the newly found shelter took a fairly solid hit. The shelter made things better for me, but Bray would still be outside in the elements. What about crabs crawling on him? All the giddy excitement waned. He must have noticed and stepped closer.

"Do you remember what I told you at the beach? I've been camping with my dad hundreds of times. We slept outside by choice."

I chewed the inside of my cheek.

"I'll get the best sleep knowing you're inside on the mattress. Speaking of that, let's go check it for bugs." He cast a long glance out to sea. "It'll be getting dark soon."

Bray

For the first time since we got to the island, things were working in our favor. Until today, everything had been moment to moment. Now we had provisions. I suspected I could scrounge more out of the buildings, but for now we needed to concentrate on what we had. I'd spent years camping with my dad, so I knew how to watch the sun and tell when the day's light was leaving. We needed to get dinner made soon.

The bed was fine—no bugs, no rodents—and would be a great place for Summer. I'd made myself a mattress out of some soft palm fronds and covered them with the tarp. I wanted Summer to use it as a blanket, but she insisted I take it. She wasn't happy about me sleeping on the porch, but I was beginning to understand Summer more and more. She really was like a wild kitten. Half fragile, half wildcat. Which meant me sleeping outside was the right thing to do, no matter how it scraped my ego and my desires. In everything I did, Summer worked right alongside me.

Exhausted from the day and preparing our lagoon campsite, we collapsed by the new fire and watched as the sun dipped lower and lower toward the horizon. The brilliant blue of the sky became a purple flame tinged with orange and yellow. Thin lines of transparent clouds raced across as if drawn by some giant paint brush. Summer sat beside me, and when the wind shifted, she wrapped her arms around her knees.

"Cold?"

"I'm okay," she said, and I watched as she tilted her head back, closed her eyes, and let the heat from the setting sun absorb into her face.

I stayed quiet for several seconds. When she opened her eyes, I said, "Keep that up, will you?"

She looked over. "What?"

"Praying. It helps."

Her eyes turned suspicious. "How'd you know?"

I shrugged. "Just seen you do it several times."

"I didn't for a long time."

"You didn't pray?"

"It's strange how in one crisis you can push God away, but in another you find Him again."

"Is that what's happening for you, Summer?"

She smiled over at me. "Yes. I'm realizing that God never designs bad things to happen to us. They just sometimes happen. In each one, we can choose to let Him help or to push Him away. I've decided to stop pushing."

"That's great, Summer."

She pulled a breath. "I miss going to church. Isn't that strange? Now that I can't go, I want to, even though I've gone a year barely giving it a thought."

"Hey, when we go home, I'll take you to church every Sunday. How's that?" I bumped my shoulder against hers and grinned.

Firelight danced across her features as she looked over at me, judging my words. She turned back to face the water, where diamonds and liquid gold fought for dominance on the low waves. I knew the moment she started to worry.

"What, Summer?"

She pulled a steadying breath. "What do you think our families are doing right now?"

Her hand fell to the sand between us as if anchoring herself to the earth could stop what was going on miles and miles away.

"We've been gone four nights, that's not that long. There are so many little islands near mainland Belize. My dad will be hiring private planes to search for us. He probably already has. I don't know the protocol for search and rescue, but the authorities will be looking too."

Her green eyes locked on me. "But we've only seen one plane."

I felt the chill to my toes. She was right.

"Think of how happy they'll be when they find us." I'd been careful not to reach down and touch Summer's hand. But my skin itched for contact with her. I placed my fingers close and pretended I could feel the warmth of hers so near.

"If they find us." It was barely an echo. She faced me. "Bray, why haven't there been *more* rescue planes? One? Only one?"

I'd been wondering that myself. "I don't know. It doesn't make much sense. Maybe something else happened in the storm and it's diverted the rescue planes. It was a pretty serious storm. The worst one I've ever been in."

She sat quietly for a long time. "We could have missed a couple planes, I suppose."

"Yeah," I agreed. "Look, Summer, my dad won't give up on us. I know him. He'll send search teams, I swear. Maybe it's just taking a little time to coordinate. We'll make it off the island."

First joy then despair. So many emotions ran across Summer's face, and I was beginning to learn them all.

"I bet you're excited to get back to college."

"Eh."

"Oh, come on. Absolute freedom. I bet girls are beating down your dorm room door." She was trying to make me feel better.

"Women love ape men."

"Did you have a girlfriend?"

"No." And I didn't really want to get into why. I liked the idea of not being committed. Getting to hook up with whichever girl tripped my trigger. And for some reason, thinking of myself in those terms made me feel ashamed as I sat by Summer.

"So what are you most excited about returning to?"

What was I most excited about? Nothing. Parties and campus fun seemed really foreign to me right now. Like they were from another life. Someone else's life. I was Bray. Survivor. Protector and guardian of Summer. And that other guy was slipping away. "I can tell you what I'm not excited about."

"What's that?" She rocked back, settling into the conversation.

"My mom and dad's divorce." Even saying it caused a spike in my gut.

"What?" Her gaze widened.

I didn't answer, just gave her a sad smile and nodded.

Her eyes roamed my face, then the darkening horizon. "That just can't be. They're so … so *happy*."

"No, they just seem happy when they're together. But they're not together much, are they?" I couldn't help the acid in my tone.

Her shoulders curled forward. "No, now that I think about it. But I never really sensed anything *wrong* between them."

"I know. They're good at hiding it. Experts."

"That's why you wanted me to leave. Were you hoping they'd reconcile?"

I scooted so the side of my hand grazed hers. "I thought if we all spent time together, they'd remember how it used to be."

Her hand flew to her mouth. "Poor Joshie. Does he know?"

I shook my head, leaning back to rest my hand behind me and give myself some space. "No. This is the last family vacation."

Her brow furrowed. "This is just all wrong. Did they tell you why?"

My head fell to one side then the other. "They said they'd grown apart, that the magic that had drawn them together had died somewhere along the way. They didn't even realize it was happening, but because they still care about each other, they want to part while things are still civil."

"That's a cop-out." Summer's hand fisted in the sand. "The magic doesn't die. It never dies. But with time, it changes. It became you, then Josh. *That's* the magic. They're just too stupid to see it."

Normally, I didn't appreciate people calling my parents stupid, but she was right, and more than a little scary with this much fire and fury sparking from every cell of her body. I leaned back a little more.

Summer flew up from the ground and began slamming things into the cold wash water. She scrubbed each utensil, dumped the water, and then carried everything into the hut. I sat quietly and watched—something akin to watching a tornado cycle through your neighborhood.

Finally, she emerged. "I'm sorry, Bray." She came down the steps and stood in front of me. "I should be consoling you ..."

"Nah. I've had months to get used to the idea."

When her inspection of my face became too much, I looked away, off to the right where palm trees swayed in the last of the fading light.

Suddenly, she was right there, hovering over me. "Bray! There's something in your hair."

Panic caused her voice to crack, and that ran down my spine like ice water. I felt something crawl over my scalp. My hands shot up, but hers were in the way.

"Spider. I got it," she said and I felt her swat at my head. A long exhale followed from both of us.

"Thanks." I expected her to walk away, but she stayed there, standing over me.

"Your hair's getting all matted." I felt one gentle tug, then another as her fingers snagged. She used her thumb and forefinger on my chin to glide my head to one side. She dove in again, pulling and tugging as knots released, leaving my scalp tingling like a live wire. My hands itched to reach up, to touch her, but I didn't. I stayed immobile, letting her have her way with my hair, scared if I moved too quickly, she'd bolt away from me. Dizziness almost overtook me, and I realized I needed to breathe. I released the air I'd been holding and it blew out in a long sigh. Summer looked down, her eyes locked on mine.

I didn't dare move, though the entirety of my body said to pull her down to me. I fought it. But for a moment we were trapped. Her lips parted and she swallowed, then her gaze went to my hairline, but not without struggle. I could see the emotion, the desire. It mirrored my own. Could it be that Summer was fighting this just as much as I was? Could it be that she wanted it just as badly? But then, she opened her mouth and shattered my optimism.

"When you love someone. Real love," she said as her hands sank into my hair again, "the magic never dies. Even if they do."

And that's when I knew. I'd never have Summer. She belonged to someone else.

CHAPTER 9

Summer

I'd made a promise to Michael and I intended to keep it. As I readied for bed, that was all I could think about: Michael. He haunted my dreams for the first month after he died. So much so, I feared going to bed. Insomnia claimed me for a time, but I knew I couldn't let something like sleeplessness rob me anymore. I told Michael to stay out of my dreams. And he'd done it.

I slipped my swimsuit off and put my shorts and T-shirt back on. The bed cracked and popped as I stretched out, but my thoughts were plagued with Michael. I felt like I'd somehow done something horrible . . . horrible and raw and he was looking down on me with so much disapproval that I wanted to just curl up in my memories and forget anything else.

I took deep breaths, trying to force my taut muscles to release at least some of the tension they held. A beam of moonlight cast a silvery glow across the room. I stared at the tiny dust particles trapped in it like glitter in a snow globe until my eyes became so heavy I could no longer keep them open. Michael's face was the last thing I remembered.

Bray

Something harsh woke me. I tried to force the grog from my mind and body, but everything was dreamlike and heavy. What had I heard? Some unnamable sound had jarred me awake. I sat up on my makeshift bed, waiting, listening. The front porch wasn't much shelter from wild animals—this was a jungle after all. I tried to remember the sound that woke me, but couldn't. It had been shrill, and close. My eyes took in the landscape. There could be jaguars on the island.

I heard no movement as my gaze trailed from the lagoon to the partial moon hanging above. Below me, the fire had burned down to fading golden coals. I stood up as quietly as possible on the tarp and waited. Nothing. I didn't bother to pull my shirt on, but knew I needed to stoke up the fire. It wasn't much, but might deter a hungry animal.

With the fire ablaze and no sign of danger, I returned to the porch and stared out over the water. It was ink-dark with silver-white moonlight catching the movement of wind-rippled sea. Stars punctured the sky, tiny holes in black canvas. For the first time since we'd been here, I almost felt like I was camping, and I felt my pulse settle. I owed my dad a lot for all he'd taught me. Things like how to build a fire and keep it burning. How to avoid using poison oak as toilet paper. Mom always packed the first aid kit, instructing me on each item from bug bite ointment to Neosporin. Every. Single. Trip. I'd tease her, saying we were manly men and just rubbed a little dirt in our cuts. She'd purse her mouth and those dimples would appear on each cheek. Joshie had those too. I missed Joshie.

It was weird to think of my mom and dad no longer living together, of times with Joshie being different from now on.

Sleepiness had finally started settling into my dry eyes, but as soon as I heard the noise again, I was wide awake. I jumped up. It wasn't an animal. And it wasn't outside. I ran into the hut right into her bedroom and started shaking Summer. She screamed once more before fear-filled eyes opened, blinked, and found me in the darkness.

She stayed still a moment, not moving, not breathing, eyes empty, hollow, and haunted. Then, the dam broke and she was crying out, body convulsing against the sorrow and pain. I dragged her into my arms and held her, fearing her entire body might come unhinged. She cried so hard her forehead would sometimes smack against my collarbone, the force so great I knew it would be bruised tomorrow. I'd never heard a sound so terrible. It ripped from inside her, shredding me with it as well. My eyes squeezed shut and I was surprised by the tears — my own tears — spilling down my cheeks.

I rocked her back and forth like one might rock a small child, but the motion did little to soothe either of us. Summer was broken, shattered, and I was finally seeing the reality of her sorrow. I wanted to help her, to quiet her. But this was too desperate for words, too deep to console. It sounded like Summer was dying inside. A groan started in her throat, and when she released it, it became a howl. Mournful, painful. Somewhere in the outcry, I heard the word "Michael."

Summer

Grief brought a weird sort of numbness. Aware, but blissfully unaware. Alive, but mercifully dead. I knew Bray held me while I cried. I knew he was bare from the waist up and that my tears had streamed down his torso. I knew he was once again being strong for me because I was incapable of doing it myself. They say that when someone loses a leg, they can still feel it. It itches, it hurts. It might even seem to move. The mind is strange. Playing odd tricks on itself. It was easier to feel nothing. I'm sure anyone who'd ever had ghost sensations in a lost leg would agree.

I scooted on the bed until my back rested against the wall. Bray didn't say anything. Just sat there with me. He scooted too, so that our faces were still close. Outside my window, the moon had moved in the sky, and a cluster of clouds held it in silence.

Bray's hand moved to my face, where hair stuck to my cheeks. I'd done nothing to clean up the mess that was me. He stroked gently, fingertips sliding along my cheekbones, hands pushing the hair out of my eyes and from my face. Finally, he whispered, "You okay?"

His blue eyes only picked up tiny splashes of the moonlight. "Yes," I said, and was surprised at how hoarse my voice had become. Upon hearing it, silent tears began again. But I had no energy to fuel them.

Bray blinked a few times and I could see him considering, weighing something. Then, he scooted even closer, placed his hands on the sides of my face and kissed my cheek with such a gentle brush, it felt like angel wings. When another tear slid onto the other side, he kissed there. Again and again his lips, soft and sweet, pressed so lightly against each tear. He'd move back, look me eye to eye, then close in and kiss another away. But as the tears continued to fall, his lips rode the curve of my face to each new spot of moisture, no longer pausing to look at me. He smelled like salt and sea and hard work, and I liked his scent because it represented how he'd protected me.

When he started to draw away, my fingers coiled around his arm. He couldn't go. Not yet. His lips parted, still wet with my tears, and I thought I saw a war going on inside his eyes. His tongue slipped out and ran slowly along the ridge of his bottom lip, then his top. He was tasting me.

I knew I needed to loosen my grip on him. But I just couldn't make my body agree with my mind. So I relaxed.

And Bray tensed. He pulled an earth-shrinking breath, his broad shoulders rising, his lungs expanding. He released it slowly and smiled. I smiled too.

"You want to go sit by the fire?" I knew what he was asking. I could say no. He hadn't pressed me to talk about my past. Not now and not before when he'd asked me what had happened to make me so strong. Even then, he'd just said he wanted to know one day. And he'd allow me to say no. But I wouldn't do that now. Bray deserved more.

He deserved honesty. So as I sat there, with my tears still on his lips, I decided to do the one thing I swore I never would. I was going to talk about Michael.

One day had come.

Bray wrapped me in the tarp and worked on the fire, then brought me a drink of water from a half coconut shell we kept in the cooler. When he went to sit near, I opened the tarp to let him in with me. He thought about it for a few seconds, donned another smile, and sat down on my right side. We closed the tarp around us and I started telling him about Michael. How a bully in first grade nearly beat him up until I intervened, how we'd gone from being best friends to being in love over one summer. Even our first kiss. It's not that I wanted to be insensitive. But when the words began spilling out, I couldn't seem to stop them. But that was all stuff people already knew. It was the stuff they didn't know that haunted my mind.

"And you broke up with him?" The sound of Bray's softened voice echoed off the tarp tucked around our shoulders. His voice was honey. Thick, rich, and vibrating with a tone that was purely male and purely caring.

"Yeah. Over the phone. He was at a party. I didn't know he had his car. I thought he rode with a friend. I just couldn't take it anymore. He'd been drinking a lot and it scared me so badly. When we were together, he was a different person."

"What happened?" Again, Bray's words soothed.

"He told me he was on his way over to my house." Heat rose from Bray's body, but I still felt a chill revisiting that night.

"I take it that he never made it to your house."

"He did. Almost. Died at the edge of my neighborhood. His car hit the entrance — it was a short brick wall on either side of the road. I heard the crash. Ran out."

Bray's expression tightened. Even from my periphery, I could see it. His arm slipped around me.

"He was trapped and bleeding from his head. I tried to pull him out of the car." I angled to face Bray and look into his eyes. "I thought if I could get him out, he'd be okay." Suddenly I couldn't look at Bray anymore, because his concern for me was readable in every micro movement he made.

"The paramedics got there, but it was too late. He died in my arms."

Bray ran a hand over his face as if trying to erase the image.

"When we got to the hospital, they said they'd revived him. But I knew he was gone. For good." The tarp held in so much body heat, I started sweating. I fanned the opening a bit and Bray readjusted it so our shoulders were exposed.

"But you were with him at the hospital?"

"Yes." Flames from the fire caught my attention, and I stared at them with tired eyes that became mesmerized by the dancing blaze. "His mom got there, but his stepdad was in China. He'd gone for business and caught some kind of virus. They wouldn't let him leave the hospital for weeks."

"I guess you and Michael's mom were there for each other, huh?"

Did I have animosity toward Rachael, Michael's mom? No, it

wasn't exactly that, but I did find myself wondering why she didn't take better care of him. "I was there for her."

"I'm sure you were both devastated."

"She couldn't ... couldn't do anything. She was in shock. When I made the funeral arrangements—"

"Wait a minute. *You* made the funeral arrangements?"

"She couldn't do it. I was supposed to meet her at the funeral home to be with her while she made plans. When I got there, the funeral director told me Rachael had called. She said I could make the arrangements. She was in shock."

"In shock for *days*?"

"For weeks. She didn't start snapping out of it until her husband came home."

"I mean, the community was there to help her, right? To help you?"

"Our youth pastor was gone on a mission trip when it all happened, otherwise he'd have been there to help me. I know he would have." I shook my head. "But I don't think anyone realized how badly off Rachael was. I tried to tell her sister. She arrived right before the funeral, but she was so busy on her cell phone, she didn't really hear me. Michael's grandparents are in a nursing home out of state. The doctors said they couldn't make the trip. She just had me. And with Michael gone, I felt so much guilt over him that it didn't seem there was anyone I could confide in."

Bray's arm closed around me. "Summer. I'm so sorry."

"I chose the clothes he wore. I went to view the body—another thing she'd decided she couldn't do—I picked out his casket. I chose the music that would play during the memorial service."

"What ... what about your parents?"

"They didn't know I was doing all of that. They just knew I was with Rachael through it. No one knew I'd broken up with Michael and caused the wreck."

"Whoa." Bray's side of the tarp dropped. "*You* didn't cause the wreck. *He* made a bad choice to drink and get behind the wheel of a car. He did that, Summer. You can't carry the weight of his poor decision."

"If it hadn't been for me, he would have stayed right there at the party. You know the last thing he said to me before his eyes closed and he was dead?"

Bray was sick. Sickened by everything I was telling him. Maybe it was hard to look at me now that he knew the truth. It was hard to look at myself sometimes. When I waited for him to answer, he shook his head slightly. "What?"

"His eyes were already going glassy, and I cupped his head as my hand filled with the blood from the gash on his skull. He said he was sorry. He was just trying to have some fun. You know, you'd think at the moment people are dying they'd say really profound things or tell the person they loved them. He just said he was trying to have fun."

The night wind whistled around us. Bray was close, so close that his leg rested against mine. My arm was cold from the wind-dried sweat, and he rubbed his hand up and down it, probably half to warm me, half to soothe.

I stood and walked to the edge of our crescent-shaped lagoon, with its flowing night water and its swaying palms. "Fun leaves a horrible wake, doesn't it?" I spoke the words to no one. I'd left Bray back at the campfire.

I knew the exact moment he stepped behind me, like a sentry. Like a strong wall to lean on. I leaned back. Into him. His arms slowly closed around my midsection. His chin rested on the top of my head. For a very long time, we stayed there. Neither talking, just staring out at the sea, the sky, the night.

Then something broke the surface of the water. "Is that a dolphin?" I asked, looking closer.

A second fin materialized, then a third. "Must be a few. Look, there's a baby." His hand left my stomach and pointed, the muscles of his upper body tightening with the movement. Farther out in the lagoon, the dolphin played.

He tugged me toward the water. "I've got an idea."

"Wait. You said we couldn't swim at night. Sharks."

He pulled again, and I didn't have much strength left to fight. "No sharks around if there are dolphins this close. It's safe."

"Wait. I don't have my swimsuit on." Instantly, I regretted saying it.

His eyes shot to my chest. I shrunk, caving my shoulders. "I'll . . . I'll just run inside and get it. I mean, I'll put it on inside." I turned and bolted, kicking sand as I ran.

I'd never been in the ocean at night. It felt like a completely different place than in the daytime. Usually, it was the heat of day and blinding sun that drove us into the water. It was to cool off and remove the sweat from our skin.

But the night breeze was cool, making the water feel warmer, like bath water. The dolphins didn't come close, but maintained a distance and seemed content to play at the outermost edges of the lagoon. With my arms out, air filled my lungs and my body tilted back, floating on the ocean's surface. Bray was close, and I didn't even jump when his hand came up from under me to rest against my back. I released the air in my lungs and let my weight fall into his capable hold. I loved floating on my back, but had to admit, this was nice. After staying there a while, I decided I was probably taking advantage of his good nature, so I started to move off his hand. His other came up and lightly pressed my shoulder.

"Don't," he said.

My eyes opened and peered at him. He hovered over me, our bodies making a cross in the water.

"Relax." The hand on my shoulder slid around to cup my neck.

He kneaded the muscles there, and as he did, the exertion of talking about Michael caught up to me. My tension became Jell-O. My weightless body was floating, drifting in Bray's arms. I'd even lost interest in the dolphin family and was content to stay right there. Somehow, I felt lighter. Not just from the water, but as if speaking about what happened that night had released some of the pain from me. What had Bray said about not carrying the weight? Maybe he was right. Maybe I shouldn't have carried it so long. It felt good to talk. I hadn't wanted to worry my parents or Becky about it. But Bray hadn't judged me. He never judged me. Just let me be Summer. Maybe the island was teaching me even more than I suspected. Maybe who we really were inside couldn't break through the surface until we were here. On the island and alone. After all, I felt more myself right now than I had for a very long time. It was liberating. And if that was true for me, maybe it was true for Bray. Maybe reckless party boy wasn't who he was on the inside. My eyes snapped open with such intensity, it made him jerk slightly.

He chuckled, looking down at me with the blue-white moon over his right shoulder. "I thought you'd fallen asleep."

I smiled. "Just deeply relaxed." My hand cupped his shoulder and I slid from his grip, but didn't move away. My feet hit and sank into the sandy bottom of the sea, warm water whooshing as my legs worked to hold me up so I could look at Bray eye-to-eye.

The moon on the water danced in confetti pieces in his gaze. I stared deep into him as if I'd be able to read all that was in his heart. "Who are you?" I whispered, my hands still latched to his shoulders.

It was a long time before he answered. At first I thought he was trying to figure out what I meant, the way his brow quirked and his mouth twitched, but with a long exhale, all the questions disappeared. "I'm just Bray."

There didn't seem to be a lie hidden in his words, just honesty. And it caused something to click on the inside of my chest, like some forgotten key turning a door from locked to unlocked. There was pressure against my heart. I looked down to see my own hand fisted there.

Bray touched my wrist, closed his fingers around it and gently lifted it to his mouth. There, he placed the softest of kisses on my fist. And all the emotion of earlier when he'd kissed my tears away came rushing into my belly like white-hot lava.

I knew I should say something. Words failed so I opened my fist and let him kiss my palm. It had calluses from the island, but he didn't seem to care. He planted two kissed there, and then moved my hand back to his shoulder.

I swallowed. "Just Bray, huh?"

He nodded. "I swear I'll never hurt you, Summer. At least not on purpose."

The words raked from my ears down into my knees, where they settled on knocking me off balance. I swayed in the water. But Bray was there, strong, holding me. "You're keeping me from sinking," I said in a breathy tone.

"I'll never let go."

Hearing those words caused my heart to squeeze. I couldn't explain it, didn't even understand it, I just knew that Bray was someone amazing. Someone I could … could …

My hands slid from his shoulders to his chest. Rock hard. There had been plenty of times my hands had been on his chest, but this was different. He wasn't rescuing me; he wasn't dragging me to safety. We weren't even wrestling in the ocean after a bucket of water had been dumped on my head. We were standing in the sea with dolphins playing behind us. There was no threat as I touched him. I wasn't surprised when his hands slid around my waist.

Something shifted in his gaze. Everything—our breathing, his look—became more intense. I felt the muscles of his fingers tighten then release almost like a spasm.

He stared up at the moon for a few long moments, and I could only wonder what was going on in his head. When he readjusted his gaze on me, he looked different. "Summer, I uh, I really want to kiss you right now."

Those words shot into the pit of my stomach.

"But—"

"But?" I echoed back to him, because I was a little confused. I wanted Bray to kiss me. And that realization rocked me.

One of his hands left my waist and ran through his hair, dripping seawater as it went. "But I just swore I'd never hurt you, and I think tonight your emotions have already had enough of a roller coaster ride. I uh . . ."

His other hand dropped from me and the water suddenly felt colder. Sadness and relief took turns on me.

He started to move away from me in the water.

"I understand." My words were barely a whisper.

We both started to wade toward the beach. Halfway there, Bray grabbed my arm and turned me to face him. His eyes were alive with a new kind of fire. "When I kiss you . . . and believe me, one day before we leave this island I will. When it happens, I want it to be about you and me. Nothing from the past. No dead boyfriends. No ghosts."

I swallowed. "That's a lot for you to expect."

"You're a survivor, Summer. It's time to let Michael go."

CHAPTER 10

Bray

I'd never been in love. It was a strange word to me, love. I mean, there were girls I'd liked and had fun with. But love? No. I'd watched my mom and dad as I'd grown up. I knew that kind of thing was possible. How my mom could calm my dad by just the gentle touch of her hand to his arm. How my dad would hold her close and kiss the top of her head. They'd been happy once. Love didn't give up on them. They gave up on it.

Summer. Summer was ... well, there really weren't words. And I'd had to use every ounce of willpower not to take a kiss right there in the water.

I used to think a kiss was just something to do in preamble to the good stuff. But all I wanted was to kiss Summer. Just kiss her. Like that would be enough to satisfy. She'd left my body aching, and the reality unsettled me as much as it excited me. I was going to kiss Summer. It was just a matter of time. But right now, she needed space. So I took off early in the morning and left her a note on the inside edge of the hut's door using coal I plucked from the fire. *Exploring north side of island. Be back soon.*

Really, I just needed space. She consumed the air around us, drawing it in and changing it like a little bit of dye changes a whole bucket of water. I was drowning in her.

I'd followed a path through the woods from the resort. A little ways down, I uncovered an outbuilding. Small, but still holding some tools and a bare spot on the floor where a riding lawn mower probably once lived. I also found an old gas can, saws, hammers, and a few nails. Everything had rusted, but looked like they would still work. I took a sickle with me into the jungle, hacking at the foliage as I went. When I heard strange sounds—foreign to the island—I stopped in my tracks.

Through the trees I saw a slash of white, so I worked my way closer, hoping, praying my eyes weren't playing tricks on me. When the death metal music floated to me, I knew it was a boat. I started to yell, though they'd probably not hear me over the music, but something stopped me. Sweat in my palms caused me to grip the sickle tighter as I closed the distance to the last line of trees and focused on the scene before me. Right on the beach beside the boat stood three men and four women who were clad in bikinis. The hair rose on the back of my neck. One of the men grabbed one of the girls and jerked her to his side. She screamed, head jolting, but didn't seem to mind his roughness as he planted his hands deeply into the flesh of her hips and kissed her.

My heart pounded. This could be our chance at rescue, but something about the men gave me pause. They were dressed in fairly normal island clothes, two with their shirts hanging open, the other in a T-shirt. But something about them just wasn't right. A little too shady looking, a little too cocky. Goose flesh spread across my thighs and arms. That's when I noticed. All the men were wearing guns.

I stayed in the brush, trying to decide what would be best to do. Maybe I could sneak onboard. Steal a radio or satellite phone. I was so intent on watching them, I only vaguely heard the sound behind me. Summer stepped near, her gaze tightly fitted to the tree line.

Just as she cupped her hands around her mouth to yell, I leapt up and tackled her.

She landed on the ground with a grunt and fought, eyes wild until she saw it was me. Still, she shoved to get me off her. I let her wiggle free, but kept my hand clamped over her mouth and whispered, "Shhhh."

Her gaze flew to the boat, then back to me. "It's not safe, Summer." I nodded toward the boat for her to watch.

Something had happened in the time I'd tackled her. The women were gone, back on the boat, I supposed, though they weren't on the deck. Then I noticed a cage sticking up from the rear of the boat—that was something you didn't see every day. On the beach, two of the three men had their guns out and trained on the other, who raised his hands and backed up until he hit a piece of driftwood on the beach and could go no farther.

Summer sucked a breath that vibrated against me where I held her mouth. Slowly, I let go. We both watched, unable to move as the three men argued. Maybe it was a game, maybe they were just messing around. But the voices drifted to us on the beach air, mingling with the loud music. The man was pleading for his life. The first guy cocked his pistol, so I grabbed Summer and put my hand back over her mouth. When the shot rang out, she jolted against me. I turned her into my chest, and her fingernails dug into the skin of my back, trying to suppress her scream. The gunshot echoed off the water and the mountains to the left of us. I'd squeezed my eyes shut. But had to look. Had to be sure.

The body landed in the shallow water, a red cloud floating around it. Arms out, legs slightly spread. *Just like in the movies.* The morbid thought entered my head, but this was nothing like the movies. A man was dead. We'd just watch him die.

I looked down at Summer, still clinging to me, and I realized this wasn't the first time for her. She'd watched someone die before.

I worried what this might do to her psyche. More than anything, I worried that we would be found. We were witnesses to murder, after all.

And stuck here on the island, there was nowhere to run.

I grabbed her and ran anyway, half carrying her toward the hut. Once I knew we were out of earshot, I started giving instructions. More for myself than for her. "I have to cover everything. We don't know if they're planning to stop anywhere else on the island. If they come around to the lagoon ..."

Summer quaked in my arms. "Stop. Just stop." She held her hands up. They were trembling. Her eyes were haunted as they darted around us. "They ... they killed him."

She probably needed a few minutes to deal, but I didn't know what kind of time we had. "I know, Summer."

"Shot him. Right there in front of us."

"I know." I squeezed her arms, hoping it would equalize her. "But right now, we need to keep ourselves safe. Okay?"

She didn't answer.

I stared into her soft, green eyes now filled with new terror at what we'd just seen. "We made a promise to each other, remember?"

She blinked, and I watched as she searched for the memory. Summer nodded, brow still furrowed, but eyes determined. "Yes. We made a promise."

I leaned in and dropped a kiss on her cheek. "I'm going to get things picked up at the hut then go over to the beach and make sure it looks like no one has been there." I knew doing so would hurt our chances of a rescue plane seeing us, but with murderers on the island, we didn't have much choice.

"I ... I'll help." Summer's voice shook with each word. But like me, she was determined. We made it back to the hut and doused the fire. Summer helped me move a giant piece of driftwood over it so that from the water, it would appear natural. I yanked the tarp from the porch and spread the palm fronds so everything looked overgrown and, hopefully, camouflaged.

Summer gathered the kitchen utensils into the large pot and we hid it behind the trees.

"I'm going to the beach. I'll take care of things there. I want you to stay inside the kitchen at the old resort while I'm gone. Okay?"

"Why?"

"I don't think they'll go to the interior of the island. Not with a half-million-dollar boat with all the amenities. No reason an abandoned resort would interest them. You'll be safest there. Safer than staying here."

But that wasn't the only reason Summer couldn't come with me. I was going to do something I couldn't tell her about. She gauged me for a long time before answering. "Okay. I'll stay in the kitchen. But promise me you won't try to get onto that boat."

I flashed her a smile. "Why would I do that?"

"Satellite phone, send a help message."

"I swear, Summer. I swear on our lives I won't try to get on the boat."

That seemed to satisfy her. I walked her to the building and ushered her inside. "I'll be back for you as soon as I can."

She nodded, squeezed my hand, and let me go. "Be careful," she said as I left. "Stay out of sight."

I took care of my work at the beach as quickly as possible—we didn't have much and with the way the place looked post-hurricane, a little disorder wouldn't look out of place.

And then I forced myself to put one foot in front of the other and navigate the island near the boat. I walked a ways before I found the body. It had drifted, just as I expected it would. Bullet hole in the chest. With a nausea born of handling my first ever dead person, I set about finding the wallet on the man who'd lost his life before my eyes. My nervousness had me glancing up and around every few seconds and — though I had seen dead animals before — my squeamishness at touching a dead human had the task taking longer than I wanted it to. I fumbled for the wallet and stepped back from the remains as quickly as I could. The waves continued to lap at the body, lifting it off the sand and up and out from the shore with each crest. Soon the body was well away from the shoreline and I felt a wash of relief that I wouldn't have to feel a sense of obligation, of ownership of these remains of someone else's life.

I collected Summer from the kitchen and we silently made our way back to the hut. The image of the dead man stayed in my head, and I saw him each time I closed my eyes. Summer didn't question me, but I felt she knew something had gone on while I was away. Many nights I'd made a silent promise to be strong for her. Tonight I needed her to be strong for me.

• • • • •

"It's different without the fire." She was sitting on the tarp, staring out over the water. Her hands had stopped shaking. We'd placed the tarp at the foot of the hut steps and were both leaning on the posts — a good spot to make a quick getaway to the jungle beyond if we heard voices or the hum of the motor on their boat.

She was right. The fire was warmth and light and life. At night, it was comfort. The sun was high in the sky, but I wasn't looking forward to the evening ahead. Right now, we still had things to do to ensure our safety.

"The toolshed I found had quite a few things in it. A lot of tools. even an old radio, but since I'm not the professor on *Gilligan's Island*, I doubt I can turn it into anything."

Her eyes widened on me. "Are you thinking we may need the tools as weapons?"

I swallowed. I didn't want to need them as weapons, but if they found us, I wouldn't go down without some kind of fight. "No, Summer. I'm just trying to redirect the conversation. We can drive ourselves mad sitting here thinking they're coming."

She pivoted, and the sun caught the highlights in her hair. "But they could be. We watched them murder a man. Just like that, alive one second, dead the next."

I *really* needed to redirect this. "Do you want to hear about the shed or not?"

This got a smile from Summer.

"There was also a box of paper."

"Paper?" She caught her hair in a mass at her neckline.

"Yeeeaaah."

"What will we use it for?"

"Good for insulation, starting fires too. I just thought we'd be able to utilize it."

"Oh." She rocked forward, and her index finger slipped into her mouth where she absently nibbled her nail.

"What are you thinking, Summer?"

"Nothing." She tilted her head. "I used to write. All the time and I haven't since ... since ..."

"I think we could spare some paper for you to write on."

Her face clouded. "I wouldn't know what I'd say anymore."

How about telling how we just watched a guy die? "Isn't that the beauty of being a writer? Don't the words kind of come to life once you start writing them?"

"I guess."

"There are pencils in one of the drawers in the kitchen. Tomorrow I'll get a couple and sharpen them with one of the knives. Okay?"

She nodded, and I could see a fresh spark inside her. Good. She needed to be ready for what we had to do. Anything that gave her a little extra hope was good. I reached behind me. "While I was gone, I got this." The wet leather wallet had a blood stain on the corner.

Summer stared at it for a long time. "You went back to the boat? You promised."

"The body floated a couple hundred yards down the beach. It followed a curve in the island. I made sure they couldn't see me."

All her horror was back, complete with bulging eyes and an open mouth.

"Summer, we had to know who he was so we can tell the authorities. Also, he may have a family. They have a right to know."

She started to take the wallet, but must have thought better of it. "His name?"

"Jamison Cavanaugh." As an afterthought, I added. "He was thirty-six."

We had a moment of silence for Mr. Cavanaugh, both of us staring out at the water and both dreading the long night ahead.

"We should say a few words. You know, have a memorial for him." Summer's hand fisted on the tarp between us.

I lay my hand over hers. "I already did. At the water's edge where I found him. But if it would make you feel better . . ."

She thought about that for a moment. "No. If you did, then it's fine. Did you . . . bury . . ."

"No. The body had already moved a bit. I just let nature take its course." I didn't want Summer to know my main concern had been some animal finding and digging him up. The thought of Summer coming across that on the island — after everything she'd already been through — just seemed unnecessary.

She gave a slight nod.

Now, on to more pressing matters. "We need a bug-out spot."

"Huh?"

"We need a place to go in case the hut is compromised. And I, uh, think I may have found one. But . . ."

Big eyes waited, the green in them filling with concern. She knew my tone, instinctively knew she wasn't going to like this.

"It's a cave."

A shudder worked its way over her upper body. "I don't like caves. I don't like anything that's all enclosed and tight."

My arm slipped around her shoulders. "I know. It'll only be used in an emergency if the people on the boat find out we're on the island."

Her hands came together, fingernails clicking against one another. She did that whenever she was scared.

"We can take some supplies to stash there."

Her breaths were coming quicker until they were only short little gasps.

"I'll go myself and get it stocked. You can stay here."

Eyes full of fury or determination — maybe a bit of both — glared at me. "No. I'll go with you. I don't think I could stand sitting alone much more."

"Okay." I didn't dare argue. Besides, she needed to know where the cave was. Also, we needed to figure out the best path to it. Since it was halfway up a mountain on the west side of the island, it wouldn't be easy to get to. And the more difficult to get to, the safer it would be from the men on the boat.

We packed up a few provisions — enough for a day or two — and headed to the west end of the island. I brought the rope we'd retrieved from our boat before the ocean claimed it and hung it over my shoulder, hoping and praying we wouldn't have to use it to get to the cave. Careful not to leave footprints on the beach, we walked just inside the canopy surrounding the shore until we came to the first outcropping of rocks. "Okay, from here on, we need to be careful. The rocks are slick, and we have to climb pretty far up to reach the cave."

"Did you go up there already?"

"Only halfway. I spotted it from below. The rocks block the view of where the boat sits, but we need to be careful. I think we'd hear the motor if they move closer, but we need to really pay attention, okay?"

Summer stayed quiet, following my steps as we climbed. The day was hot and muggy, with the heavy scent of mold hanging in the island trees. I supposed the rocks created a barrier for the west side, never allowing the moisture to dry completely. The heat was stifling but neither of us complained. Climbing would take us a while, but eventually we'd be above the line of shrubs and brush that anchored this part of the island. I stopped at the foot of the blue-black mountain we'd have to climb; it jutted into the sky and made me realize what a miracle it was that I'd spotted the indention of the cave from the ground below.

"Doing okay?"

"Could use a drink." Summer carried the lidded plastic container—the kind you'd see in restaurant kitchens usually filled with nonspecific foods like coleslaw. I carried everything else we needed to keep us alive if we had to hole up in the cave for a few days. We'd filled her container half full of water so she could manage it easily. Slender fingers gripped and peeled the plastic lid open. A half coconut shell floated on the water's surface. She scooped it up and offered me the first drink. I drained the shell and handed it back to her. She did the same, letting a bit of it dribble down her neck and disappear into rim of her gray T-shirt.

The mountain loomed above us. I worked to figure out the best way to navigate the rise.

"How'd you find the cave?" Summer said, breaking the silence.

"Half luck. Half searching."

"It wasn't luck."

I looked over to find a hint of a smile and a spark in her light green eyes. I mocked a frown. "Have you been praying again?"

"Guilty."

"Could you hurry up and pray for a rescue boat?"

Summer sighed. "I have been. But ..."

"But God's awful busy?"

"No. I mean, sure, I imagine He is, but we're going to be rescued, Bray. In my heart, I know that. But sometimes I think God doesn't rush in so quickly because maybe there's something we need to take away from the experience. Does that make any sense?"

"Maybe." I wasn't sure. We were in a horrible situation. Summer claimed God didn't put us in it, but if He had the power to get us out, why didn't He? I'd always wondered how people could have faith in bad situations. "I guess you could maintain your faith if you knew at the right time God was going to get you out."

"Exactly." She smiled. She stared up at the black rock. "Now give me my mountain. I'm able to handle it."

"No fear of heights?" I was remembering her hesitation to climb the Mayan ruins.

"Yes, the fear is there, but our answer is on the other side of it. If I really believe God is going to get us out of this, then I'm not going to die on this mountain."

"Yes, ma'am."

She looked over at me. "When did you see the cave?"

"After I retrieved the wallet, I decided we needed a place to go if ... you know ... if the boat men figured out we were here. So instead of using the island interior to get to the beach where camp was, I started climbing over the rocks. The cave is pretty shrouded from the beach, but it sits high enough we wouldn't want to build a fire there or anything. It's not going to be easy to get to. And I'm not even sure how far it goes back into the rock, but they'd have to really be searching to find it."

The vein in Summer's throat throbbed. She swallowed. "You really think they will find us, don't you?"

I dropped the pan of provisions and turned to face her. "No. I'm just being extra careful." She hadn't seen the guy grab the girl and kiss her. I had my suspicions about what those two guys would do to Summer if they found her. Me, they'd kill. But her, they'd abuse. I wasn't willing to take any chances with her life.

She forced a tiny smile.

"Maybe we should just stay at the cave until they're gone. Not go back to the hut at all until they've left the island."

Fear entered her eyes and her voice. "Bray, we can't. They could be here for days, weeks."

"Probably not. More than likely, they'll move on in the next day or two. They killed a man here, Summer. They won't want to hang around too long, just in case."

"Can we just wait until we get up there to make any decisions? It might not even be big enough for us."

I could tell Summer didn't like enclosed places. I'd watched her voice tighten with fear as she'd talked about Michael being trapped in his car. Maybe this stemmed from that incident. Whatever the reason, she was going to have a difficult time if the cave was as small as I suspected. Smaller meant safer in my opinion. But to Summer, smaller meant more terrifying.

"Ready to climb?"

She nodded, but paused as I started placing palm fronds and brush around the pan. "Aren't we taking those up?"

I was a little nervous about navigating the mossy, wet rocks. "I'll come back down and get them. Right now, we don't need the extra weight. We need a path first. The mountainside will be slick, so promise me you'll be careful. You might try using the same footholds and handholds that I do."

She nodded, clustered her hair at her nape and tucked it into the neckline of her shirt. Since one of her shoes had come untied, I knelt to tie it. "Going to double knot these. I already did mine. Are they snug on your feet?"

Toes wiggled inside her shoes. "Yes."

I rewrapped the rope into smooth loops and placed a couple of slip knots near the ends. After that, I rested it on my shoulder. "Let's go."

The first section was easy to climb, though slippery. I figured the condensation on the rocks would lessen as we rose higher. At the lower quarter of the climb, the rocks were moss-covered. I reached a flat spot large enough for both of us and sat down. Over the edge, I reached for Summer. So far, she'd kept up well, but I could see the exhaustion in her face, sweat sliding down her cheeks and onto her neck. The sheen on her skin caught the sunlight, and I wished I'd brought the water bucket with us. With a grunt, she was on the narrow ridge with me, our legs dangling off the side. She dropped her head back to rest on the mountain. In front of us, we could see nothing but rock as if we were cocooned in a jagged, stone womb.

"My legs are twitching."

"Mine too," I agreed. "Maybe I should climb back down and get the water."

Summer tilted back to look far above us, one eye closing as she squinted from the sun's glare. "No. Let's just get to the cave, and then we can come down for things." I knew she was anxious to find out what our bug-out destination would offer: a sprawling room or a tiny crevice. I assumed we could fit inside easily, but who knew?

She stood and offered a hand. "Ready?"

We soldiered on until I could see the opening. "Summer, look up." She'd climbed like a monkey, but I knew it was getting to her. Her gaze trailed above me.

She was plastered against the rock. I looked down. Big mistake. Below her, the jagged spikes seemed to go on forever, like skewers waiting to impale us. It was more than a little creepy.

Summer didn't notice. She'd locked her gaze on the cave opening then dropped her head forward, resting against the sun-hot rock.

I lay down on the ground at the entrance to the cave and reached my hand over the side. "Here, let me help you from there." The idea of her having to navigate that last large step scared me. She clamped her hand around my forearm and I did the same, surprised at how slick she was. I started to pull, but the rocks bearing her weight shifted. I watched pebbles drop from beneath her feet and plummet down, down, down until they cracked at the lower ridge where we'd stopped to rest. My hold tightened, as did Summer's. She scrambled for a new foothold, but the weight on my arm grew heavier and more intense as her feet faltered.

Her other hand gripped a small protrusion on the rock face, but with her feet dangling, she couldn't hold on. Her fist began to loosen on the rock. I shifted my weight to get a better hold, the toes of my tennis shoes digging into the ground. My side hadn't been bothering me, but as I tried to lift, pain shot into my ribs, weakening my strength.

Summer's hand finally gave way and slipped off the rock. She screamed. The sound echoed, and amplified in my skull. I jerked my arm to drag her up. Pain ripped through my side. My eyes slammed shut as desperation gripped me by the throat. At the base of my slick arm, Summer dangled. Nearly blinded with pain, I called to her. First, screaming her name. Then calmly saying it. I had to get control of the situation. I had to calm her down. "Summer."

Terror-filled eyes found me and pleaded.

"I'm not going to let you go."

The words seemed to work. She stopped fighting against gravity and hung there, unmoving.

"In the water, I told you I'd never let go. Remember?" The ligaments or tendons or muscles in my arm started tearing. Maybe all three. With each slow movement, I could feel something ripping. "I swear I won't. Never, okay?"

She nodded and pressed her face to the rock as if able to hold on vertically.

"Find the spot for your hand." Without looking, her fingers, bloody now from raking against the rock, began to feel along the cliff. When they touched a spot she could grip, she clamped on it. "Good job."

The rope still rode on my shoulder, but without two hands, I wasn't sure what good it would do. Then, I remembered the slip knots. With my free hand I shook the loops from the rope and arranged it so one end was wound around my waist. Pain seared my arm at the extra movement, but I tried to ignore it. The other end of the rope I tossed over the side. "Summer, I'm going to need you to let go of the rock for a few seconds and slide your hand into the rope. Then, use your mouth to tighten the knot. Can you do that?"

She nodded, but still hadn't said anything.

My grip was slipping, so I tried to hold tighter as I dangled the knot against her hand. "I've got you. Go ahead." She'd found a tiny crevice with her left foot and tried to jam her toes inside. It looked like this took just enough of the weight off for her to release her hand from the rock, and she slid the rope over until it rested against her wrist. Summer drew it to her mouth, caught the dangling end of the rope, and jerked it tight around her.

I released a tension-filled gust of air. "Okay, we're connected now. I can pull you up." Really, our situation hadn't improved that much—I still lay prone at the cave opening, and she was still dangling below me—but panic was gone and the fight to survive settled over me. "When I let go, I want you to grab the rope with your other hand. Okay?"

"Okay," she said softly. The sound crawled over me. I wouldn't let her fall.

I glanced behind me. There was a spiked boulder just beyond my reach. Slowly, my hand slid free from Summer's. She tried not to jump, but I felt the jolt on the other end of the rope. One tiny knot was all that kept her from falling. I forced that from my mind and shimmied around the edge of the boulder. Placing my feet against it, I hollered, "Hang on."

My feet planted, I pushed with every ounce of force inside me. Though already tired from the climb, somehow I managed to draw the rope. Summer's face appeared at the ledge, fueling me. I repositioned and pushed against the boulder again. This time, her shoulders appeared. Her free hand released the rope and she scrambled to grab the ground. One more pull and she was close enough to throw a dirt-covered leg onto the ledge. I reached forward, grabbing her with one hand while holding the rope tight with the other. Another grunt and she was beside me.

My mind screamed to hold Summer, but we were both too exhausted to move. I lay on my back, staring up at the sky. Summer was lying on her stomach, both of us breathing hard. I worried about the damage I may have done to her wrist. My forearm was screaming like someone had slit it open and poured hot acid inside my veins. And if mine was that bad, I could only imagine what her wrist must feel like.

And that led me to another question. How in the world were we going to get down?

CHAPTER 11

Summer

Several thoughts occurred to me at once, fighting for dominance inside my head. But the biggest of all was, "How are you going to get the supplies?"

"I'll make it," he said, and smiled. "Down is always easier than up."

My arm felt like someone had held it in a washing machine and turned on the spin cycle. Bray inspected it, his hands working in smooth motions over my fingers, palm, wrist, then up my forearm and settling on my shoulder. "All this okay?"

I nodded, bent my wrist back and forth. "Seems so. I mean, it hurts."

His index finger traced the red lines left by the rope. "I don't think it's out of place. You did a good job holding some of your weight with your free hand."

But I was concerned for Bray. He kept holding one of his arms to his ribcage, like someone would do if their arm was broken and in a sling. "What about you?"

"I'm good." Such a liar.

"What if I wasn't telling you the truth?" I said.

His gaze narrowed, concern knitting his brows together. There were dirt smudges on his cheeks and forehead.

"What if I really was hurt but I didn't want you to know?"

"That wouldn't be okay, Summer." He moved closer so that I couldn't escape his inspection. "We're alone out here. We have to depend on each other. It would be *really* unsafe for you to be hurt and not tell me."

I grinned victoriously.

When he scanned my face for an explanation, I nodded to his arm.

It only took him a second to understand my meaning. His eyes rolled. "It's hurting."

I took his arm and turned it palm-side up. Red snaked from his wrist up to the bend of his elbow. "Oh, Bray." I placed my hand flat against it gently. "It's hot. Like it's on fire."

We stared down at the bright-red skin. "I scraped it climbing. Some of that might even be inflammation. My dad has arthritis in his knees, and when we play tennis, they look about like this."

"Inflammation?"

"Yeah. And I felt something tearing while I tried to lift you over the side. It wouldn't have been difficult—you hardly weigh anything—but I couldn't really use my stomach muscles because my ribs are still sore. Guess whatever I did was the wrong thing." Then he switched tactics. "Come on. Let's check out the cave."

That stole my focus. I couldn't believe I had climbed a mountain to do something I never, *ever* wanted to do. But Bray felt we were unsafe as long as those men were around, and I had to agree. They had killed a man.

I stood at the mouth of the cave—and that's exactly what it looked like: an open, hungry mouth fitted with tiny, jagged teeth, smiling sadistically, inviting us inside where the gums would clamp down around us and crush us into powder.

"You gonna be able to do this?"

My head shook back and forth. "Yes."

There were a few hanging vines blocking the entrance. Bray pulled his dive knife from its sheath. He cut some near the bottom, but folded them back rather than cutting them from the top too. "Camo."

"Good thinking." I tried to be supportive. But my heart was beating so fast, it felt like a steady hum instead of individual beats.

As Bray finished folding the vines back, light flooded the cave. "Listen." He put his hand out to quiet me, but I wasn't making any sound.

Then I heard it. The white noise of distant running water. Before I could answer, he grabbed my hand and led me inside.

We had to bend at the waist to keep from scraping our heads on the roof of the cave. "Wow," I said. "It's about twenty degrees cooler in here."

"Right?" Bray turned and smiled at me. We both raised our arms to allow the cooler air to dry the sweat we'd accumulated on the treacherous climb. I watched as he stopped at the first wall. He placed his hand against it. "Cold. And wet. Look at this, Summer."

I moved over to him and peered down into a small puddle of water.

As he took a step to get closer, his foot clinked against something on the ground. He knelt and picked up the empty Coke bottle.

"Someone's been up here before?" I asked him.

"Probably when they were going to do the eco-resort here. I'm sure they explored the whole island. We can use this to get a drink, if you're game."

"Is it fresh water?"

Bray spread his hand across the wet rock, moistening it then bringing it to his mouth. "Yeah. And it's cold." He disappeared from beside me and returned with a small piece of bamboo he'd cut with his dive knife. Bamboo of different lengths and widths dotted the whole island, but I hadn't thought of using the hollow branch as a straw. The small piece of round wood rolled between his fingertips. "Still game?"

We took turns kneeling down to drink from the tiny pool. It tasted slightly different from the lake water we'd been living on. Somehow, this water was more alive, earthier. "This tastes like the well water I drink when I visit my cousins in Missouri," I told him.

Bray nodded. "I think it might be mineral water. It's probably better for us. Tastes good, that's for sure."

We still hadn't inspected the deeper part of the cave. It looked like it went back a ways, but our eyes hadn't adjusted to the dim light enough to tell.

"Let's drink as much as we can. I think it will improve our energy."

It was hard to imagine water as any kind of miracle cure, but I had to admit, I was feeling better, less lethargic. Bray's lips were bright red from the cold drink, making it look like he wore lipstick. The giggle stayed in my throat. He placed the water bottle along the wall and positioned the bamboo straw inside. Instantly, the bottle began collecting the water that dribbled from the rocks.

"Smart," I said. "I give you an A plus for ingenuity."

"How you doing with the whole cave thing?"

"Not bad. It's pretty open. If I have to go back farther, I don't know how I'll do, but up here is okay. It's better than hanging out with murderers. Do you think they were drug dealers or something?"

"I don't know. Drugs, human trafficking, paid killers. All I know is we need to stay away from them."

"I still hear the water."

His hand cupped around his ear. "Hear how deep and hollow it sounds? There's got to be something farther in. Plus—"

I spun, hearing the change in his tone. "Plus what?"

"Well, I just need to make sure there's no sign of an animal living in here. If there is ... or if I decide climbing that mountain again is worse than fighting off armed killers using our garden tools, we may have to find a new place."

Oh. I hadn't thought of animals.

"I'm just trying to be safe, Summer. If we have to bug out to this location, I don't want any surprises when we get here."

Behind him, the dark cavern loomed, ready to swallow us. My eyes had adjusted somewhat, and I could see the cave split off in two directions. Slowly, I moved to the back where they spread, one left and one right. "Hey, is that light?" It was hard to tell, because the water on the cave walls bounced tiny bits of light around inside.

Bray took a few steps deeper on the right hand side. "It is."

From my vantage point, it only looked like a thin trickle of light, but hopefully it was enough that Bray wouldn't fall into a pit or something. My fingers itched to grab him as he moved deeper into the cavern.

"Summer, there's plenty of light back here. Must be an opening somewhere in the top of the mountain."

His words grew faint as he went deeper, bouncing and playing off the cave walls, like the cave was stealing him and turning him into an echo.

"Whoa," he said, voice filled with awe.

"What? What did you find?" The Loch Ness Monster, maybe? Jimmy Hoffa? Amelia Earhart?

But my words bounced off the rocks and returned to me unanswered. "Bray! What is it?"

"It's ... it's ... You gotta see it."

My feet stammered at the crossroads between the two directions. Off to the left, I could see the cave ended just a few feet in. But the other went far enough to cause Bray's voice to sound foreign.

"Come on, Summer. It gets a little squeezy, but I swear it will be worth it."

There was so much excitement in his tone; I knew I couldn't let him down. Pulling a hard draw of air, I dove into the cave, my feet making tentative steps as the rocky walls tightened around me until I saw what lay ahead. My lungs squeezed. I had to nearly bend into a pretzel to get through one part, but I did it, expecting an opening on the other side. Instead, I was met with a blank wall. That's when I couldn't keep the panic at bay any longer. Palms sweaty, heart hammering, ears red-hot and ringing. I grabbed the rock in front of me in a futile attempt to push it out of my way. My lungs weren't getting any oxygen, and tiny spots appeared before my eyes. This was an anxiety attack. I recognized it. And I was all out of paper bags. Something dropped onto my left shoulder and I screamed as the sound bounded off the rocks and back to me, filling my ears with my lonely roar of fear. Something else closed around my waist and tugged.

Bray. He was dragging me from my frozen spot. The tight enclosed space widened as he pulled me to him. I knew I was trembling, but couldn't help it. Then he turned me around and held me in a tight embrace. My eyes squeezed shut, and I breathed him in. Just feeling him calmed me. He held my head to his chest and mumbled, "That's my girl."

I felt the soft kiss on the top of my head and knew that what had frightened me wasn't so much the cave, but my own inability to control my situation. To have to bend and twist to get through to the other side. But I'd done it. Which in some tiny way, meant I'd conquered the cave.

"You're gonna love this," Bray said, his words a low rumble in my ear.

I opened my eyes and sucked in a giant, cool breath. Rays of light shot through the roof and down into a round pool. The liquid ran from the cracked sections in the walls, accumulating at the bottom. All around it, smaller pools—some the size of our wash pan, some larger—sat holding crystal clear water. Where the light hit just right, you could see the bottom of each little pool. And I swear it looked like the place was glowing.

"It's beautiful."

Bray knelt down in one corner of the room. "Mud." He brought his hand up to show me the dark stuff. Before I could say, "Gross," he started spreading it up the inside of his sore arm.

"Uh ..." was all I could manage.

"You next?"

I took a step back. "No thanks."

"I think it will help your wrist." He seemed really sure of himself and I wondered if the cave had somehow swapped his brain for mush.

"It's *mud.*"

"Didn't Mom take you to the spa? People pay high dollar for this."

I did seem to recall a mud mask on the spa menu. "You really think that will help?" I couldn't believe I was falling for this. It was probably some kind of joke, but I shuffled toward him.

"Mud has great healing properties. Seriously. We can slather some on, and then rinse it off in one of the little pools. Or ..." He let the word hang in the air.

"Or what?"

He wiggled his brows and pointed to the large pool. So fresh, so inviting. And right there waiting for us. I slipped my lower lip between my teeth and bit down.

"The water's nice and cool. Would feel great right about now."

Before I could change my mind, I pulled my T-shirt off to reveal my bikini top—which by now I was growing more accustomed to. "I don't want mud on my shirt." Of course, it had become a darker shade of gray in the time we'd been there. I dropped to my knees next to Bray and we hovered over the mud hole.

Bray plunged his fingers into the muck and brought up two handfuls, then spread it on my wrist over the rope burn. The half liquid, half solid pressed against my burns, soothing them, cooling them.

I sighed and dropped from my knees onto my bottom. Bray scooted beside me.

"It's good for sunburns too."

Suspicious eyes met his all too innocent ones. I just couldn't get a mental picture of Bray spreading mud all over my body. Or maybe I *could* get a picture of it and that's what bothered me. "I'll stick with just the wrist."

We really weren't that sunburned anymore. Bray was a little worse than I was. The burns had become tans and we were both about five shades darker than when we had arrived. At least the tan seemed to help us tolerate the sun and unforgiving temperatures on the island. But even if I didn't want the mud, the water in front of us was practically calling, and I could imagine it cool and clear, caressing my sun-tightened skin. My eyes trailed from the mud pit to him. "Last one in is a rotten egg."

I leapt up and removed my shoes and then my shorts, leaving them right where they dropped.

My foot hit the water and I froze. Behind me, Bray was yammering about it not being fair, that he wasn't ready and his entire arm was covered in mud, slowing him down.

"It's *cold*. I mean, *really* cold." I snatched my foot out like it had burned me.

Bray carefully pulled the T-shirt from his body, but it got stuck around his head as he tried to remove it without getting the whole thing covered in mud. "Could use a little help here."

Hands over his head, face blocked by his shirt. I stepped closer and noticed the lines of muscles in his stomach, like chains under flesh. He really was beautiful, even when covered from elbows to fingertips in mud. "Uh, Summer?"

He couldn't see me inspecting his chest and stomach from such close proximity, so I did the only thing I could do. I plunged my hands into the mud and brought it up to his chest. When I first touched him, he tensed. Then quivered. Then a long sigh left his lips.

I could imagine his eyes closing, his mouth slightly open. I don't know why it was easier to do with his face covered, but it was. The mud was cool, but warmed as it made contact with his hot skin. My fingertips ran over his pecs, leaving dark smears wherever they touched. I moistened my hands and placed them along his sides, then slowly drew them upward until I felt his lateral muscles tighten at my touch. I grabbed his arm and turned him around so that he faced away from me. He moved easily as if not wanting to break the contact. With one tug, I stripped the shirt from him. His hands lowered, shoulders rising and falling, but in an uneven manner. I spread a generous helping of mud over his shoulders, fingers and palms moving with more and more confidence as I learned the curves and contours of his body. I covered his back, taking note of the way his waist dipped slightly inward and the indention of spine ridged with muscle. He could be a model if he wanted. He was perfect. Bray made all other guys seem like little boys. He made them smaller. I could lose my heart to him. And that wasn't the only thing on the line.

After I finished, I doused my hands over and over again in one of the small pools until they were clean.

"You next?" Bray said, coming to stand just behind me, his voice hoarse against my ear.

I closed my eyes. He wasn't touching me, but he felt so *there*, so in my space, and I didn't want him to move but I also couldn't take his hands on me. My body had reacted to his as my hands roamed freely over him, and right now, I wasn't sure I could resist. I swallowed.

"I probably shouldn't have done that." The words were a whisper on my mouth. Until he answered, I wasn't even sure he heard.

"I'm glad you did."

I turned to face him, water still dripping from my fingertips.

"You just looked more burned than me. You're the one always out in the sun, and I didn't want you to be uncomfortable if the mud could help ..."

He placed a mud-caked finger over my lips. Luckily, the mud had hardened. "Summer. Don't apologize. Don't *ever* apologize for touching me."

"Stop it!" I slung the remaining water from my hands.

Bray took a step back and raised his brows.

"This isn't *fair* to you, Bray. You have ... you know ..." I turned to face the pool because I couldn't look at him and say it. "Needs."

Beside me, he tromped a couple steps into the water. One quick glance told me he was dousing his hands. A moment later, he stepped in front of me, blocking the pool.

I chewed my lip. "I told you, it's cold."

"Yeah." I couldn't bear to look at him. My gaze flitted everywhere else. He tilted my chin with his finger and thumb. A long moment stretched. "Needs, huh?"

I would have thought he was making fun of me if he hadn't sounded so tender. I had once placed a purity ring on my hand and promised to wait.

"Summer, I'm not going to lie to you. I want that. In fact, I'd love that. But you're not punishing me by sticking to your convictions. I think I have a good idea of what that means to you and I'm okay with waiting."

I was all geared to defend my position. "What?"

"I can wait for you, Summer. You're worth it."

I was speechless, trying to digest that. "No. You don't understand because it's not just about waiting. Bray, I made a promise to myself a long time ago that I wouldn't until my wedding night."

His hand dropped, but his face was unreadable.

"I have a vision for my wedding day, Bray. I put a purity ring on my finger and made a vow."

When he didn't speak, I had to continue, had to try to make him understand. "It started in my freshman year when Michael's mom married. It was the most amazing wedding I'd ever seen and it made me want to wait. Waiting is the only thing that could make a day like that more special. More unforgettable. I went and talked to my youth pastor. He'd been wanting to take us through the class about waiting for marriage. Michael even did the class with me."

"But Summer, are you waiting for Michael? Because if this vision is wrapped around him, that can't happen. If that's the case, you're going to end up really disappointed."

He wasn't being cruel. Just honest. And it deserved honesty in return. "I ... I don't know."

His chilly fingertips slid up and down my arms. "Okay, then. We have some decisions to make."

I frowned.

"First, you need to figure out how you really feel about it. And second, I need you to know that whatever you decide is okay."

My heart did a little flip. "It is?"

"Yeah." He ran a hand through his hair. "I gotta admit, I'm not always going to like it. You're a really beautiful woman, Summer, and I wouldn't be human if I didn't want you. But ..."

"But?"

"I've learned something from you. I want a deeper relationship, a *real* relationship. One that looks nothing like what I've had in the past."

"Oh." I didn't know what else to say.

"So let's just take this one step at a time, okay?"

I knew what he meant. *This* was that thing, that chemistry, that intensity that had grown since we'd arrived on the island. "How do we do that?"

"Can I take you out on a date?"

I almost laughed, part from relief, part from the silliness of it. We were shipwrecked on an island together.

"If you need some convincing, I'm a pretty good date. Flowers and everything. Besides, we've witnessed some horrible things today. A date would make life feel — at least a little — more normal."

"Flowers, huh?"

"Or chocolate."

I narrowed my gaze on him, fighting the smile.

"Okay, chocolate might be difficult to find, but flowers I can manage. Will you meet me at our place tonight at dusk? That is, if we survive climbing back down the mountainside."

I crossed my arms over my chest. "Sure."

At that moment, the stillness around us intensified. Bray leaned toward me and brushed a kiss across my cheek, causing my eyes to close. "Guess what?" he whispered.

"What?"

"You lose. I'm in the water."

My eyes snapped open. And just like that, he clamped me in a death grip and dragged me into the frigid pool.

CHAPTER 12

Bray

"Bray look!"

We'd started our way down the mountainside moving slowly. I'd slipped once, but regained my footing quickly. Standing on a flat rock just below Summer, I tried to see what she was pointing at. All I could see was rock. She was perched on one a few feet above and motioned for me to come back up to her.

When I did, I saw a path that cut through the rock moving downward, but at a much easier slope. Her eyes lit. "Do you think it goes all the way to the bottom?"

"One way to find out." We redirected ourselves and headed down. We navigated the terrain smoothly until we reached a mossy, flat surface. It was about ten feet wide and dropped straight down.

"Can we jump?" Summer's tone was helpless, and I felt about the same.

"Yeah, I think we can make it." We both peered over the edge to the forest floor below. It *looked* soft enough. "I'll go first." I sat down on the ledge and inched my body over, hoping to slide down, but gravity took hold and I landed with a thud, my feet beneath me and my body jarring.

Summer followed and I caught her at the bottom, clamping my hands around her waist just in time to soften the landing. "We made it," she whispered.

I was out of breath, but not sure if it from was the descent or having Summer trapped against the rock wall.

When her arms came around me in a quick hug, I knew. It was her. All her.

Before we could make it back to the hut, I heard the hum of a far-off boat engine. Either the killers were leaving, or more were joining the party. Either way, we had to be careful.

It was still hours before dusk, so I had time while Summer busied herself setting up the hut so that we could stay hidden there in the daytime if we needed to. She'd brought containers of water inside and made sure the entrance looked uninhabited. I figured it was unlikely anyone would venture into the hut unless they suspected people were there. And really, if they suspected that, we were as good as dead anyway.

But my curiosity wouldn't let me rest. I'd heard a boat motor, and I needed to know if it would be best for us to just go back to the cave where I was certain they wouldn't find us. But the climb and its dangers made the decision for me. While Summer was working, I ran as quickly as I could, being as quiet as possible, to the beach where the boat had been.

Through the trees, my eyes scanned first the beach and then the horizon in both directions. They were gone. No boat. No murderers. At least we could sleep tonight. The problem was, I'd been thinking about how my dad had told me the islands and the cays were used for all sorts of illegal things. This might be a regular stop for these guys. Really, we weren't much safer than we'd been with them on the other side of the island. But it was unlikely they'd return tonight, so at least we had that.

I returned quickly. I'd spotted a swing on the end hut, but the chain was broken. With the tools I had from the shed, maybe I could repair it and hang it on the hooks on our front porch for the evenings. I could take it down each morning and cover it with brush. But having a real place to sit might help us hold it together. As if being stranded here wasn't enough, now we had to worry about who might show up and slit our throats.

Summer didn't want me sleeping out on the porch anymore. On the one hand, being out there meant a lookout, someone to stay guard. On the other, it was hard to be a guard when you were asleep. Plus, if someone happened to wander by, they'd see me. Whereas if I was inside, they may not give the old hut a second glance. Neither was a great option, but I scavenged one of the other huts and found a mattress. Summer had her own room. I'd be in the living area.

The mattress I found was ripped on the top and covered with vines, one growing all the way through, but the bottom side was intact, so I dragged the thing back to our hut and hoped any resident critters would get out on the way. I returned for the swing, and found it in good repair other than a couple of cracked slats. The chain was easy to fix, so after manhandling it back to the hut, with one good arm and one at half power, I fixed it. It now dangled a couple feet off the ground. I lowered my frame onto the new seat, hoping the rafters weren't rotten. They groaned, but held my weight even as I bounced a couple times. All good.

"What's going on out there?" Summer called from inside.

"Nothing. A surprise."

I heard her move to the window. "Well, which is it?"

"Nothing."

She huffed, and I heard pans clanging. "Can I come out yet?"

"Nope."

I stepped off the porch and stood back to look at the hut. A warm fire billowed smoke up over the roof while the sounds of the lagoon serenaded me. I'd created a place of at least pseudo-peace.

I fixed dinner quickly, using a grate from the kitchen as a stove top on our fire. I'd just set the pot aside when Summer yelled through the window for me. "I'm done waiting."

"Okay, but close your eyes. I'll lead you." She was dressed in her same T-shirt and jean shorts, but she'd twined tiny flowering vines into her hair. Her skin glowed and as I took her arm, the scent of coconut filled my nose. "You look great," I said.

"Coconut. The brown ones work the best because the fluid inside is more like thick milk than water. Your skin soaks up the oil. You'll have to try it one day."

"I have my mud."

She flashed a smile. "And a treacherous hike to get to it."

"True." My hands remained on her. Couldn't help myself. "Take a look at the hut."

She turned and her eyes grew round. "Where'd that come from? I wondered what those hooks were for. And all that banging around you were doing."

"I carved it while you were inside."

She glanced over at me, feigning annoyance. "You did not."

"Okay, fine. I got it from one of the other huts. There's also a window intact on one, so I can repair the broken one in our place."

Summer filled her lungs. I fought the urge to stare. "Bray, this is incredible." Her eyes skated across the landscape. Fire blazing, scent of hot food, the swing. It was good, normal. We needed a dose of normal right now.

"The boat's gone," I told her. "I checked. But that doesn't mean we're out of the woods. They could come back."

I watched the relief then the apprehension spread across her face. She took a small step toward the swing.

"Want to try it out?" I offered.

"A seat. An actual seat." I watched Summer shake off her earlier tension and run up the porch steps with me right behind. We lowered our bodies onto the swing like it was something spiritual. She leaned back. "Aaaahhhhh."

I rocked us slowly. "We can eat dinner up here if you want."

Her eyes opened at the very moment the wind shifted and tossed the smell of cooking food to us. "No. You made such a nice table by the fire. Let's sit there, then come up here and watch the sunset."

I'd poured water into two coconut halves and coconut milk into two large oyster shells. Our plates were pie pans from the kitchen and we had actual utensils, making this almost feel like a real dinner. We sat on either side of our cooler-table, close enough to the fire to hear the creaks and pops of wood being consumed. I ladled up a generous helping of the beef stew.

Summer took a bite. "Mmm."

I never thought canned stew could taste like a gourmet meal, but right now I didn't think anything could taste better. My plan was to keep the conversation and her thoughts away from what we'd seen earlier.

"I'm more aware of flavors since we've been here," Summer said.

I wiped my mouth with the back of my hand. "What do you mean?"

"This, for instance. Back home, I would have just tasted beef stew. Here, I notice the carrots, potatoes, even the small bits of onion. It's like I'm savoring all the flavors."

"Yeah. That makes sense. Going without anything to eat for the first few days made us appreciate food more."

"Maybe that's it. Or maybe we actually slow down enough to taste it." The breeze from the lagoon worked its fingers into Summer's hair. I reached over and touched it.

"Did you mean what you said about taking me to church?"

"Of course." If God got us out of this, back home to our families—like Summer was so certain He would—I'd want to explore this whole thing that made Summer filled with faith against such difficult odds. At the same time, I would keep watch over her. Faith could be tested. Right now, she was solid, but what if things continued to work against us?

"I wanted to tell you thanks for earlier, Bray."

Her hair was soft. I slid my fingertips through the strands. "For what?"

"My commitment to wait. I've been thinking about what you said."

"And?"

"And I'm really getting back in touch with my relationship to God. How did I let it slip so far away from me?"

I propped my hands on my knees. "You tell me."

"I thought I was mad at Him. I thought I blamed Him for Michael's accident. Now I realize, I blamed myself and pushed God away because I knew He would forgive me. But I couldn't forgive myself."

"And now?"

"I know it wasn't my fault. But that doesn't stop me from feeling and acting irrationally some times. Old habits die hard."

We finished eating, sitting in comfortable silence and watching the sun sink lower on the horizon, our cue to start clearing the table. I stood and took the pie plates to drop them into a pan of water. Summer started helping clean up, but I stopped her. "Go sit on the swing. I'll join you in a couple minutes."

"If you're sure." But before she left, she reached over, planted her hands on my arms, rose on her toes, and kissed me on the cheek.

I finished in record time, knowing she was waiting for me, only pausing to feed the fire that had died down while we ate. Bright burning flames rose, casting soft light on the porch and Summer's face.

I joined her on the swing and knew the moment the tension of the day left her. "Summer?"

The sun was a far-off orange glow, throwing shades of rainbow colors onto the sky and the lagoon water. Deep reds bled into purple and eventually faded back into softer orange and yellow. "Yes?"

"I think you should write."

She pivoted to look at me. "What?" Her green eyes glowed in the flame's light.

"Write. You told me you used to do it a lot. I think you should write. In fact, I put some stuff by your bed in case you wanted to start tonight."

The atmosphere changed around us. "I don't know, Bray."

"Why not?" It's not like I was asking her to pen the great American novel.

Her hands kneaded together on her lap. She was quiet for a while. "I used to have story ideas. You know? They ran through my head all the time and wouldn't go away until I sat down and wrote them."

"Like short stories?"

"Yeah, some. Some were longer, novella length. But the point is, they were *there*. I didn't try to make them up; they were just there in my head."

I brushed the hair from her face. "And now?"

She shrugged. "Nothing."

"When did the stories stop coming?"

She looked out over the water. A seagull tilted his wings, searching out a last meal before nightfall. "When Michael died."

I laid my hand over hers where they rested on her lap. "I think it's time for the stories to come back."

She pulled a deep breath. "I'd like that." So much sorrow filled those few words. I knew Summer wasn't just grieving for Michael—she was grieving for the loss of everything she used to be.

I couldn't help but press a little deeper. "What did it mean to you? Writing?"

She blinked at the question as if never really considering it. "It meant ..." She tucked her hair behind her ears, a look of longing on her face. "For me, writing was the warm cup of hot chocolate after getting caught in a cold rain. It was rushing down to the tree on

Christmas morning and knowing you got that one thing you'd been hoping for. Writing was the strong hand holding mine when I felt off balance. In some ways, it completed me."

Our fingers interlocked. I lifted them to my face and kissed her knuckles. "I think you should write. You have a poet's way with words."

She gave me a sad smile. "Thank you."

"Will you try?"

"I don't know if I can."

"I know you can, Summer."

She turned to look straight at me. Fear and determination mingled. "Okay, I'll try. No promises, but I'll do it."

My hand slid out of hers and brushed across her cheek. She'd try. Because I asked her to. Heat pooled in my stomach. Summer's skin was silk, and rather than pull away from me, she nuzzled into my hand, her eyes drifting shut. When she opened them, there was nothing in the world but us. No island, no hut, no lagoon. Just Bray and Summer. Who we both were had been stripped down to the barest of essentials. There were no walls stopping us or causing us to be anything or anyone but ourselves. And that was something worth fighting for. Summer was someone worth fighting for.

I leaned closer and her eyes smiled. Green and beautiful, filled with mystery and magic. She ran her tongue over her lips, and I knew I had to kiss her. But I didn't want to break the spell, didn't want this moment to end. When I didn't move, she leaned toward me, her intention as crystal clear as my own. Our lips met. Held. Neither of us moved except for the pounding of our hearts. We stayed like that for several seconds, her lips so lightly on mine that the slightest breath could make it all disappear. The intensity of the moment became too much for me and I sank my hands into her hair. Summer responded by opening her eyes for the briefest of seconds and locking on my gaze, then her eyes closed as if knowing, seeing whatever it was she needed to see. Her body, tense from the interaction, softened and she moved in, closing her lips on mine in a longer exploration. She melted against me. The kiss became a rush, something inexplicable and primal, and I knew I'd have to break the bond or we'd both end up somewhere I'd sworn I wouldn't take her.

Already aching, I broke the kiss, having to cradle her face in my hands to create the needed space because I just wanted to continue, to consume.

She blew out several quick breaths, her eyes widening as the moment settled around her. She opened her mouth to speak, but no words came out.

A slow grin spread on my face.

She huffed, swallowed. "That was um … it was …"

Why she felt she needed to verbalize *everything*, I didn't know. But it made me chuckle. "Yeah, it was."

We stayed on the swing for a long time. I'd turned her into the crook of my arm and she nestled against my collarbone. Around us, the beach was alive with crickets and various bugs making a hollow hum that played off the lagoon's gentle waves.

And even though we were lost and alone on a deserted island and had no idea when or if we were going to be rescued, all seemed right with the world. I was learning what it meant to be a man. With Summer in my arms.

Summer

I hadn't kissed anyone since Michael. And since Michael was the first and only boy I'd kissed, what I'd shared tonight with Bray was monumental. He'd swept me away. There'd been electricity, one that zapped my strength and left me tingling like I'd just grabbed a frayed wire. With Michael, we'd both been awkward, new at the whole *couple* thing, and it all had a sweet innocence to it that, looking back, I guessed I'd treasure forever. But this was different. And somehow the same. Bray didn't have the awkward innocence, the sense of discovery. But that didn't make it any less new or fresh—at least, if the look in his eyes was any indication of what was happening inside him. But it wasn't just discovery.

There was something else. Something more. Like he'd been searching for a long time and finally found what he'd been looking for. With Bray, there was easy companionship intensified by that sudden crackle of fireworks when we touched. How could I be so comfortable with a person one second, then edgy and needy and tingling only moments later? I didn't know.

It was beyond my understanding, and from Bray's reaction, it was beyond his as well. We both felt it. The chemistry. The power. But it was okay because we'd made a commitment to each other. Bray had saved my life over and over again, often at his own suffering. I could count on him to not let me down. I could count on him for everything. Even life.

What Bray and I were building went far beyond human comprehension. It was deeper than the ocean that held us captive from the mainland. It could be more powerful than the crushing water on the rocks. We deserved to give it a chance.

• • • • •

"Hey, Summer," Bray said, voice drifting through the bedroom door from his spot in the living room.

"Yes?"

"You writing?"

My face flushed hot. If he only knew what I'd been thinking about. "No. Too dark in here."

"There's moonlight." His voice sounded groggy, as if he'd almost fallen asleep.

I turned on my side and stared at the door, sliding my hands beneath my head. "I, I couldn't think of a story."

"Once upon a time ..."

I laughed.

"Do you want to hear this story or not?" I heard the clicking and popping of his mattress—louder than mine because only half of its cover remained intact. Bray must have turned onto his side as well—that's what I imagined. Him, right there on the other side of the wall.

"Yes, I want to hear the story." There was no disguising the smile in my voice.

"Once upon a time, there was an enchanted kingdom with a very, very, *very* handsome prince named Bray."

I giggled.

"One day, a maiden rode into town on a black stallion so beautiful, it made the town folks cry."

"Wait. Who was beautiful? The maiden or the stallion?"

"The stallion. No one knew what the maiden looked like because she was covered from head to toe in chainmail and leather. The prince called for her to come to the castle because the town was in such an uproar about the amazing horse."

"This is a strange story, Bray."

He ignored me. "But the prince didn't have much time because he was putting an army together to go out and hunt a dragon who'd been terrorizing the town and burning the crops. But when the prince saw the maiden, saw her face, he couldn't move. Couldn't even breathe."

"She was that ugly, huh?"

"No. She was beautiful. With hair the color of autumn streaked with gold and pale green eyes so alarmingly gorgeous, he couldn't look away."

"Let me guess. She gave him the strength to go slay the dragon."

"Wrong. She was in fact, a dragon slayer herself. The best in the entire world."

"Oh! I love this story." I scooted my hips so that I was more comfortable and settled in to hear the rest. "What happens next?"

"Hmm." I heard him yawn. "Let me think."

I waited, but didn't hear anything else from the other room.

"Bray? Bray, what happens next?"

Silence.

I sighed. After a moment's consideration, I swung my legs off the bed quietly and slipped to the door. My hand fell on the knob and clicked it open. There on the mattress on the floor lay Bray, shirt off, one knee bent, flat on his back, one hand resting on his stomach. I listened for a few seconds and heard the faint rumble deep in his throat. My head fell against the doorjamb and for a short time, I watched him sleep. It was his first night on a real mattress. I smiled. My own personal angel, too exhausted to stay awake.

I tiptoed over to him and knelt down. With a butterfly touch, I moved the hair from his forehead and swept it aside. His exhale became a moan. I ran a finger gently across his eyebrow and he stirred, so I lifted my finger quickly, not wanting to wake him. Just wanting to watch him. More deep breaths, so many, my eyes were getting heavy from the constant hum of his breathing. But then, his face pinched into a frown. His shoulder jerked. He pulled a lungful of air, and on the exhale mumbled, "Summer. Be careful."

My eyes filled with tears. Even in sleep he was watching over me.

CHAPTER 13

Summer

The next morning, I wrote a story about a handsome prince and the young woman who'd come to his kingdom to slay a dragon. When I left my room, I could smell coffee.

Outside, Bray was stoking up the fire and lifting a pot from the grate we used as a stovetop. "Ready for a cup?"

My eyes closed and I pulled the morning into my being. The sun rose slowly off to the side of the lagoon, but the beach remained cool. A hint of fog lay around like a transparent blanket, making everything dreamlike. I took the coconut shell from Bray and lifted it to my lips. He'd made this one specifically for coffee by only whacking off the top quarter of it and hollowing out the meat. No easy task, but it was that or drink coffee from a small saucepan—which would have been fine with me, but he said this would seem more normal. The only problem with the coconut was that you couldn't really set it down. But I had to admit, coffee tasted great in it. Rich, kind of nutty.

After a long swallow I said, "I wrote a story this morning."

A slow smile formed, and he pointed to the swing. "Tell me about it."

We sat and he instantly set the swing in motion. "Nope."

The seat screeched to a halt. "No?"

"You have to read it."

The swing started moving again. "Even better. Is it done?"

"Almost. I'll finish it tomorrow and give it to you." I took a long drink of coffee, steam rising from my island mug and clouding my view. Around us, the island awoke with all the sounds and sights of a living, breathing ecosystem. Fish jumped, seagulls and pelicans searched for breakfast. A crab left crisscrosses in the sand as he navigated the shoreline. Neither of us spoke about the boat men. I sensed that Bray wanted to steer my attention away from the horror, and I appreciated that.

"Bray." Even as I said his name, a cold chill passed over me. I cared about Bray. So much. And inside I was terrified of what our future held. He must have noticed the tightness of my voice.

He turned and searched my face, eyes crinkling slightly at the edges. "What, Summer?"

"What's going to happen to us?"

A strong arm slid around my shoulders. "You mean if we don't get rescued?"

I couldn't answer.

"We're alive, Summer. We have shelter, water."

"But our food will eventually run out." This wasn't what I'd meant, but it needed to be discussed too. What if they never found us?

"I've been thinking about the food situation. I'm going to try to repair an old fishing net that I found in the toolshed. Also, I'm carving a spear for spear fishing. I've made a couple while you've slept, but the wood hasn't been strong enough. If we can fish, we can live." He swallowed. "Long-term if necessary."

"It's probably stupid, but I'm not concerned about if they *don't* find us. What happens if they *do*?"

He blinked, dark blue eyes settling on me. "We go home."

My heart ached. "Home," I mumbled. Him back to his world and me back to mine.

His fingertips made circles on my shoulder. I reached up with my free hand, touching his for a moment, and then clinging to him. Going home meant me returning to the Summer I was and him returning to the Bray he was.

"It'll never be the same," I barely whispered.

He squeezed, drawing me even closer in that safe place I knew so well. "Of course it will. You'll see." He tilted his head back, closed his eyes, and pulled a deep lungful of air.

"What are you doing?"

He glanced over at me with one eye open. "I'm capturing it. I learned that from you. At Cory's party."

Bleah. Did he have to bring up the party?

"I didn't understand what you were doing then. But I do now. Everything is so much richer and, I don't know, more real, since I met you."

I almost choked on the words, but they needed to be said. "And you'll take all that home with you?"

"Yes."

"Why?"

"Summer, don't you realize what you mean to me?"

Panic set in because I knew what I meant to him here, on the island. I popped up off the swing, sloshing my coffee. "What about the girl at the party?"

Confusion ran over his face. "What? I hardly knew her."

"Right. And you hardly knew me until we got here. You seem to switch gears pretty quickly." Would he return home and forget everything that happened here? Could he turn his emotions on and off so quickly? I couldn't, and I was falling fast and hard for a guy who would soon leave me, just as suddenly as Michael had, of that I was certain.

"Summer, I *care* about you. I didn't care about her."

"You cared enough to step in and punch that guy when he started hitting on her—the guy who'd been hitting on *me*—you punched him in the face as soon as he turned his attention to her."

Bray rubbed a hand over his face and looked out at the lagoon. "You don't know anything about it, Summer. Please drop it."

Anger scalded my throat. "I think I have a right to know. As far as I could tell, you guys had just met earlier that day, but she was sooooo important that you had to protect her honor. You certainly didn't do that for me. The guy had been bugging me for about fifteen minutes."

Bray stood and faced me. "Stop it, Summer. Just stop. You want to know why I punched the guy?" Flames lit his eyes, and I didn't know if they came from the fire or some combustible thing within. "Because of you."

I took a step back.

"I punched him because of you, okay? I saw him when he first approached you."

"You did not. You were all entangled with your beach bunny."

Heat rose off his body in such palpable waves, it made me want to move farther away from him. But I stood my ground.

"Really?" he said. "That's what you think? I saw *everything*, Summer. You were standing down at the water's edge, and he'd been watching you for about ten minutes. After a few shots of liquid courage, he went down there. Tried to put an arm around you, but you ducked. When he wouldn't leave, you spun and headed for the house, but had to go back to get your shoes."

I was speechless. Bray really had seen what happened.

He grabbed my arms, my coffee mug sloshing again between us. "It drove me crazy, Summer." His face was red with heat, eyes hard and ablaze. "And the fact that I even *cared* drove me crazier."

What could I say to that? "You didn't even like me."

"I know." His hands on my arms softened marginally. "But even back then, I wanted to protect you. Even then, there was something ... inexplicable between us. You had to feel it too."

Did I? Had I felt anything for Bray besides animosity? I didn't really think so. I'd hated him on sight. "You were so much like Michael."

"Stop it!" he ground out. His hands tightened for an instant, hurting, and then he released me with such force, it caught me off guard. "Stop blaming Michael. Stop blaming me. Stop hiding, Summer. You didn't die in that wreck. Stop acting like you did."

A dark, dark cloud passed over me, so tangible that for a moment I thought it had blotted out the sun. But the burning ball still hung in the sky, and I realized this wasn't a physical cloud. It was an emotional one. All this time, all that had happened, and Bray thought I was just hiding behind Michael's death. Which indicated that all the things he'd said to me about giving me time to get over Michael, maybe he hadn't meant. Maybe everything I was feeling, the hope of a life after the island, the hope we'd even get rescued at all ... maybe it was just a pipe dream. And maybe Bray'd tricked me. As that dark blanket of self-security closed over my heart, I made a promise I'd never let him trick me again.

The fact was, he was Bray and I was Summer, and once we returned home — if we returned home — we'd both go right back to who we'd been before the island. Him, a party boy. And me, the girl who'd lost both her faith and her hope.

"I'm tired," I said almost mechanically. "I'm going to go lie down."

I shuffled into the house quietly and found my way to my bed. I lay down and closed my eyes, feeling more alone than ever in my life. Michael was gone and Bray was right here on the other side of the wall. But I'd lose him too. He'd be just as dead to me as Michael was because one day we would be rescued.

Summer hadn't emerged from the house, so by late afternoon, I went to check on her. She was sound asleep, or acting like she was. I filled a coconut shell with water and perched it on the floor near her bed, propped by oyster shells.

Once out of the hut, I constructed a spear out of heavy wood and retraced our conversation, trying to decide where it had gone so wrong. It all started with me saying we would go home. Something about that had panicked her. Or something right after. I didn't know. All I knew was Summer looked at me with hurt and suspicion—just like she used to. And I hadn't done anything to deserve it. Well, except maybe for blaming her for hiding behind her dead boyfriend.

In the early evening, the air cooled and I made a pan of tomato soup. I took a coconut bowl into Summer's room. The water sat untouched on the floor. That alarmed me. You just couldn't go without water here. Careful not to spill soup on her, I used my free hand and shook her shoulder. "Summer," I said quietly, but when she didn't rouse, the panic caused my voice to constrict and get louder. I turned her to face me. She moved easily, and when her heavily lashed eyes fluttered open, I breathed relief.

Her stare was blank.

"You need to eat. I brought you some soup."

Her eyes closed, slamming me out. "Not hungry," she mumbled.

I shook her lightly. "Summer, you can't go without food." When she didn't respond, I rose from the side of her bed and replaced the soup with the shell of water. "Here."

She exhaled a long, frustrated sound, but allowed me to lift her slightly off the bed to get a drink. I held the shell while she took several long draws from it.

"Now, time to eat."

But she turned over on the mattress, curling into a ball facing the window. "Not hungry."

I fisted my hands in my hair, not sure what else to do.

"Leave it," she muttered. "I'll eat it later."

But I knew she was just trying to get rid of me.

"I'll be right outside the door. Holler if you need me."

But Summer wouldn't need me. Careful as I'd been, the wildcat had finally run off.

Summer stayed in bed for the next three days. She hadn't eaten enough, and the lack of nourishment fed the exhaustion. Something had to happen. Something had to change. Quick. But this wasn't just exhaustion. I'd taken a psychology class my first semester. This was textbook depression. Problem was I didn't know how to fix it.

I had to do something drastic.

I'd spent a few mornings trying my hand at spear fishing and had landed a couple of prize guppies, neither one was more than an inch long. I almost gave up, but having no one to talk to made me even more determined than ever to spear a real fish. My first came on the fourth morning of Summer's downward spiral. It was early, and I'd checked on her to find her sleeping. What she did about seventeen hours a day now. The rest of the time, she'd stare out the window or at the ceiling. Except of course, when I was pestering her to eat. After getting her to eat a bit of canned peaches, I took spear in hand and waded into the lagoon.

Something moved near my left foot, stirring up the sandy bottom. It was a flounder, fins flipping lightly as he reacquainted himself with the seafloor. I was in water to my knees so his outline was easy to make out. The two eyes on the upside of his head closed, and I held my breath, raised my spear, and then shoved it into the water and through his flesh. I lifted the end with a scooping motion, so he wouldn't slide off. I got so excited, I practically fell in the water, but steadied myself and carried him to the shore, yelling for Summer as I went. Once on land, he flopped, catching me off guard, and I dropped to my knees, so elated I could barely remember what to do next, so I stood up and ran toward the front door. "Summer!" I yelled it again, and looked to find her standing in the hut's doorway.

She looked awful—her eyes dark and sunken. I shuddered to a stop.

She swayed one direction, then the other, as if caught by invisible waves. There was no smile and when she spoke, her voice sounded far away. "That's great, Bray." Then, she turned and disappeared back into her room.

A horrifying thought struck me, dropping me to my knees again. She was going to die. If I didn't do something, Summer was going to die. Fear clawed its way over my flesh and into my system. She was half dead already.

I tossed the flounder by the fire and paced, chewing up the ground in front of the hut. I'd thought back over the last four days. When I'd asked her what was wrong, she'd repeatedly told me she just wanted to go home.

Confusing, for sure. It seemed the idea of going home brought on the depression—still something I didn't understand—then after a couple of days, she was saying she *wanted* to go home.

I left the area and walked back to the beach where we'd spent our first nights on the island. No signs there of how to fix her. I knew I was just burning off nervous energy. My gaze fixed on the horizon. White-blue light sparkling, searing my eyeballs. Something flashed at the far edge of the water where it met the sky.

I sucked in a breath and squinted, then turned and ran back toward the hut, screaming Summer's name.

Summer

Far away, I could hear Bray. As he neared, I knew there was a different pitch to his voice than I'd ever heard before. It roused me, if only a little, then I curled back on my side, letting sleep take me. But the voice continued, getting louder, closer, and I just wanted to clamp my hands over my ears. He was screaming my name. But something else too. I couldn't make it out, and the effort just seemed too great.

"A ship!"

I sat straight up in bed, mind and head spinning. I had to have imagined it.

"Summer! I think I see a ship on the horizon."

The whoosh of my blood surged through me as I stood from the bed. Feet stumbled as I zeroed in on the sound. Bray yelled it again, this time louder, close enough to the hut that every word was audible.

When I flew to the door, he caught me. Grabbed me off my feet, kissed my cheek, and said, "Come on!"

"But what if it's the murderers?"

"It's not. It's a huge fishing vessel."

I don't know how I was able to keep up with him, but as we ran to the beach, my legs grew stronger and stronger, something quick and powerful spiking through my veins. Soon I realized it must be adrenaline, because I'd barely been able to get to the front door earlier. Now and then, when I slowed, Bray turned to me as we ran and said, "A ship, Summer. There's a ship on the horizon."

We reached the beach and both of us ran straight into the water, stopping about knee high. I lifted my hand to shade my eyes and searched. First right in front of me, then to the east, and the west.

Tears from the sun's intensity smeared my vision, so I brushed them away over and over. It was several minutes before I realized Bray had stopped searching.

My gaze fanned over to him. He stared down at the water below us. "Bray, where is it?"

He wouldn't look at me. "It's gone, Summer." Instead, he turned and walked out of the water and onto the beach.

"Gone?" I echoed.

He remained silent.

Something inside me shifted. "What aren't you telling me?" I knew him well enough to know when he was lying.

"Nothing. There was a ship and now it's gone." His eyes blinked several times, and I realized what a lousy liar he really was.

I stomped out of the water to him. "What aren't you telling me?" I repeated. My eyes scanned the water again, and then went back to him. Anger began to slowly boil in my gut when he couldn't meet my gaze. "There … there wasn't any boat, was there?" A sudden flash of heat rose to my head, making it spin.

He lifted his hands, dropped them. "No. Are you happy? There wasn't a boat. I mean, I saw something. It flashed at the edge, but I don't know what it was for sure."

"You made me think it was right here." I tried to pull a breath, but no oxygen met me. "How could you …" My hand fisted over my heart where a lightning bolt of pain struck. "How?"

"I had to."

My knees became Jell-O. Before I could drop, he grabbed me. I refused to look at him; instead, I found my strength, shook my head, and backed away.

"I had no choice, Summer. You were dying on that bed. I had to get you up."

My hands rose to my face where the sudden rush of heat and anger throbbed like flames licking up the world around me. "And this helps how?" My voice rose to a squeak, and even to me, it sounded alarming.

"At least you're up. At least you're moving."

I dropped to my knees. "That's cruel." My eyes widened as I said it because I wanted him to look inside me and see exactly what he'd done.

"So hate me. But Summer, *live*. You can't die. I need you. I can't do this alone, be here alone." He knelt in front of me so we were face-to-face.

Sobs overtook first my stomach then my chest, then my throat. It was no use hiding it. Bray had both rocked and changed my world. Everything had escaped from that deep place where I'd locked it all away.

"I don't want to go back to my world, Bray. I ... I did something so stupid here. I fell in love with you and I can't lose another ..." Words were coming between short gasps for air because I was drowning. "I can't ... lose you. I can't lose another ..."

"Is that what you thought?" He tried to pull me, drag me into him, but I fought. "That we'd go back to the real world and everything that happened to us—*between us*—would be gone?"

He scooted closer to me on the sand. "Summer. I can't live without you. Here or there. I don't even want to try. When I said we'd go home, I meant both of us. Together."

My addled brain tried to work out what he was saying. But it was all wrong. He was supposed to be telling me I'd be okay once we were back to civilization. That we'd keep in touch, maybe visit each other on occasion.

"What?"

For the first time in days I saw his smile appear. "You're gonna make me say it, aren't you?"

My eyes closed and opened multiple times, trying to sort out what was happening.

Strong arms came around me gently. "I'm in love with you, Summer. I haven't felt anything like this before. So I may not do everything right, but as far as I'm concerned, you're stuck with me for the rest of your life."

I melted. Right then. Right there. Because I had been in love before and knew exactly what it was. Knew exactly what losing that person could cost. But it didn't matter because every day was a treasure whether you had only a few or a whole lifetime together. Love was worth it.

Bray was worth it. And he deserved someone who would stand strong beside him.

Bray

We ate the flounder as a celebration of Summer's return to life. She had a voracious appetite, and within four days was back to her normal weight and looking better. Great, in fact. Being in love agreed with her. It agreed with me too. Neither of us spoke of the incident again—there just didn't seem any reason—but we both had settled into a nice routine that included moonlit walks around the lagoon, the occasional night swim when the dolphins appeared, and as much kissing as I could get from her.

I was careful, though. A gentleman. I had to be. Wanted to be. After all, if I couldn't accomplish this one small thing for Summer, I really didn't deserve her. So, it wasn't always easy, but if I thought we were getting too close, I cut it off. Or she did. We were strong for each other, neither of us hitting a moment where we were both too weak. But the longer we were on the island, the harder it became. Sometimes I hated myself for being a guy. It didn't seem as difficult for Summer. But being with her 24/7 never really gave me a break from the hormone push. In college, I'd been taught that sex was a basic need of humanity. Food, water, shelter, sex. What idiot came up with that? He'd never been deserted on an island, having to survive with lake water, a hut, and canned food. And he'd probably never been in love either.

Sex wasn't a necessity. I was controlling the beast because I needed to. For Summer's sake, but also for mine. It was making me a better man—more frustrated perhaps—but better. We'd wait until our wedding night. I was strong. I could do this. As long as we got off this stupid island soon.

And the need to get off the island quickly had to do with more than just my sex drive. I'd been using debris wood from the resort to keep the fire up, and now there were actually places where you could see all the way to the floor. I'd discovered a reservations desk and searched inside to see if anything was left. A stack of brochures and envelopes inside a plastic bag remained my biggest discovery. They were a little worse for wear, but not too bad. I cut a piece of the plastic and wrapped a brochure inside to show Summer.

She'd been cleaning the hut. Sand crept through the floorboards, so it was an endless battle, but that was good. With a permanent shelter, food, and a solid supply of water, days were long, and when you didn't have to hunt or forage for dinner, they were even longer. In fact, we entertained each other by telling stories from our childhoods, talking about our favorite movies, and the things we loved and hated. When I stepped through the worn path of vegetation and rounded the corner to the hut, Summer was humming. I stopped, listened.

"Bray?" she yelled from inside.

"I'm here."

"I thought I heard someone walking, but then it stopped." Her face appeared at the clean window. She smiled down at me.

"Guilty. I heard you humming. Hey, you're getting pretty good at the hearing thing."

She giggled. But it was true. When we first arrived at the island, every sound freaked us out. Now we knew the distinction between the island's normal noises and those that were uncommon. We were adapting to our world. But there was another waiting for us. One that seemed to be slipping farther and farther away.

"I've got dinner ready." Summer told me as she greeted me at the front door.

I pulled her into a hug. "Great. I'm starved."

She busied herself at the fire, filling two coconut bowls with food. We sat down on the swing.

"I've got something for you when we're done eating."

She eyed me suspiciously.

"Nothing big. Just thought you might like to see a picture of this place before the hurricane hit it."

"Oooooh."

After we finished, I carefully opened the plastic. I'd stuck the brochure in one of the envelopes. She unwrapped it like a treasure.

"Wow. No wonder your dad wanted to bring you here. Gorgeous." She carefully unfolded the pamphlet. "Look! It's our hut!"

"Well, it's a hut. I don't know if it's specifically ours." I guided her hand holding the brochure closer to my face to inspect the picture.

"There are only a few. I think it's ours." A strand of hair kept flying in front of her face, so she handed me the paper and gathered her hair at her nape. I pulled the pencil from my pocket—I now always kept one there for this very reason—and had her turn. I wound the pencil in the hair, and Summer sighed. Yes. We were adapting.

"Is this the only brochure?"

"Nah. There's a whole stack wrapped in plastic."

She fingered the envelope. "Why'd you bring the envelope?"

"Well, I was thinking that maybe we could take a few of our glass bottles, put a brochure inside with a note, and send them out to sea."

"A message in a bottle?"

"Yes. We just have to weigh the pros and cons. Is it worth giving up a provision like a bottle with a tight-fitting lid? We need to think about it. We don't have a lot of those, and odds are it may never be found."

"Technically, we could have done that before you found the brochures. Just add a note and send it off." Summer was still perusing the pamphlet.

"Could have. Didn't think about it." I must have sounded a little ashamed, because she placed a flat hand against my cheek.

"We can decide what to do in the morning."

The brochure slipped back into my hand and I folded it, wrapped it in the plastic, and then slid it into my shorts pocket.

"I have a confession," Summer said after a moment. "Today's my birthday."

"What?" Summer's birthday? Why hadn't she brought it up before?

Long fingers brushed at the few remaining strands of hair, pushing them from her face. "At least, I think it's my birthday. I've lost count of the days."

"Why didn't you let me know so I could—?"

"What? Run to the bakery and get me a cake?"

"Summer, it's important." My finger wound around the ends of a strand of her hair.

"You already gave me the hut, the swing. I don't want anything else. Plus, I already made a wish."

"What was it?"

"That they'd find us so we can go home. Together."

I took her in my arms and pressed a kiss against her cheek. Then another on her lips. "Happy birthday, Summer." We stayed on the swing until night closed around us.

"Considering our situation, is it okay to say it's a really good birthday?"

"More than okay. Been writing?"

"Yes," she answered and yawned. "Thanks to your never-ending bedtime stories. One of these nights you will have to actually finish one."

"That's your job. I start them, you write and finish them." I drew her up and accompanied her into the hut, stopping at her bedroom door to lean against the doorjamb.

She turned to face me. "In case I don't tell you later, thanks for everything you've done for me since we've been here, Bray."

Our fingers wound together, making our arms a V between us. When she started to let go, I tightened my grip and tugged her close. Our hands stayed locked together as we kissed. "I love you."

"I love you too," she whispered.

Reluctantly, I let go and watched her disappear into the room. Stretched out on my mattress, I said, "Summer?"

I could still hear her moving around in her bedroom. "Yes?"

"If we don't get off this island, what do you think you would regret the most that you missed?"

Her voice sounded a little self-conscious. "I guess the one thing I've always dreamed about and couldn't wait to make happen was my wedding and what my life would be like married and with kids."

"Tell me about your dream wedding."

She sighed. "Guys usually aren't too interested in stuff like that."

"I am. I want to know what you want. Everything. Every detail. Start with your dress."

"It's charmeuse."

"Char ... what?" My back pressed into the mattress, and I imagined Summer lying on the other side of the wall.

"You know what satin is, right? How it's so shiny? Well, charmeuse has a sheen to it, but isn't as shiny. The dress is strapless, fitted through the midsection and flared from the hips down to the floor—sort of Cinderella-like."

"You have an exact dress picked out already?"

"I have everything *envisioned*. Oh, it's not really a bright white; it's a soft winter white. Very fairy tale, with tiny pearls on the bodice."

"You look beautiful in it," I mumbled, crossing my hands behind my head.

Summer was silent for a long time.

"It's going to happen, Summer. I swear you'll get your fairy-tale wedding."

"I love you, Bray."

"I love you too."

I drifted off, dreaming of Summer and an event I'd never dreamt of before. A wedding. Soft and whimsical and perfect. Like her.

Something startled me awake. First, I thought maybe Summer had stepped into the living room, but nothing moved inside the house. I waited. When the scraping, stepping sound came again, I bolted upright. Something or, worse, *someone* was outside.

I grabbed my fishing spear from the corner and silently opened Summer's door. I expected to find her still asleep, but instead, she was sitting up, eyes wide and sparkling in the moonlit room. A finger slid to my mouth. She jerked a quick nod.

Neither of us moved for a few seconds. Then we heard the rustling again. Summer had drawn her knees to her chest, and now her grip tightened as she split glances from me to her window, where the sound drifted inside.

I took a slow step toward her, hoping my movement wouldn't cause the floor to creak. The noise came again, louder, closer this time. It sounded like someone was dragging a body past the hut. My heart started pounding at the bump against our wash pan, a clunk of metal followed by a slosh of water. I tried to look out her window, but with the dense foliage beyond the hut, I could see nothing.

The boat men. They had to be back. And maybe they were dragging another murder victim right outside our door. My grip tightened on the spear. I could surprise one of them. But if there were more, my spear was no match for their handguns.

We remained frozen for a while longer, Summer's eyes wide, the whites glowing in the shaft of window light. I wished I could calm her, but needed to remain close to the door. Slick palms slid down the spear, so I swiped them against my shorts and adjusted my grip higher on the wooden weapon. Why hadn't I made more of these? Summer was completely unarmed, incapable of protecting herself against an attacker. And all the knives were outside. We'd have to remedy that. That's when her hand slipped off the edge of her bed and under her mattress. I saw the blade of a long butcher knife catch the moonlight as she drew it from its hiding spot. *Way to go, Wildcat.*

Within minutes, the sound moved away, crushing hard, fallen leaves as it went. I waited. Counted to a hundred. Waited again. Summer looked like her breathing was slowly returning to normal.

When I was sure whatever it was had gone, I exhaled all the air and adrenaline I'd drawn. "I think it's okay now."

"What was that, Bray?" Her eyes pleaded with me for an explanation I didn't have.

"What or who?" I went to her bed and sat down.

"You think the boat men are back, don't you?"

I hated to admit it, but yeah. "Probably. I just don't know why they didn't come in. The fire was still burning, if only a little. The pan was at the edge of the cabin."

Summer ran a hand over my shoulder. We were both slick with sweat. "Why didn't they kill us, Bray?"

"I don't know. Tomorrow we have to find out what it was. And from now on, be more careful."

"What are we going to do?"

The thought of taking her to the cave entered my head, but right on its heels I saw her dangling from the rock face, hanging on by one hand. My eyes squeezed shut to close out the memory. "I don't know."

Frightened eyes searched me, and I wanted to have the answers, but I didn't. I always had the answer. Always had a plan. She tried to offer me a weak smile.

"Get some sleep, Summer. I'll keep watch."

Hair fell over her shoulder as she shook her head. "There's no way I can go to sleep now. What if they come back?"

"I'll watch over you. If they were going to kill us tonight, I think they would have done it already. But, if it would make you feel better, we can take the tarp out onto the beach somewhere and sleep there."

Her eyes darkened. "But no campfire, right?"

I nodded. "Right."

"Without a campfire anything could crawl over us."

"Yes." Which is why I hadn't suggested sleeping somewhere in the jungle.

"I'll try to sleep." She snuggled down on her mattress. "For a couple of hours, then we trade places and you sleep. Okay?"

"Deal."

• • • • •

I didn't wake her until morning.

I ran a hand through the hair that splayed across the mattress. It was cool to the touch, like silk. Like *charmeuse*.

She nestled into the bed, her long tan legs stretching out, ankles crossed. Her face and body had tanned to such a rich, deep color that she looked like someone who'd been raised on the island. Her hair had grown slightly wilder and it had a hint of curl to it now, making it even more beautiful.

Summer opened her eyes, stretched and smiled. "We survived the night," she mumbled.

I should have stopped looking at her body, legs, torso, face. Her stomach was flat beneath the threadbare T-shirt. It had a rip in the hem, where the edges frayed.

I swallowed and knew I needed to get out of there. I'd stayed by her bed all night and watched her sleep. With the moonlight casting a shaft of light across her body, she was even more beautiful. The road to hell really was paved with good intentions. My gaze rose to her face and held.

"Bray," she whispered, and I felt her hand land on my thigh.

Oh boy.

"There's not really anywhere to hide if they know we're here." Her hand moved on my leg, only a few millimeters, but it sent my heart rate spiking.

She's right. If they *knew* we were there, we were as good as dead. Even the cave couldn't save us. Maybe they were just playing with us. We were stranded. Where could we go?

The crystal rays of early sunlight shone down on her through the window, highlighting every curve. She arched her back to scoot closer. The pounding of my heart stopped. As did my breathing. "You told me that you don't believe God puts people in bad situations, right?" I didn't wait for her to answer. "But there can be things taken away from the experience that will make us better people. We're building our foundation for a life together right now, Summer. Right here on the island."

She listened, but I couldn't read her thoughts.

"I swear, I'm going to get you home. Okay? There's only one thing left to do." When I opened my mouth, words failed me. I jumped off the bed and paced. Three strides to one end of the room, three strides to the other. Wall to wall. And again. Three steps. Turn. Three steps back.

"What are you doing?" Summer stood slowly, but didn't come near me, just remained there, standing at the edge of her bed staring at me like I'd lost my mind. I probably had. I continued to assault the floor.

Finally, I stopped and spun to face her. "I didn't want to do this now. But I do."

The flash of a frown appeared on her face. "That doesn't make sense."

"No. I know." Nervous energy ran down my arms, settling and humming in my fingertips, so I flexed my hands repeatedly, but it didn't help. "Um."

She waited.

My mind blanked. Why was this so hard? I knew what I wanted. "Summer? I, uh ..."

Her chin tilted down ever so slightly, urging me on.

"I love you."

Her smile lit the room. "I love you too, Bray."

Those words seeped into my skin, through my system, and right into the deepest pit of my heart. They gave me courage. I fumbled in the tiny pocket just on the inside waistband of my swim shorts. My fingers clamped around the small rope. "I wanted to do this later. After a nice dinner, maybe standing near one of the palm trees at the edge of the lagoon."

"Bray, what are you talking about?"

I wasn't sure if I should kneel down or not. Did people still do that? One knee bent slightly, or gave way, unable to hold my crushing weight anymore. My knee hit the floor. Already the rope ring was sweaty in my hand.

I closed my eyes for a second but when I opened them, Summer was face-to-face with me on her knees as well. *Oh no!*

Her eyes searched mine. "Bray, are you okay?"

My head shook, lips forming the word *no*, but nothing came out. I clamped my hands on her hips and shoved her up.

She stood, but threw her hands up in frustration. Then, shock stole the place of her facial features. She looked down at me, there on one knee, then her eyes scanned her own posture, then back to me. For a girl with such a deep tan, she paled. Swayed. Grabbed her heart. *Great. I killed her.*

I swallowed. "I need you to listen to me, okay?"

She jerked a nod.

"Close your mouth," I coaxed. It was hanging open like a barn door.

She snapped it shut.

I pulled a breath of courage. "I might not be much of a handsome prince. And heaven knows it's been no fairy tale since we met, but, Summer, I can't imagine walking through life without you beside me. Every day. Every moment. You know what writing is to you? That's what you are to me. *You* are the cup of hot chocolate after a cold rain. *You're* the Christmas morning gift I hope for. I love you, Summer and I want you to marry me."

Her legs gave way, and she fell down into my arms, our knees bumping. But that's how our relationship was. Face to face. Eye to eye, breath for breath. She was right there with me. Ready to meet every challenge. Ready to fight side by side. Me with a fishing spear and her with a butcher knife, ready to take on the world.

Her hands came around my neck and I held her there, letting the elation take us both for a moment. "Hey, you haven't answered."

She tilted back and took my face in her hands. "Yes. Yes, of course, Bray. I love you. I will marry you."

I opened my hand to reveal the rope ring I'd made. "I swear when we get home, I'll exchange it for real gold." I slid it onto her finger.

It fit.

She squeezed her hand closed and pressed it to her heart. "I love it."

Bray

Outside in the morning light, I could tell something had been dragged along the edge of beach from the jungle. But the wind had left only small indentions in the sand. "No footprints," I noted.

Summer sipped a cup of coffee I'd heated on the coals. We were too cautious to make a blazing fire this morning.

I turned to her. "I need to see if it's them."

"You're going to the north end of the island?" she said, face pinching into a worried frown.

"I have to, Summer. What if it's someone else? Someone who could help us?"

She nodded then drained her coconut shell. "I'm going with you."

Actually, I thought that would be best too. I wasn't about to leave her here when whoever had come knew there was a campsite and people. We could stay silent in the jungle.

We walked the forest without speaking, making little to no noise. But when we got to the beach, there was no boat. I waited for a time, searching through the trees, scanning one end of the north beach, then the other. Quietly, I moved through the last bit of cover and could plainly see where the boat had been, its deep grooves on the sand still visible through the approaching tide. I also noticed the cage they'd left behind.

"What is that?" Summer stepped around me.

I shrugged. The end was blocked open, and from the beach, you could barely see the metal contraption. Deep grooves of footprints told the story. Someone, probably several people, had dragged it to its spot along the close tree line. It would take a handful of pretty tough men to get it here if it had an animal inside. And given the flattened bit of sand at the cage door, something had crawled out.

The prints, though they were hard to see in the shifting sand, were deep, clawed, and large. Four giant paws almost the width of the cage. "Bray," Summer said, latching onto my arm. "What kind of beast came out of there?"

"I don't know." I had my suspicions, though. After all, we lived in Florida when we weren't summering in Belize.

We left the cage and returned to the hut. Summer fixed breakfast.

"We're almost out of water," I told her. "I'm going to go to the lake to fill the cooler."

She stood from where she'd been feeding the fire. "We usually do that together."

"Yeah. I'm leaving my spear here for you. In case."

Her hip and her head cocked in unison. "I've got a knife. Besides, I'm going with you, Bray."

I knew she'd put up a fight. "Okay."

I grabbed the cooler and rope and handed her the spear. For good measure, I slung the fishing net over my shoulder and took the dulled machete I'd been using to hack through the jungle.

"Why are you taking that?"

"Don't know. Just seems like a good idea."

We made it to the lake, and Summer slid out of her shoes. When she headed for the water, I stopped her by placing a hand on her arm. "Let's not swim today."

She stared at me for a few moments, then nodded and put her shoes back on. Cooler in hand, I approached the water cautiously. When I dropped it in, I heard the growl.

It rose from somewhere along the water's edge where brush and plants flourished. The low, guttural roar bounded off the water. Summer materialized beside me, gripping my arm with one hand and the spear with the other. "What is that?" she hissed.

Movement off to the right and a splash forced us into motion. Carrying the cooler, we booked it to the edge of jungle. "It's exactly what I feared. It's the reason I didn't want to risk swimming. I dropped the net."

Summer grabbed my arm when I turned from the edge of the trees. "You're not going back to get it!"

I scanned the lake. "Summer, look!"

The long nose came out of the water first, right at the spot where I'd filled the cooler. A mouth full of sharp, jagged teeth. Then a body, a good two and a half feet across at the shoulders, and a long, long tail. "It's a crocodile."

Summer dropped onto the cooler. "It's huge."

"Yeah," I agreed, and as if the beast heard us, he turned so we could see the entire length of his gnarled green-and-brown body. His mouth opened wide and stayed that way. I shuddered. It was big enough to kill either of us.

"I've seen alligators at home. But they don't look like this." Summer remained on the cooler. I don't think she trusted her legs to hold her.

"Alligators steer clear of people for the most part. Unless you're in the water after dark, then you might be on the menu."

"What about crocodiles?"

If I remembered my high school science, crocodiles were a whole different story. "Very territorial."

Summer grabbed my arm and used it to drag herself to her feet. "That's what was at the hut last night."

"Yep."

"So the boat men don't know about us." There was a little hope in her voice.

"No. They must not."

My arm started to fall asleep from the grip she had on me.

"Why did they have it? Was it the same people?"

I worked my fingers to encourage blood flow. Summer noticed. "Oh, sorry." She loosened her grip.

"I saw a cage on the boat. I'm guessing they're trafficking exotic animals."

"Is that a big business?"

"Huge. I watched a special about it on the Discovery Channel. Dad and I, since we fish and hunt back home, had to take a hunter safety course, and they told us what to watch out for with poachers." My eyes stayed on the croc. I couldn't look away. The creature was surreal.

"Poachers and animal traffickers are the same thing?"

"Well, poachers can just be someone who kills an animal illegally. We get quite a bit of that in Florida with the alligators."

When the croc slipped back into the water, I took one side of the cooler and waited for Summer. She stayed there a few seconds more, staring at the settling ripples. "Will he come back to our hut?"

"I don't know. I don't think so. Looks like he may have found his honey hole."

She twisted her face. "Huh?"

"Sorry. Fishing term. No. I don't think he'll come back. But we should still be careful."

She nodded and latched her fingers around the cooler. "How are we going to get water now?"

"I don't know. We'll have to be careful." The reality of our situation hit home as we carried the cooler back to the hut. With the croc there, I didn't know when we'd get water again.

Summer

Bray started getting sick three days after we found the croc. We had been rationing our water, and the cooler was still half full. Enough to last us a couple more days, but not too long. On the first day of his illness, I noticed he seemed weaker than normal, and then his skin started looking gray. By late morning, he'd broken out in chills. From my calculations, we'd been on the island for over two weeks, and both of us had escaped illness until now. "Let's get you inside," I told him when I noticed him napping in the late morning. Bray never napped in the morning. We'd often nap in the heat of the day, but never this early.

He stumbled in and started to fall onto his bed.

"Nope." My grip tightened on him and I led him to the bedroom. "If I'm going to have a patient, I want him up off the ground."

He nodded and let me take him to my room.

I helped him pull the shirt from his body. Beneath it, he was slick with sweat. We had our fair share of sweat here, no doubt, but this was different. A cold sweat. As soon as he stretched out, the chills started again. I tried to gauge his fever, but really couldn't tell how bad he was.

"Where does it hurt?" My eyes scanned him from head to toe.

"Everywhere."

"Do you feel like you're going to throw up?"

A glassy eye opened and looked at me. "Yes. Can I have your shirt?"

I swatted at him. "You're not *too* sick."

A light smile tilted one side of his face. I assembled all the medical items we had. Our lip balm was long gone, but I kept an oyster shell full of coconut oil nearby. I had fresh water, a pan in case he puked, and lastly, I shook sand from the tarp and dragged it inside.

Bray's hands clutched his arms as he shivered, the muscles covered with gooseflesh. I stroked a hand across his head. My palm was slick when I drew it back. "Poor baby."

"So cold." I grabbed his shirt to put it back on him, but it was soaking wet. The breeze on the front porch would dry it quickly. Back inside the room, I tested Bray's temperature again. Placing my hand to my own forehead told me he was feverish, but not drastically so.

"Okay, I'm going to cover you in the tarp, but if your temperature goes up, I'll have to uncover you."

He nodded, eyes closed and lined with dark circles.

I started to cover him, but he looked so miserable there, lying in his own sweat. "Bray." I shook his shoulder a little. "Bray, I'm going to bathe you first, then cover you, okay?"

His teeth were chattering, but he managed to mumble, "You'll get no complaint out of me."

My instinct was to use the sea water, but I knew it left the skin sticky and sometimes irritated, so I scooped a small amount of the fresh water from our cooler. When I entered the room and stripped off my shirt, he was already on his side facing the window. I doused my T-shirt in the water and began on his back. When the cool cloth made contact, he arched and sucked a breath through his teeth. I knew he didn't want to complain, but cool water when you're already chilled isn't fun. I wiped down the mattress before turning him over, and then continued with my work. The fresh water was drying faster than the sweat, and by the time I'd finished he was no longer shaking. I pulled the clean tarp up over him. Stretched out on his back, I dunked my shirt once again, this time wringing it with more force. I folded and placed it against his forehead.

"My mom used to do that for me when I was sick." I whispered the words, so they wouldn't disturb him in case he was close to sleep. My thoughts turned to my parents, what they must be going through with us missing.

He mumbled something back at me, but it wasn't audible, so I sat still and watched him breathe.

When each inhale and exhale was long and deep, I slipped from the room. The sunshine outside scorched my eyes, so I paused on the front porch. The lagoon pushed a salty breeze to me, and I lifted my hair from my shoulders to let it cool the sweat I'd accumulated working on Bray. It was strange how sweat was just a common, normal part of our world here. We didn't usually give it much thought anymore. But Bray's sick sweat had been different. And I hoped he was through the worst of it because I hated to see him so miserable.

I scrounged through the canned soups we'd collected at the kitchen and chose a chicken broth for him if he got hungry later.

But later came and went and Bray slept on. I'd been sitting in the swing finishing up my latest story when I heard him cry out. I bolted upright and realized I must have gotten lost in the story, because the sun had been high in the sky and now it was nearly dusk. Long shadows stretched from the palm trees out over the water. I dropped my pencil and paper and ran into the hut.

He was drenched in sweat again and the chills rocked him from head to foot. I stripped the tarp away. His skin was cold and clammy and pale-looking. This was getting worse, not better. The fever was gone, but his flesh felt like cold leather. I cleaned him as quickly as possible with another small pan of fresh water. After I finished, I tucked the tarp around him, but he continued to quake. I didn't know what else to do. I knew that people could go into shock if their body temperature dropped and couldn't rise. This sent a spike of fear through me causing me to shake his shoulder. "Bray, how can I get you warm?"

His lips were blue when they parted. "Do, do you have any paper left over?"

"Yes."

"T-t-tuck it around me under the tarp."

That's right. I remember him telling me paper was a great insulator. I ran around the hut gathering all the paper I could find. It stuck to his body like a mummy suit. "Could you drink a little hot broth? It might help."

He shook his head. "No."

"I could help you. I can make a bamboo straw—"

The more forceful shake of his head stopped me. "No. Can't keep it down. Just need to get warm."

I paced back and forth a couple times trying to figure out if I could somehow bring a little of the fire inside. We just needed a heat source. Then, I realized. *I'm* a heat source.

I pulled the tarp back and stretched out beside him, then tucked us both under the crinkly fabric. Instantly, heat began to pour off me.

"Th—thanks," he mumbled, teeth chattering. "But I'm not that kind of guy."

"Very funny. Just shut up and get warm." Bray angled on his side and laced an arm around me. He pulled me close, and I was so aware of him, his body, his essence, that I closed my eyes. It wasn't long before he was sound asleep. Me, on the other hand, I was wide awake and right beside the man I loved. Fueling him with my heat.

Over the next two days, Bray's fever returned, left, and returned again. I'd force-fed him enough water to keep him alive, but the supply was dwindling and he lost so much when he had the bouts of sweating, I knew we were hitting a danger zone. After the first two baths, I switched to sea water, but the damage was done. Our fresh water supply was almost out. If Bray didn't turn the corner soon, I'd have to go to the lake for more. He couldn't live without water. I'd even rationed my share, and drank as much green coconut milk as possible. Still, as I stared down into the nearly empty cooler, I knew there was no other way. I waited until early evening to leave the hut. Bray had been tossing and turning all day, and I knew he'd be exhausted and sleep while I was gone. There was no way I could carry the cooler, so I grabbed the rope and the plastic container we often carried water in and headed toward the lake. After just leaving the campsite, I returned, grabbed the spear and the machete, and went into the jungle.

I didn't love traversing the jungle alone, but didn't hate it either. The only thing that really bothered me was knowing a hungry crocodile had claimed our lake as his honey hole. Maybe he'd moved on … not that there were a lot of places to move to, but I kept hoping.

When I paused at the edge of the clearing, his evidence was everywhere. Long, swirling lines leading in and out of the water, brush disturbed and flattened at the edges. Oh, yes. He was here to stay.

I stepped out and waited. There was no sound, so I crept a little closer to the lake. I'd just decided to run, dunk the container, and get out of there as fast as I could when the trees to the right of me shifted. It came charging forward, hundreds of pounds of muscled green monster up on all fours and moving fast as lightning. I bolted to the tree line, tripped over a stump, and half expected its jaws to clamp down on my leg. I'd bleed to death. Or be eaten. Neither option sounded good, so I dug my fingers into the ground, catapulted myself to my feet, and ran, in the process dropping the machete and spear. The croc stopped. A tall palm became my leaning post as I contemplated my next move. After long consideration and knowing my likelihood of success was minimal, I trekked around the left side of the lake. But when I started to enter the clearing, there it was, running me off again.

Hands to my knees, the tears came. We could do this all night and I'd still not end up with any water. I stepped just inside the clearing to grab the machete. Angry, I shook it at the croc that waited at the water's edge, daring me to try again. "There's no other water!" I screamed. "Stupid animal! We don't have any other water!" My screams became sobs, and I was thankful no one was around to hear.

I'd failed. I brushed the angry tears from my eyes and added in a defeated whisper, "We were here first." What was I going to do? I didn't know if Bray could make it through another night without fresh water. Shoulders curled forward, I headed for the hut. The far-off cry of some unknown sea bird caused me to lift my head just as I entered a clearing. It squawked, tilted its wings, and landed on the mountainside in the distance.

The mountain.

I dropped everything at my feet, planning to come back and get it later. With only the plastic container and the rope, I ran full speed to the mountain cave.

CHAPTER 15

Summer

It was nearly dark, but I'd already considered my options. This was it. I knew it would be dark inside the cave, but there was no other way. With any luck, I could fill the container in the front room where the water dribbled from the cave wall. But there was the possibility that I'd have to go all the way inside through that tight, frightening section. I wasn't sure I could do it. But first, I had to climb the mountain. And this time I was alone, already tired, and in the dark.

I closed my eyes, said a prayer, and started climbing. A half-moon cast enough light that I could see each handhold above me, but not enough for me to tell how far I'd climbed. Beyond a few feet above or below, everything faded to black. Probably just as well. When I made it to the first landing, I knew how far I'd come and how far there was to go. Hair had slipped from where I'd tucked it in my shirt, so I gathered it behind me, did a quick braid, and tied it with a piece of vine.

It was fully dark now, no sun, just moonlight and stars above. My legs ached already, so I gave myself a minute to rest, head against the rock behind me, hands splayed on either side. I closed my eyes.

Something tickled across my neckline, and I first thought it was the vine, but when it crawled beneath my shirt, I leapt up, screaming. My hand flew into my shirt, clawing first at the neck, and then at my shoulder as it moved. I grabbed it, dragged it out, and flung it to the ground, still wiggling in my hand. The spider crouched on the rock for a few moments, its stick legs spread. It was half the size of my hand. I kicked it off the ledge.

Maybe something in me snapped right there. Rope around my shoulder and container dangling from it, I climbed. I didn't look down, didn't think, just concentrated on each step and each handhold. It felt like it took forever, but knowing I could help Bray fueled me. With every step I found, I made certain I was solid before moving to the next foothold. This made the trek a little slower, but having traversed it before helped my confidence. By the time I made it to the top, I was exhausted. But I didn't dare rest for long. There was no telling what might crawl into my clothing, so I stood, hands pressed hard against my knees, and pulled breath after breath.

There was only the smallest shaft of moonlight inside the cave, meaning I'd have to feel my way to the wall where water flowed. I mustered. Hands flat against the rock, and ready to shake off whatever night crawlers I might come in contact with, I found my way to the dripping wall. The trickle of water wasn't as loud as it had been, and dipping my finger into the small pool told me what I expected. Only the tip of my index finger was wet. I closed my eyes.

There was no choice. I'd have to go into the other room. I'd have to go through the place where I'd panicked until Bray dragged me from the entrance. Baby steps led me deeper until I reached the crossroads that would direct me through the winding, ever-closing tunnel. I tried to visualize it in my head, how I'd had to twist and turn to get through. And the wall. The spot where my lungs closed for business and shrank to the size of a pea.

My best defense was to stay calm, but as I crept along and the tunnel became smaller, tighter in the pitch-dark, and my hands had to press around me just to find which way to go, my calm slipped farther and farther away. It was hard to breathe. Each breath was saturated with the carbon dioxide I'd just exhaled, and I knew my blood was filling with it. Spots appeared before my eyes. Hands trembling, I shuffled, but hit a wall. Frantically, my hands moved, first searching, then pounding the rock around me, trying to make the space bigger. It was crushing me. My fingers found their way up above my head. I stretched each digit out, groping for the surface. Air. There was the slightest flow of air. My concentration centered on it. I couldn't tell where I was. How far I'd come. It seemed I'd been right here in this spot forever just waiting for the rocks to shift and crush me. Hands slick with sweat grew colder on the back side. The air came from behind me. With a ten-point turn, I shuffled my body until I'd completely spun around. Hands flew out in front of me where, to my side, I saw the opening. One strong shaft of moonlight entered the ceiling of the pool room, and with a grunt I was in it and out of danger.

I paused for only a minute, then filled the container, lifted it to my lips, and drank my fill. The water ran down my chin and over me like a cleansing rain. I filled the container again, placed on the lid, and headed back. Having navigated the tunnel in the dark, I had a strong mental picture of the twists and turns. I left my eyes closed and imagined each protrusion, each swell of cave wall. Before long—and without panicking—I was in the first room of the cave.

Using the rope, I secured the container to my waist and headed down the mountain. The moon had shifted, so there was a bit more light going down. Having the extra weight of the water worried me at first, but after I reached the landing near the bottom, I'd grown accustomed to the unbalance. I'd taken the express route down, but worried that the last jump would jar the water open. I wrapped my

T-shirt around it for a little extra padding, cradled it against me as much as possible, and leapt. The water sloshed inside, but the lid remained intact.

On solid ground, I started to take another drink, but decided not to. Bray needed as much as I could give him, and I could drink coconut milk when I got back. Maybe, if he was feeling better, he could drink some of it too. Coconut was full of nutrients. As of yet, he hadn't been able to keep it down.

Back at the hut, I ran inside the bedroom and lifted the drink to his lips.

He took tiny sips and lay back.

Throughout the night, I roused him every fifteen minutes. Each time he was able to drink a little more.

"I thought we were running low on water," he said, voice scratchy.

"I got some."

"You can't go off alone. Too dangerous."

"Yeah, well. I thought I saw a ship on the horizon."

He chuckled.

"Feeling better?"

He nodded.

"Good. Try to get some sleep."

I didn't bother to tuck him in. Just rose, put the lid on the water, and headed for the door.

"Summer?"

"Yes?"

"What paper did you use to keep me warm?"

My eyes closed, hand clamping on the doorjamb. "Why does it matter?"

"What paper, Summer? I found a piece and it had writing on it."

Man. I thought I'd cleaned it all up. "The stories were put to good use."

"Why?"

"Because I'd used up *all* the paper, written on every last page. Isn't that crazy?" I turned to face him.

"But they're all gone now." He sounded so sad that I turned and headed back to the bed.

"No. They're not gone. They're here." I took his hand in mine and spread his fingers. I pressed his open palm against my heart.

Heat flashed in Bray's eyes, and I realized he was definitely feeling better. I plucked his hand from my heart and lifted it to my face. "It's the *writing* I love. Not having the stories. Besides, you would have done the same thing for me."

"Nah. I would have depended completely on body heat."

"Oh. You remember that, do you?" My face warmed. I'd sort of hoped he wouldn't.

"In fact, I'm feeling pretty chilled right now." He tugged at me.

I fought. It was no contest, he had no strength. "Okay, Tiger. Time to rest. You can prowl tomorrow."

He took my hand, kissed it. "Promise?"

"Promise."

"Okay, then. Goodnight, future Mrs. Garrison."

My heart squeezed. *Future Mrs. Garrison.* Wow. That would take some getting used to.

Bray rolled onto his side and slept. Me, I stayed wide awake, staring at my future husband.

Bray

By morning, I felt human again. Summer had saved my life. But at the same time, I knew the water wasn't from the lake. It tasted different.

The thought of Summer making that trip stopped my heart. We couldn't live like this, survive like this. The mountain was too dangerous. Sooner or later, one of us would fall. There was only one choice open to me, and I wasn't looking forward to it.

I spent the morning in the ocean bathing the general gunk of sickness off me. Summer kept a steady supply of coconut oil on hand—she'd taught herself how to extract it by placing a small pot into a large pot with the coconut meat between, then she'd fill the smaller pot with rocks and press until oil gathered along the edge. She'd pour off the drops of oil and begin again. We now had a glass bottle half filled, so I used the fragrant stuff on my skin and some on my hair.

The sun was already high in the sky when Summer emerged from the hut. "Good morning, Princess."

She pointed toward the jungle. "Off with his head."

I met her on the porch and handed her a shell of coffee. I didn't want to tell her, but the caffeine supply was running low.

She took it and forced a smile through her morning grumblies. "It's good to see you up and around."

I slid my hands to her waist. "It's good to see you anytime."

"You're definitely feeling better." She leaned closer and sniffed. "Smell better too."

"So, you'll sit with me?"

She nodded, letting the morning breeze work in her hair. "Since you made coffee."

We nestled onto the swing, Summer tucking her feet beneath her. "What was wrong with you, Bray?"

"I have no idea. It was like the flu. But, uh, since there's no one here but us, I don't see how I could have caught it."

She curled both hands around her shell mug—just like she did every morning. I loved it.

"I'm sorry about all your writing. Did you try to salvage any of it?"

"It was all soaked with sweat, Bray. But I don't care about the paper. I wish you would get that through your thick head." For emphasis, she deemed it necessary to reach up and knock on my scalp.

"Come in," I said.

"Got your sense of humor back, I see. That's what that was, right? Humor?"

I slid an arm around her and chucked her shoulders. Coffee tilted dangerously close to the top of the shell, but she salvaged it. "Watch it, bud. I lost *my* sense of humor days ago."

I pulled a breath. "Okay. Serious then. We have to be able to get water."

She shuddered. "We have the cave."

I tilted her chin so she had to look at me. "We can't depend on that. There's no way we can get the cooler up and down that mountainside. Which means we'd have to climb almost every day. You know it's too dangerous. Speaking of that, what were you thinking?"

She blinked. "I was thinking that my future husband was severely dehydrated and dying. I won't apologize for going. And I'd do it again in a heartbeat." Her gaze became steely.

"That's what I'm afraid of. We have to kill the croc."

"What?" Her green eyes melted from the ice chips they'd been and grew wide. "We—we can't."

"We have to, Summer. We need fresh water and not just a plastic container of it every day or two. We can't survive without the lake."

She buried her head in my shoulder. "Are you sure that's the only way?"

"Yeah, I'm sure." *Note to self: Don't take your future wife hunting.*

"Okay." But the word dragged out and I knew her heart wasn't in it. She popped off my shoulder. "How do you kill a ten-foot crocodile?"

"That's what we have to figure out."

Together, we worked out a plan. I'd been on a couple of alligator hunts during hunting season in Florida with my dad, so I hoped crocs had the same soft spot just behind their heads. Getting close enough to drive the spear into his brain was another matter.

We'd sharpened several pieces of hardwood, and Summer was good at chiseling them to a wicked point. Her upper arms had toned with the rigorous work, but it just made her more beautiful. She caught me watching her and lowered the kitchen knife. We'd already dulled half of them. "Maybe we don't have to kill him. We could coax him back into the cage. You know, with fish or something."

I'd been spearing fish for the last two days. Rather than eat them, we were storing them in the fishing net and hoisting them high into the air each night so rats or other opportunistic animals couldn't easily get to them. They'd be bait, but just to get it where I could kill it. "And what, Summer? In the cage, it would just die slowly. We can't feed it." I pointed to the pitiful number of fish I'd collected.

She brushed the sweat from her brow where little strands of hair stuck. "You're right."

"If the cage wasn't so tightly woven, we could coax it in and spear it there."

Her expression turned troubled at the thought.

I dragged a hand through my hair. Nothing about this would be easy on Summer. "You want to go over the plan again?"

"No. We've been over it a thousand times."

"We have, but I thought it might make it simpler when the time comes."

She stopped what she was doing. "You can count on me, Bray. I'm strong."

I chuckled. She was certainly strong. "I'm not worried about my wildcat."

Summer scrunched her face. "What?"

"Wildcat. It's a little nickname I have for you."

She cocked her head and her jaw, and then shrugged. "Okay."

"I'm glad you don't mind it."

The knife tip made little swirls in the sand around her. "Who's gonna hear?"

"Good point. You ready?" I brought the last fish onto the shore and dropped it on top of the others.

"Now?"

"I thought it would be good if one of the fish was still alive. This one's pretty big. I think the croc will go for it quickly."

If crocs were anything like Florida gators, they fed at night. But even a good old Florida gator wouldn't turn down an easy meal. This would be an easy meal. And with any luck, its last.

We didn't see it when we first entered the lake clearing. I hated that. With its natural camouflage, it could hide almost anywhere in the thick foliage. For safety, we didn't drift too close to the water. I'd cut the rope into the sections we needed and lashed the machete to my waist, my dive knife to my leg. The machete wasn't worth much, dull as a rock and half rusted through. Still, I took it along. The net was all but worthless, with giant rotting sections, but it wasn't really meant to hold the croc, just slow it down and hopefully create enough of a diversion so I could run the spear — or several — through it from above.

I positioned myself in the crook of a low tree after Summer climbed higher. She'd hand me a spear once we'd drawn him close.

"Showtime," I hollered up at her and dropped the bait line practically to the ground. The freshest fish had died on the trip over, but he swung there on the end of the line, so I jolted the rope up and down to get the croc's attention. I was stretched out prone on the tree with both feet planted firmly. The branch was a good four feet off the ground, and I hoped the croc didn't possess some unknown leaping skill, or I'd be dinner.

When I heard movement above me, I glanced up. Summer was on the other side of the tree but still in reaching distance. Staying out of the line of fire.

The croc slid out of the water silently and headed for the bait. My heart picked up. When it reached up to snag the fish, I dropped the net on its head. As soon as it left my hands, I grabbed the first spear. With all my might, I drove it into the croc's neck, but it had already started twisting and turning in the net. Summer handed me another spear, and I sank this one by the first. The croc stopped for a moment. Summer reached to quickly hand me another, but the branch she leaned on broke. She jolted forward and tumbled out of the tree. She landed on her back behind the croc. Fear stole my focus. "Summer! Get back into the tree."

She started to, but turned and grabbed a spear, then another. They'd landed splattered around the croc. Only a few feet of grass and shrubs separated her and the beast. She tried frantically to climb. The croc growled and whirled in her direction. I grabbed her hand and jerked her up just as it snapped its jaws.

She stood on my branch, and when I heard the crack, I knew we were in trouble. Summer must have sensed it too, because she dropped the spears and grabbed a branch above her head. Using her whole body, she hoisted herself up, out of danger for the moment, but how long could either branch last? The croc was bleeding, but hadn't slowed down. It continued to thrash. I looked around for a weapon and saw one of the spears lodged in tree vines. I grabbed it, stretched out as far as I dared, and sent it down into the croc's neck. It tried to stumble away, but had gotten caught in the net tied to the tree. At the time it had seemed a good idea, but now we were trapped in a tree with an angry croc lashed to the trunk.

Eventually, it would break through. This was our last chance. I stood on the low branch and jumped out away from the trunk, aiming for the spears. "Bray, be careful!"

I landed, snagged one, and pivoted to get behind the croc. It sensed me closing in and stopped moving. The blend of hiss and growl crawled over my flesh.

I reared back and sank the spear with everything I had. It broke in two as the croc twisted into a death roll.

"Here!" Summer was behind me. She held out another spear and I took it.

"Back into the tree."

She nodded, but I knew she wasn't leaving me.

I sank that spear and knew the croc was slowing. Its stagger gave me confidence. I reached out for another spear and, just as I suspected, Summer slid one into my hands. Maybe I'd gotten too confident. I thought I was out of reach, but it spun hard, rope snapping, tree shaking. Something brick-hard hit my ankles. I saw a blur, then trees above me as I landed flat on my back. I tried to inhale air, but all I could do was gasp. The croc was practically on top of me, and its mouth filled my vision. Rotting, jagged teeth snapped once and opened wide. Summer screamed.

"No!" She struck out, lightning fast, and the broken spear lodged lengthwise in the croc's mouth. She jerked on my arm, helping me scramble to my feet.

In the blur of adrenaline, I don't recall seeing Summer grab another spear, but one was in her hand, and she sank it deep, using all her strength to drive it, and then twisted.

The croc shuddered to a halt.

Summer and I groped for each other, stumbled a good fifty yards away from the monster, and collapsed on the ground.

It was at least ten minutes before we moved. I led Summer to the water's edge, where we drank our fill without fear. Then we stripped to our suits and entered the water, both still a little shell-shocked.

"We did it," she finally said.

"You did it."

Her eyes welled. "I killed it."

I nodded. The protective part of me wanted to take this off her shoulders. But I wouldn't. This was important. It was her kill and she'd have to make peace with that. Her gaze drifted to the dead beast. It was no longer a monster but an animal, and she'd taken its life.

"I'm proud of you. You want to go talk to it?"

Sorrow-filled eyes found me. "What do I say?"

"Thank it for dying so we could live."

Her tears flowed freely, and she jerked a nod. We approached from the croc's tail. She held her hand far above it, thanking it, but soon, she was on her knees, stroking the creature and dripping plump tears on its flesh.

Over and over she repeated, "Thank you. Thank you for dying for us." Then she patted it, wiped her eyes, and stood.

I searched her face. "Okay?"

She nodded, rolled her eyes sheepishly.

"It's the same with hunting. Especially a first kill. Would it make you feel better if we use what we can?"

"How?" A frown darkened the green in her eyes.

"I think we can salvage some of the meat. At least the tail. It won't last long in the heat, but maybe we could rig up a way to smoke some of it."

She chewed her bottom lip before answering. "Yes."

And right then and there, the future Mrs. Garrison experienced her first hunt. Complete with field dressing a crocodile.

By the end of the next day, we had several long thin strips of croc meat, and I'd made a teepee for smoking. We'd use the tarp to cover the smoker.

Several feet away from the hut, we inspected my handiwork. "You don't think it will catch the tarp on fire?" Summer asked.

"Don't know. That's why I made the base so large. I've only seen one of these on TV, so we'll see. The first night, I'll stick pretty close, keep an eye on the flame."

She peeked inside the teepee. "What do you mean?"

"We can only smoke through the night. So the men on the boat won't see."

"What if they come back for the croc?"

I shuddered. "They ditched it here. Hopefully, they won't."

Her eyes narrowed. "But you don't believe that, do you? They obviously tracked and caught it once, which means they could do it again."

I took her by the hands. "We have to be extremely careful. Are you okay here for a while? I'm going to head over to the lake and gather some wood."

Her nose crinkled. "Why the lake?"

"Green wood will give us more smoke. Those small trees around the water will be great, and I think I can work them out of the ground fairly easily."

"I can go with you. You might need my help."

"If you stay here and finish stripping the branches to make the rest of the shelves, we can start smoking tonight." Our bottom shelf of the smoker was made out of our fire grate. It sat a couple feet above the sand where I'd make the fire. The rest of the shelves would have to be crisscrossed branches tied with vines. So far, it looked pretty good. Sturdy even.

"We need two more shelves, each getting smaller as they go higher in the teepee," I explained.

She nodded. "Okay."

I didn't want Summer back at the lake. I'd already dug a hole and buried what was left of the croc, but being there was difficult for her, so I felt she should sit this one out.

"Be careful." She leaned up and kissed my cheek.

I gathered my various knives and tools for taking down the trees and headed out.

Summer ran to catch me just as I passed the tree line. "Here. In case you forget your way home." She pressed the brochure into my hand and stayed planted there, beaming up at me.

A slow smile formed on my lips. "I think maybe that was just an excuse to get a good-bye kiss."

She cast her eyes heavenward. "Maybe."

I dropped everything I was carrying and took her face in my hands. She was soft as velvet, and I let the sensation of touching her, knowing she was mine, wash over me. My fingertips grazed her hairline. Looking intoxicated by my touch, her eyes drifted shut.

She tilted her head back.

"What are you doing?" I whispered.

"I'm capturing it." She pulled a deep breath, and I knew her mind was taking a snapshot of this moment. Life was comprised of moments. The really brilliant ones you remembered and stored deep inside the gallery of your heart.

A chill passed over me, some strange sensation I couldn't name. "We have a lifetime of these moments ahead of us, Summer."

Her eyes opened and she smiled.

But deep inside me something twisted, like maybe we didn't have a lifetime. Like maybe our time was running out. I stepped in closer, my thighs spreading apart, and pulled her into me. She came willingly. There was no fight, just agreement. Her hands rested on my chest and when I bent to kiss her, her fingers slid up around my neck. She tasted like coconut and salt and was the most gratifying thing I'd ever had on my mouth.

Drowsy eyes opened slowly. "You better go, Tiger. Or I might keep you right here."

I kissed her forehead. "I'll be back soon, Wildcat. Try to stay out of trouble." But before I could let her go, I wrapped my arms tight, dropped my cheek onto her head, and captured what it felt like to have her in my arms. Then I gathered my stuff, complete with the brochure in my pocket, and headed to the lake.

Downing the first two trees was easy. They were barely as big around as my wrist and planted in the loose, moist earth surrounding the lake. After dragging them to the edge of woods, I decided to take a break. The water beckoned, so I stepped in. I almost dove under when I remembered the brochure in my pocket. I dropped the contents of my shorts onto the shore, and just as I turned to dive back in, I stuttered to a halt.

There, across the lake, a woman stood.

I blinked, thinking my eyes had to be tricking me. It was the sun, the shine of rays through the trees across the water.

But then she moved, a fight or flight look obvious in her body language. She turned to head back the direction she'd come from.

"Wait! Please!" I dove under the water and swam across the length of the lake, knowing she may be gone when I came up.

My head cleared the water and I pulled myself onto the shore, but couldn't see anything except a narrow path of flattened grass where she'd gone. I dropped my head in my hands as hope and water trailed in rivulets off of me. Nearby, a branch snapped. I spun. There she stood, not ten feet from me.

For a few seconds, we both stayed unmoving. She shuffled a few feet closer. Her hair was long and dark, matching her eyes. White shorts and an orange bikini top graced her body. Off to the right, her trail waited, and she threw a glance to it, then back to me as if trying to figure me out.

My mouth opened, but the whole thing was so surreal, I couldn't quite muster what to say.

Then, her eyes narrowed, head tilting a millimeter. She sucked a breath, eyes widening with understanding. "You're him."

"I . . ." She spoke English, but there was a Belizean accent to her words.

Her feet carried her closer. "You're one of the American kids who went missing in the storm."

Hearing those words—about me—made my knees buckle. I leaned forward, feeling like the air couldn't reach my lungs. For stability, I planted my hands firmly on my thighs, trying to shore them up.

She came closer and placed a flat hand on my back. "You and someone else. A girl."

The mention of Summer cleared my thoughts. "Can you help me?" But that's when I realized I recognized this girl. She'd been with the boat men.

Her gaze shot off toward the north end of the island. She shook her head.

"Please."

She took a step back. "I'm not in charge. They'd kill you."

I knew as much. My eyes scanned the area and dropped onto my pile of stuff across the lake. "Can you come with me?"

She hesitated, but after a fleeting moment of empathy entered her eyes, she dipped her chin in a nod.

Once we made it to my stash, I turned to face her. "What are you doing here by the lake?"

"Don't worry. None of the others will come this far in. There was a croc. I just wondered if he'd found a home."

"He did. Unfortunately, it was the only fresh water supply. I had to kill him."

This seemed to disturb her. She looked sad. "I see."

"Why was he here?"

She chewed her lip. "Authorities followed us from Belize. The guy that has the boat dropped her here in case they caught up to us and wanted to board."

"Are you going back to Belize?"

She chewed the inside of her cheek. "Yes."

I grabbed the brochure from the ground and pressed it into her hand. "Please. Tell them I'm here."

Her gaze narrowed. "You and the girl?"

I knew what she was doing. She'd spoken of us in plural tense. I spoke in singular. She knew I didn't want anyone to know Summer was with me. I could either trust her or not. And maybe my decision right now would determine if she did or didn't help. "Yes," I answered, and prayed I hadn't just signed our death sentences. "The girl is with me."

She seemed to absorb this. "I can't go to the authorities."

"I know. I understand. But could you just drop this off at my parents' house?"

She stared into the tree line as if waiting for the boat men to pounce.

I took the time to kneel down and place the brochure against a rock. I usually carried a pencil in my pocket for Summer to use in her hair, but didn't have one, so I used my dive knife to scratch the address onto the paper. "Can you read it?"

She nodded, repeated the address twice, and then used my rock to scratch out the letters. "I can't make any promises."

Hope drained from me, my shoulders curled forward.

"But ..." She folded the brochure and tucked it into her white shorts. "I'll do what I can."

I reached for her hand, took it in both of mine. "Thank you."

"What else have you seen here?" It was a very direct question and I knew I needed to be careful with the answer. "There was another man with us, last trip."

"Yes," I said. "His name was Jamison Cavanaugh."

Her face lit with understanding. I'd either given her exactly what she needed to help us or I'd given her what they needed to kill us.

"We'll be in Belize in the morning." The woman turned and started walking away.

Before she could get far, I said, "My name is Bray Garrison."

She half turned, chuckled. "Yeah. I know. You've been all over the news. After the cruise ship went down—"

I ran the few steps to her to close the distance. "What?"

"In the storm. A cruise ship hit the coral reef and sank trying to come into Belize. Huge mess. Three days to get all the people out of the water."

So that was why we didn't see or hear any rescue boats or planes for the first few days. They'd probably all been diverted to the cruise ship.

"I can't believe you drifted this far from the mainland. They were searching for you north." Her brown eyes looked troubled as she seemed to try to make sense of our location.

"Why?"

"The current."

"Are they still searching?"

She shrugged. "I don't know." Hearing those words brought a hopelessness into my heart. Had our families given up on us?

"Please help. I don't know how much longer we can do this."

Her gaze dropped to the ground. I didn't know what she would or wouldn't do. I didn't know if I'd helped or hindered our situation. After I watched her disappear, I ran back to the hut, pausing only long enough to grab my stuff. The trees stayed where I'd dropped them. Tonight we weren't going to be smoking anything.

After returning to the lagoon, I doused the fire—which was little more than a few glowing coals. Still, there was no need to draw attention. "The boat men are here."

Summer's eyes widened as she came down the hut steps and stopped at my feet.

"I met one of them, a woman who was with them when they killed Cavanaugh."

She sucked a breath and her fingers flew to her face.

My hand captured them and raised them to my lips. "Don't worry. I think she's going to help us."

But her eyes were saying everything her mouth couldn't.

"She was at the lake. Actually worried about the croc. She recognized me, Summer. Said she'd seen our pictures on the news."

Her green eyes blinked, mind taking in and processing the information. "Bray, what if she tells the boat men?" Summer sank into me.

"I don't think she will, but tonight we need to keep everything put away and dark. No fire."

She nodded, face tucked against my chest. Then she popped up to look at me eye-to-eye. "We may actually be going home to our families, Bray. By now, they must believe we're dead."

"I can't wait to see Joshie. Mom and Dad. This has to have been so hard on them."

"I know, my parents too. We may actually be going home."

"Yes, future Mrs. Garrison. We can plan that wedding."

Her fingers closed around my face and she kissed me. "Yes we can. I think I see a ship on the horizon."

I held her close, shards of that strange feeling I'd experienced earlier in the day rolling back toward me. I forced it away. "I told you I'd keep you safe."

"At the risk of sounding like a cliché, Bray, you're my hero."

I kissed both her cheeks, the tip of her nose, then her mouth. "No, Summer. You're mine."

CHAPTER 16

Bray

We'd cleaned up and stashed everything the night before, so when the sun rose, I walked to the north end of the island to make sure the boat men were gone. I was almost back when I heard the deep rumble above and knew either a helicopter or plane was nearby. My heart kicked up. She'd done it. The woman I met yesterday had done it. I ran back to the hut, screaming Summer's name and running through the trees like a wild man.

The sound muffled slightly, and I knew they must have landed. When I ran the last little bit, I could see the edge of the float plane in front of the hut.

My eyes darted around for Summer as I entered the clearing. She was immobile. Standing with her hands up and fear filling her features. When I made it all the way around the hut, I saw why. A man stood on the leg of the float plane, a handgun trained on her. I ran, shouted her name, and dove toward her as the shot rang out. Something ripped my side. I landed on a soft carpet and could hear the scream tear from Summer's throat. More shots. *Bang, bang, bang.* Like fireworks on the Fourth of July. I realized I couldn't see. Maybe my eyes were closed.

Shuffling. Whimpering. My soft carpet was moving beneath me. Beyond us there was commotion. Someone yelling instructions. I forced my eyes open. Sand had caked them and my eyeballs burned, but I blinked around the bits of sand and tears until I could see giant wings on the beach. Men in black jackets with white letters left the helicopter and moved onto the beach, weapons trained on the float plane. Others headed straight toward us. Words flew around me.

"Get the kids."

"All clear."

"Is Maria in the plane?"

"Yes, sir. She's been shot."

Someone touched me. Soft hands. Then, stronger ones. Lifting me from my spongy bed on the ground. I tried to form her name on my lips but couldn't. How had it become so cold? A giant bird hovered over my head, its pounding wings startling me, waking me from my forced slumber and slicing the bright sunlight. But it wasn't a bird, it was a helicopter. *Summer, where are you?*

She didn't answer. I was too weak to keep my eyes open any longer. Darkness closed over me, blotting out the light, the cold, everything.

CHAPTER 17

Summer

I woke in a hospital room.

To my right, the sun poured rays of heat through the window, but I couldn't feel its warmth. I reached toward the pane, only to have my arm tingle with goose flesh from the air-conditioned chill. My long hair was matted, a tattered splash against my shoulders, ends frayed from too many hours in the unforgiving sun.

I closed my eyes and imagined him. Like me, his skin was sun-darkened against the sterile bed. I saw him standing at a campfire, reaching down to take my hand. He had so much more right to live than I.

Yet I was saved. My throat closed, and the smallest of sounds escaped my lips because I'd felt this pain before.

Can a person survive losing both boys she loves? If so, I didn't see how. I squeezed my eyes tight and wished for the one thing I never believed possible.

I wished I was back on the island.

But I was in a sterile room. "Please," I begged as a nurse entered from the left. The door was held open by an armed man in a black uniform. My gaze closed on his weapon, and everything else disappeared. I remembered the feeling of stepping off the porch of the hut and seeing the plane. The man, stepping out onto the leg. Raising the gun to my face. My body frozen as I waited to die.

Bray ran around the hut screaming. He jumped at me at the same time the man fired. Bray landed on top of me, protecting me with his body, covering me with his blood. Flat on my back, I saw the helicopter. It rounded the edge of the lagoon, and someone inside opened fire on the float plane. The man who shot Bray bucked, tried to lift the gun, bucked again and again, and then toppled backward into the water.

I pressed my hands on Bray's gushing wound, but its force was unstoppable.

Bray was dying.

They pulled him from me, and I was whisked away with a blanket thrown around my shoulders and rough hands closing on me, dragging me to the helicopter and out of the pool of Bray's blood. Within minutes, we were lifted from the island. I watched as it grew smaller and smaller. I held Bray's hand while they worked, four men hovering over him, stripping things from packages and speaking words I didn't understand. He was on a gurney. We were off the island.

And I watched as blood from the man I loved pooled in the bottom of the rescue helicopter.

The nurse paused at my bed. This was the third time she'd come in. "Please," I said through a raspy throat. "Is Bray okay?"

"I'm not authorized to release any information." Her English was broken, but understandable. She patted my hand. "I'm sure someone will be in very soon."

I gripped her hand. The force must have surprised her. Her eyes widened, and her gaze dropped to our clenched hands. "Please. Just tell me he's alive."

She swallowed, stared at the door a few seconds, and leaned closer. "He's in surgery."

Bray was alive. My heart nearly erupted through my ribs. He was alive and we were back on mainland Belize. I released her hand, and she clutched it to her chest. I'd hurt her. "I'm sorry. I didn't realize how hard I grabbed you."

Her brows rose. "You're strong."

Yeah. Thanks to the island. That's when I noticed my rope ring was gone. "My ring!"

"The rope? It's in your side table drawer. I scrubbed it for you."

Oh. It would have been covered in blood. I didn't remember them taking it off of me, but the whole morning was a blur. I reached to the drawer. "Please, can I have it back?"

She drew it out and handed it to me, then said, "Don't you dare tell them I told you about Bray."

I cast a glance to the door and nodded.

"Sleep if you can. Someone will be in soon."

The door swung open, causing us both to start. A man, round-faced and with a belly that pushed hard against the bulging buttons of his shirt, stepped inside. "Can she talk?"

I answered for myself. "Yes."

The nurse shot me a glance, and I knew this man had the answers to what happened. I leaned up on the pillow. "Is Bray okay?"

He cleared his throat, stepped closer, and looked at me from head to toe, as if gauging something.

"Sir, please."

He sniffed, causing his shoulders to rise and his shirt to groan under the pressure. I'd noticed he also spoke perfect English and looked as American as Bray and I. His eyes cut to the nurse. She hurried to finish and left the room.

"My name is Orlin MacAbee. What I'm about to tell you cannot leave this room."

I nodded.

"Maria Sosa is a U.S. Fish and Wildlife undercover agent. I'm a colleague of hers. Maria met Bray at the lake on Sovereign Island."

The woman with the boat men was an undercover agent?

"Three years of hard work have gone into bringing down the trafficking ring the two of you encountered. She took a great risk letting us know you were there and alive."

I remembered back to when the shots rang out. "Someone yelled the name Maria. She'd been shot."

Orlin pulled a breath, and scrubbed at the scruff beneath his chin. "Yes."

"She was there when they came to kill us this morning?" My mind tried to wrap around it. "She was with them?"

"Held at gunpoint. Your uh ... incident blew her cover. She'd snuck off their boat and made a call to me. I contacted Bray's family. After torturing her, then drugging her, they made her give up your location."

It was getting hard to breathe. I splayed my hands flat on the sheet, fingers spread and trying to feel the solid surface beneath me. "How ... how did we get here?"

"The helicopter. We swarmed the island just as Raul opened fire on you. We brought you straight to the hospital here."

I hadn't been shot. "Brought in the helicopter?" Why were the details so blurry? The frown on my face deepened.

"Yes in the helicopter. You were in shock. On another note, you two killed a croc on the island?"

I nodded, a little surprised by the change of conversation.

"With the croc dead, Maria'd lost her chance to meet the head of the organization. It was to be a gift for him. Three years down the drain."

Okay, so was Orlin MacAbee just here to tell me how badly we'd messed things up? "Look, it was the croc or us. We didn't have a real choice. Is Maria okay?"

"She'll live." He stared down at me like this whole thing was my fault.

"I'm sorry about what happened to her. About your investigation."

I focused tightly on his small round eyes and watched them change. Disapproval turned to empathy. Mechanical equipment hummed around us, hospital machines whirred—I'd never noticed them before.

Orlin reached out and patted my hand. "No, I should apologize. You were just trying to survive. Glad you two made it."

"Who shot Bray?"

"A man named Raul. He also shot Maria. I expect them both to make a good recovery."

I let out some of the tension that had settled in my lungs, my heart. Eyes closed, I focused on those words. A good recovery. But with my eyes squeezed shut, all I could see was Bray, the horror on his face, him diving on top of me. The feeling that he was gone, dying, bleeding out as I tried to hold him together.

He's alive. I said the words over and over in my head, praying they would take root, but each time I tried, there he was, bleeding, dying.

"I'll leave you to get some rest. No word of any of this, okay Summer?"

They'd hooked me up to an IV, though I wasn't injured. Fluid drained into my system. I toyed with the tube. "Yes sir."

"We'll be in touch. Until then, no one except the Garrisons will be allowed in. If you leave the room, you don't go alone."

A tremor ran the length of my spine. Was I still in danger? Then I remembered the armed guard just outside my door.

MacAbee left, but I couldn't sleep. Not with this living nightmare running through my head and not until I knew Bray was out of surgery. But my eyes grew heavy, and I wondered if they'd slipped some medication into the IV. The room grayed around me, sounds muffled and grew farther and farther away.

I woke to commotion.

Markus and Sandra stood at the foot of my bed and little Joshie ran to me from the door, arms out and a smile as big as Texas on his face. "Joshie!" I gasped and pulled him to me in a bear hug.

Sandra pitched forward. "Oh, Josh, don't hurt her. She's been through a lot."

"I'm fine," I said and held him so close. I closed my eyes and tucked my head into his hair, breathing in the life and light that was Joshie. He smelled like strawberry shampoo and little boy sweat, and it was such an amazing scent that all I could do was hold him.

With tears in her eyes, Sandra came around the bed and dropped beside me. She pulled me into a hug, and before I knew what was happening, all four of us were tangled up there on the bed, crying tears of joy and laughing between the sobs.

I pushed back. "Is Bray going to be okay?"

She nodded. "He came through surgery like a champ. The bullet nicked a vein. He lost some blood, but he's going to be fine."

Some blood. That was an understatement. My head fell back against the pillow and I closed my eyes. Bray was going to be okay.

"Now, what can we get for you?"

"I'd like to talk to my mom and dad."

"Can't." Markus grinned. "They're on a plane right now."

"They're coming here?"

Markus stood beside his wife. "They're coming *back* here. They were here for the first two weeks after you disappeared. Your dad had to return home for work. Your mom went with him. She was planning to come back next week."

"Summer, we're so sorry this happened to you." Sandra let go of Markus and took my hand in both of hers. I wondered if things had changed between them.

Joshie curled into a ball on my lap. I was the link to his big brother. He nuzzled deeper. He probably hadn't seen Bray yet, so I was getting all the love. I hugged him hard. This was my family now.

I toyed with the rope ring on my finger. It now sported a pink tinge. I'd wait for Bray before saying anything about it.

A doctor slid the door open and addressed the Garrisons. "Bray is out of recovery and awake. He'd like to see you." The three moved away from my bed and the world felt a little colder.

The doctor turned his attention to me. "I'll get a nurse in here to remove that IV, and as soon as she does, we'll walk you over to see him too."

But it was too late. I grabbed the needle and ripped it from my arm. Blood came out in a quick spurt, causing Sandra to gasp and Joshie to yell, "Ewww, gross!"

Markus grabbed a washcloth from the sink nearby and pressed it to my arm. He turned to the doctor. "Guess there's no reason to leave her behind now. Come on, Summer. You can lean on me."

I didn't need to lean on anyone. I was strong. What I lacked before going to the island, I'd gained while there. I'd killed a crocodile. I'd climbed a mountain to get water. I'd let go of my dead boyfriend and found love.

I was Summer Mathers. And soon I'd be Summer Garrison. Life had been hard up to this point, but now it was going to be perfect.

We entered Bray's room as silently as possible for four people so excited they buzzed like a lightning storm. As soon as Sandra saw her son, the tears started. I didn't think he looked too bad, but they hadn't seen him in over three weeks. Markus tucked his wife beneath his arm the same way Bray had tucked me so many times when I needed shoring up. He gave her the strength to make it to the bed. Joshie stood back too, so I slid my hand in his and coaxed him forward.

Markus touched Bray's hand.

His eyes drifted open. A slow smile spread across his face. "Hey, I missed you guys."

Sandra dropped carefully on his bed and hugged him. His arm, still trapped by the IV, came up around his mom. Markus bent and kissed the top of his head. "We missed you too, son," he said, and I had to fight tears because it was hard to see a man like Markus, so strong, so in control, crumbling at the sight of Bray.

They were careful not to touch his stomach. "Where's Summer?" The rasp in his voice disappeared.

"I'm here."

He blinked then found me at the door. From across the room, our eyes locked, and I knew that everything—Bray included—was going to be just fine. I held Joshie's hand out in front of me. "Go see your brother."

He'd been squeezing harder and harder, little boy nerves all jangled. He undoubtedly didn't like seeing his big brother—his larger-than-life hero—weak and confined to a hospital bed.

"Yeah, come on Joshie." Bray patted a spot by him on the bed.

A nurse entered the room, passed by us, and busied herself checking monitors. "He just received pain meds, so he'll be out soon. He needs to rest."

"We won't stay long," Markus told her.

Josh walked toward his brother. Bray winked at me. His gaze dropped to my arm where I held a washrag in the crook of my elbow. "Summer, what happened?"

I glanced down at it, but it was Markus who answered. "They weren't going to let her come over to see you, so she ripped the IV out of her arm."

"Come here, you." Bray motioned for me. I swallowed. Joshie wasn't the only one who idolized him. My knees were weak, but I could do it. Go over and let him hug me or maybe just squeeze my hand. He was like that, always needing to touch me. But as I took the first step, everything that had happened welled up, pressing against my heart.

"What were you thinking? You could have died and I never would have forgiven you." I wiped a smear of tears from my face and closed the distance to his bed. "I still might not." No one in the room seemed surprised by my hysteria. Except me, of course. I wiped another smear, and then folded my arms.

Bray chuckled, grabbed my hand and leaned back into his pillow. "Yeah, that's my wildcat. Your arm?" He pointed to the cloth.

"It's fine," I added, embarrassed. "Not even bleeding anymore."

Joshie turned to look at me. "Can I see?"

"Later." Markus reached to touch his son's leg, but Bray's eyes were growing heavy and he had to use more and more force to hold them open. "We never gave up on you, Bray. None of us. Especially Katie."

His eyes closed, but he mumbled, "Who's Katie?"

Both Markus and Sandra laughed. And I felt oddly out of the loop. Who was Katie? I didn't remember Bray ever mentioning someone by that name. A cousin maybe?

It didn't matter. We were home and we were safe. And we belonged to each other.

Bray fell into a deep sleep, so we left the room. Sandra turned to me. "Would you like to go down to the cafeteria and get something to eat? Mr. MacAbee said that would be okay."

I'd really hoped to have my first meal back with Bray, but the thought of real food was irresistible. "Yes." What else did they know? I decided not to discuss it, since MacAbee told me not to.

We traversed the hall and passed the armed guard. After we were inside my hospital room, Markus nodded toward the guy. "He'll probably follow us down. But that's okay. Whatever we need to do to keep you both safe."

Sandra grabbed an overnight bag from inside a small closet. "I took the liberty of packing you a couple changes of clothes, Summer. I think it's safe to say the ones you were in should be thrown away."

I laughed, hardly believing we were there.

Sandra handed me the bag. "Everything you need. Even shampoo so you don't have to use that horrible hospital stuff."

Any shampoo was a blessing. Didn't she know that? "Thank you. Thank you both for everything. I'll be quick."

"We're going to speak with Bray's doctor, so take your time, Summer," Markus said.

"Yeah, you smell like feet," Joshie added, and we both laughed.

"Josh!" Sandra brandished him with a look. "Actually, you smell like coconut."

"Yeah." Joshie's face sparkled. "Coconut feet."

"We'll be back shortly to get you."

I watched them leave, surprised by how much energy it zapped from me to have a conversation with all of them. It was like my body had gotten so used to it being just me and Bray that I didn't know how to react to multiple people. I felt tired. The shower would help. I scrounged around in the bag to make sure I had everything I needed and my hand fell on something cool and hard in the bottom corner. I lifted it out. My favorite Bible. But I hadn't brought it with me to Belize, just a small one. Tears stung my eyes. My parents must have brought it with them when they came. Slowly, I pulled it to my chest and thanked God for getting us off the island. I opened the cover and a piece of paper slipped out, landing silently on the floor. I opened the paper and my breath caught. It was from my dad.

Baby Girl,

You've always been the sunshine in my life. Your mother's too, although she's more internal about her words and feelings than me. Summer, we know you're out there. We know you're alive and we won't give up. We won't stop searching until we find you.

My heart is breaking, but it won't let me down. I know what a survivor you are. I've watched you rise above such hard circumstances. I wish I could have helped you last year. But you shut us out. You're a little like your mother that way, carrying things without asking for help.

We will search every island and every port until we find you. The Garrisons are as determined as your mother and I. I'm sitting in your room as I write this. It feels so empty here without you. Through the window, the world keeps turning, and I wonder how it can with you gone. And then, I think maybe there were times you sat in this same spot and wondered the same thing with Michael gone.

Come home to us, Summer. Come back.

I love you, Baby Girl,
Dad

I wiped the tears from my eyes and stepped into the bathroom, heavy with the weight of all my folks had gone through in the last three weeks. I forced my focus around me. I flipped on the light. I flipped it off. Then on. Then off again. One switch. All it took to illuminate the whole room. I flipped it on and stared up at the bulb; what a magnificent invention. In the small room, strange sounds echoed to me. The hum of mechanical things around this world replaced the one I'd left—these were sights and sounds I'd never noticed before. The scent of metal in the air, the stark whiteness of the light. The chill of the floor against my bare feet.

I turned on the water, and then angled to look in the mirror. My hands came up to my face. It was so dark. Was that even me looking back? The light streaks in my hair had intensified, brighter than before the island. I ran my hands through it to make sure it felt like mine. Yes, it felt right, it just *looked* wrong.

When I got tired of looking at the mess that was me, I grabbed the toothbrush and toothpaste. I brushed, and then brushed again. My hospital gown dropped to the floor and I stepped into the shower. My body couldn't take the sudden heat. I usually loved hot showers.

Sandra had also sent a bodywash, so I used up the whole four-ounce bottle, scrubbing myself from head to toe, rinsing, and scrubbing again. I almost felt clean. The water finally ran clear.

I dressed in the white shorts and black tank top and slipped on the sandals. I was glad to see Sandra had added a gray hoodie. I shrugged it on and pulled it around me like a blanket.

I walked with them to the cafeteria, where so many smells melded in the air, I wasn't sure if I'd pass out from euphoria or if I'd puke. We got our plates and sat down with the guard hanging nearby.

Sandra nodded toward him. "At least he's not making a fuss and hovering over us."

A plate of pot roast sat before me. I really wanted a hamburger, but felt like I needed to wait for Bray for that. I had also slipped off my engagement rope ring and kept it in my pocket. It could cause questions and it wouldn't be fair to Bray to not save the news. We should tell them together.

The roast melted in my mouth. I savored each bite. I noticed a girl a couple tables away staring at me. When it became too much, I dropped my fork to my plate. "Why is that girl looking at us?"

"Maybe she recognizes you." Markus shrugged when he said it. "You and Bray have been big news."

I wasn't hungry anymore. "What happened while we were gone?"

"First, a cruise ship went down in the storm, and that's all the news was covering for days. We were so frustrated because we wanted people to be looking for you guys. You know, aware you were out there. Then, Katie showed up."

Sandra picked up the story when Markus took a bite. "Katie and Bray know each other from college. Her dad is an anchorman for

CBS. When she got word, she put the news wheels into motion. You might say she became the face of the search for you two."

"Your pictures, information about your lives, all over the news. Every time they stopped talking about you, Katie came up with some reason to get your faces back on TV. She wouldn't back down."

This whole thing seemed so surreal. Us. On the news. "The woman Bray met on the island, she said she recognized him."

"Thanks to Katie," Markus said, his appreciation evident.

"I guess I owe her a lot." But it was weird to think of my life being broadcast for the whole world to see.

Sandra reached over the table and took my hand. "You'll get the chance to thank her. She'll be here day after tomorrow."

Markus's cell phone rang, the mechanical chirping sound causing me to jump. He answered then stood, placing his hand over the bottom half of the phone. "It's MacAbee. I'll be right back."

He exited the cafeteria through a set of glass doors and stood outside in a courtyard. The foliage was lush, and part of me wanted to join him. Just stand there in the sunshine with the trees whistling over my head and the sand beneath my feet. I shook the thought from my system. *What was I, crazy?* I was finally back. Back to the real world. Concrete and asphalt. Sturdy walls and safe streets. Showers, mirrors, shoes. All of it. I loved all of it. But . . .

I had to admit, there were things about the island I loved too. The quiet. The solitude. I'd worked through my issues there. Worked through Michael's death. Maybe it was okay to appreciate the island for what it gave us. In time, I'd get used to this world again. But being a news item . . . that I was sure I wouldn't get used to.

Markus entered the cafeteria with a smile on his face. "Great news. They caught the animal trafficker and are in the process of breaking down the entire ring." He reached over and grabbed my arm. "You're out of danger, Summer."

I nodded. I was tired. Overloaded. I pushed my plate away. "Do you mind if I go back up to see Bray?"

Sandra stood. "I'll come with you."

I held out my hand. "No, you guys finish eating. I know the way."

"Really, it's no trouble." She started to gather her things.

Markus placed a hand on hers, stopping her. "She might like to spend a few minutes with Bray, honey. The guard will walk her up. Let's give them a little time."

Sandra nodded slowly, came around the table, and hugged me tightly, almost like she was scared to let go. It was wonderful to be so cherished. "We'll be up in about fifteen minutes."

I headed for the door, guard in tow.

• • • • •

"Hey there, Wildcat." Bray's voice was still groggy from the pain medicine, but his smile grew as I drew closer and reached for him.

He took my hand, turned it over to inspect my ring finger. "You didn't give up on me, did you?"

"Never." I bent at the waist and kissed his cheek. Wincing, he scooted to make room for me on the bed. "I just thought we should tell our families together. Is that okay?"

"Whatever my princess wants." His eyes closed for a few seconds.

"I just want you, Bray. How are you feeling?"

"Hurts like crazy, but the doctor said I can probably go home tomorrow or the next day."

"That's great."

"We're here, Summer. We're home."

"We're safe. It looks like the guys who tried to kill us have all been arrested."

His hand came up to rummage through my hair. "You smell different."

"Well, let's *hope* so."

"I loved the way you smelled." It seemed like a sick thought, but I knew what he meant. Our bond was birthed in survival and sweat. "How weird is it out there?"

"Being back? It's weird. I mean, everything sounds so different. I grew up with these sounds, so you'd think I'd be comfortable, but it's strange for sure."

"Yeah, we'll get used to it again."

"Yes."

His blue eyes settled on me in that way he had of looking right into my soul. "I love you."

"I love you too."

Markus, Sandra, and Joshie entered the room. "You're released, Summer. Your mom and dad gave me permission to speak with the doctor on your behalf. They ran some blood tests, but everything looks fine."

Markus placed a hand on my shoulder. "Your folks will be here around seven this evening. We have a room for them at the house. I thought we'd leave here in a couple hours and pick up dinner on the way home for all of us."

I didn't want to leave Bray. At the same time, I really wanted to see my mom and dad. Sandra must have noticed my hesitation.

"It's okay, Summer. I'm going to stay here with Bray. He won't be alone."

I opened my mouth to protest, but what could I say? Bray was her son. She deserved this time with him.

Bray leaned up. "You don't need to stay, Mom. I'm fine."

He got three dirty looks in answer to that. His mom cupped his face. "I'm staying. No argument. Besides, Summer's parents have been here so much, they're practically family now. They'll understand why I'm not there to greet them."

When she said that, Bray's eyes skated to mine. The spark of excitement was undeniable. "Speaking of almost family—"

I cut him off. "Yes, speaking of that, it's so gracious of you to let them stay at your house." I reached for Bray and gave his hand a warning squeeze.

He bit back the smile. Poor guy. He was bursting at the seams to tell them. But I really wanted my parents there when we told them. "We'll all be together by tomorrow evening or the next," I squeezed again, "so we can *really* catch up then. Tell you guys everything that happened on the island. But we'll *wait*. Until we're all together. Agreed?"

He rolled his eyes.

The doctor came in to check on Bray and seemed pleased with his post-surgery recovery. We stayed at his bedside while he drifted in and out of sleep. At six, Markus suggested we go ahead and leave. I felt like I was abandoning Bray, though I knew I left him in Sandra's capable hands. Before leaving, I bent down to kiss his cheek. He turned and caught my mouth with his in a quick peck. I froze. His *parents* were in the room. I glanced over, but neither of them saw. They were chatting with each other, and I watched Markus take his wife's face in his hands and kiss her on the lips. It was just a peck, followed by a long, slow smile as they looked into each other's eyes. I didn't think Bray and I were the only ones in the room who were in love. With a hand against my neck, Bray angled his lips to my ear and whispered, "Good night, future Mrs. Garrison." My heart soared.

"Good night." We left, and I couldn't wipe the smile off my face.

CHAPTER 18

Summer

My mom and dad trapped me in a hug that lasted a good five minutes. We ate at the long dining table in the Garrison home with flickering candlelight playing against the windows. Beyond the pane, I heard the roar of the ocean working its way to the shore.

We talked and joked, but when the conversation turned to the island, I told them I wanted to wait for Bray. We'd tell them everything together. They seemed satisfied with this and with the fact that we were back and safe. For them, that's all that really mattered. By nine, I was exhausted. I slipped upstairs and found my favorite T-shirt to sleep in, tempted, *really tempted*, to take yet another shower. But my body wouldn't comply, so I settled on sleep.

The soft rap on my door surprised me. I'd already told everyone good night. I slipped into a pair of sweatpants. "Come in."

My mom entered the room with a glass of water. "Markus told me the doctor said you should continue to drink lots of liquids. You were both dehydrated when they admitted you."

She busied herself at the bedside, folding back the covers and fluffing my pillow. Moms are great. When I crawled under the blankets, she tucked them around me. "Thanks, Mom."

A light kiss brushed my forehead. "Need anything else?"

The bed was heaven and it instantly made my eyes drowsy. "No. Wait, could you open the window? I'd like to hear the ocean."

Her fingers fumbled with the latch, and then finally managed the small hook. Window opened wide, a salty breeze gushed into the room. Aaaahhh. That's what I needed. "I love you, Mom."

Stopping at the bed, Mom hugged me again. "Love you too, sweetie. Get some sleep."

I waited for her to leave, but she stayed there with me, probably watching me like Bray had watched me so many nights. I wanted to stay awake with her, but exhaustion claimed me.

As I slept, I dreamed of a white wedding.

I didn't wake up until three o'clock the next afternoon and stared at the alarm through the haze, unable to imagine being in bed that long. Outside my door, voices drifted up the stairs. I ran into the restroom and tried to corral my hair, then headed down to see what was going on, wishing I'd set the alarm. Why didn't anyone wake me?

The living room was crowded with people. My parents, Markus and Sandra, Orlin MacAbee and a woman I didn't know.

Markus turned to me. "Ah, Summer. Great. I'd like you to meet these folks."

Sandra headed into the kitchen. "I'll get us some drinks."

"How's Bray?"

Orlin spoke up. "He's great. On his way here, in fact." His face was splotchy, and I noticed he didn't mention that we'd already met, so neither did I.

"He's coming home? Now?"

Everyone nodded.

"Summer, this is Special Agent Orlin MacAbee and Special Agent Maria Sosa."

I went straight to her and first noticed a partially covered bruise around her left eye. She'd done what she could with makeup, but it didn't fully disguise the swollen purple flesh. "Hello," I mumbled trying to hold in my emotion. She'd saved our lives. Almost at the expense of her own.

"Maria is the woman Bray met on the island."

I tried to act surprised. "You're the one."

She nodded.

"You saved us." The tears came quickly and hotly down my cheeks.

"Yes, she did," Markus said.

She was beautiful. There were tears in her eyes too. "All I did was make a phone call. It was Orlin who got things into motion."

"It could have cost her life," MacAbee added, and I detected a hint of awe as he glanced over at Maria Sosa.

She chuckled. "Everything worked out in the end. I was on the floatplane, Summer. I watched Raul shoot Bray. You did a great job thinking quickly and snapping into action."

"Thanks," I mumbled. "I don't remember doing anything."

"You rolled him onto his back, stripped off your T-shirt and used it to apply pressure to the wound until the helicopter could land and the paramedics could get to him. You may have saved his life."

Splinters of that horrible memory materialized with her words. "Well, we saved each other multiple times on the island."

She smiled, eyes crinkling. "I'm sure you did."

Sandra rounded the corner from the kitchen with a tray of iced drinks. Everyone took one and settled in the living room. "Who's bringing Bray home?"

Maria spoke up. "Our operatives. We didn't want to make a fuss about him leaving the hospital until we had a chance to brief all of you on what lies ahead. The media doesn't know he was shot or the connection with the trafficking ring."

What did she mean? I thought the nightmare was over.

Orlin jiggled the change in his front pocket. "It looks like the croc incident might have leaked to the press. Honestly, we were hoping your rescue wouldn't get a lot of media coverage."

"I was hoping so too." I didn't say it loudly, but really, I just wanted us to be able to move on.

"Unfortunately, Katie Van Buren has already alerted the media, and she's called a press conference for tomorrow afternoon. We'll need you and Bray to speak. And we need to brief you both on what you can and can't say. Do you understand, Summer?"

My mind began to spin, and I wished I'd eaten something before I talked to them. "I don't want to speak to the media."

"Well," Orlin said. "I'm afraid that's out of the question now. What we don't need is reporters poking into the situation. I know this is difficult to understand, but Maria is an undercover agent. As far as we know, the only suspects who knew her identity were the man who was killed on the island and his pilot. If you're too secretive, it might look like you've got something to hide."

My drink clinked on the glass coffee table. "Something to hide? We were trying to survive."

"I know, Summer. If you appear and make your speech, the media will undoubtedly lose interest quickly. We're already working on damage control. Keeping Maria out of this media fest is imperative."

Maria brushed her hair back. "Also, if you tell the media the wrong thing, it could jeopardize the case we're building against the traffickers."

I touched my fingers to my temple. My head was pounding. "Won't they lose interest if I just *don't do* the press conference? I mean, no one *asked* me."

Orlin gave me a sympathetic look. "You could do that, but it might actually be worse. For you. If you refuse to give a public statement, reporters will hound you, hoping to get an exclusive."

I pressed my palms into my eye sockets. "This is a nightmare."

"The best way to make this go away quickly is to smile and play nice with the reporters. Answer as we instruct. Tell them how happy you are to be home. Half hour, forty minutes, then you're done. If they don't sense anything out of the ordinary, they'll leave you alone."

My hands came down with a clop. "Okay, whatever I have to do."

"Great. When Bray arrives, we'll give you all the info." Maria excused herself to take a call.

· · · · ·

I finished eating breakfast at three thirty in the afternoon, just as Bray showed up, looking fit in a pair of sweats and a white T-shirt. After hugging everyone again, they settled him on the couch. I headed over to sit beside him, but Sandra slid into the spot. He sent me a pleading look, but I just winked and gave him a soft smile. Maria and Orlin explained about the exotic animal ring, and as I listened, I noticed how good they both were at giving only minimal information — which was what we'd be expected to do. I tried to learn what I could from them.

If anyone could get us ready for this press conference, they could. The spectacle was to be held in a convention room adjacent to the hospital, leaving people under the impression that Bray was still there. It was all very spy-ish and seemed bizarre and over the top. But hey, what did I know?

"What about the murder?" Bray asked.

Maria's eyes darted to Orlin's. "We know you found the body on the island, Bray."

"We watched the murder."

Maria popped up from her seat. "What?"

"We were hidden in the tree line and we watched them shoot and kill Cavanaugh."

Orlin leaned forward. "Could you identify the man who pulled the trigger?"

Bray nodded. "Easily."

For the next two hours, we went over what Bray and I should and shouldn't say. I took notes because I'm a visual person and can't remember anything if I don't write it down. Rather than tell about Bray meeting Maria, we were to say a couple of fishermen found us and alerted authorities in Belize. The Belizean police would confirm they received an anonymous tip from someone fishing in the area.

It wasn't the truth and that bothered me, but I knew lives were at stake if we gave up Maria's identity. Plus, it was helpful that we would have no information about the person who called. If the reporters wanted to dig around trying to identify the fishermen, so be it. Maybe they'd leave us alone.

When the intensity became too much, I slipped into the kitchen for a drink of water and grabbed a bottle from the counter though I knew there were several in the fridge. I wasn't surprised when warm hands came around me as I stood at the kitchen sink. My eyes drifted shut.

"I miss you," he whispered against my hair, and my whole being came alive. I stayed there a moment, savoring him, the heat of his arms, the brush of his chest against my back.

He turned me to face him. "I miss you too, Bray. But we just have to get through this stupid media circus tomorrow and we can move on."

"Are we going to tell our parents tonight?" He nuzzled into the hair covering my neck.

"I wanted to, but now I just want this whole thing to be over. Can we wait until after the press conference? Tomorrow night?"

He held me at arm's length. "You aren't backing out on me, are you?" Those blue eyes searched deep. Eyes I knew so well. Eyes I'd watched in almost every imaginable circumstance.

"No. Never. I swear. I just want it to be a celebration. I don't want this press conference hanging over our heads."

He threaded his fingers through my hair. "You want it to be perfect. I get it."

Of course he did. He knew my feelings almost before I did. I never knew there could be someone on the planet so perfectly right for me. He pulled me in an embrace. "I love you, Bray."

"I love you too, Summer."

· · · · ·

At noon the next day we were escorted back to the hospital in an SUV with darkened windows. Our entourage entered through a back loading area, and I hoped the whole thing would be over quickly. Nerves started getting the best of me, so Bray reached over and took my hand. We waited in a small room and could hear the reporters on the other side of the wall. Orlin had instructed us to talk freely about life on the island, even the croc if it came up since that may have leaked, but not to mention how it got there. Or the boat. Or the men. Or Maria.

I leaned over and whispered to Bray, "I don't think we should talk about the crocodile."

"Orlin says they may know. We don't want to get caught in a lie."

"But let's not volunteer it." Killing the croc was still raw and painful. I knew people would understand, but I just wasn't ready to talk about it.

He squeezed my hand. "Just keep bringing the conversation back to life on the island. It'll all be fine. I'll do most of the talking, okay?"

I dipped my chin in a nod. "Okay."

"You can do this." And looking into his eyes, I felt like I could. "You're strong, Summer."

"Because of you."

Orlin rubbed his hands together. "Showtime." He turned us over to another set of handlers and left through the back door.

Bray pushed the side door open, and I was instantly blinded by flashing lights. Someone led us to the podium where a microphone angled toward our faces. I did my best to hide behind it, but that was futile. As soon as we stopped, the room erupted in a barrage of questions coming from every direction. With a set of bright lights before us, I could barely see beyond the first few rows of the crowd. I felt like a piece of bread thrown in front of a bunch of pigeons.

Before I really knew what was happening, Bray started answering questions. I calmed, listened to him explain about losing power in the boat and drifting for hours. He said thanks to me we were both wearing life jackets; that he'd tried to refuse but I'd insisted.

"Do you think you'd be dead right now if you hadn't had the life vest?" one asked.

"I know I would. We almost didn't make it even with the jackets. We were being crushed against the rocks and the jackets not only kept us afloat, they were a cushion from the rocks."

Well, that was sort of true. Actually, it was Bray who protected me from the jagged boulders.

I concentrated on his profile, his sandy hair curled slightly against his neck, how the muscle in his jaw moved. This was going to be okay. Bray did all the talking, and I just stood there and smiled when I felt the need to tear my gaze away from him.

"Summer, can you tell us what it was like to be on the island?"

I couldn't tell who had spoken. "It was terrifying at first. Bray was amazing. He protected me. Stayed awake at night to make sure crabs didn't crawl on me."

Another voice from the back said, "The two of you must have become very close."

I looked up at Bray to find him looking at me. We both smiled. "Yes. I don't think you could be in that situation and not become close to the person you're with."

Another voice, "Are you in love with him?"

My gaze snapped back to the crowd. Had I just imagined that? Surely someone wouldn't ask.

Bray answered. "We're here to talk about the island. Let's not put Summer on the spot like that, okay?"

I closed my mouth. He was really good at this.

The same irritating voice came again. "Was it hard, being alone with Bray *knowing* he had someone waiting at home for him?"

Bray and I both shot a look to each other, his expression as confused as mine. That's when the man who'd led us through the side door leaned over the microphone. "We need to keep the questions limited to the experience Bray and Summer had on the island. No more speculation about their relationship."

Another voice. "Can you tell us how you killed the crocodile?"

The tone of the questions had changed, accusatory now, where moments before they were friendly. A little shell-shocked, I could hear the tension in Bray's voice as he explained that the croc had blocked our water supply. The reporters seemed excited about the croc, and we both released a little of our former tension. "Who actually killed it?"

Bray squeezed my hand. "Summer. I had fallen and she was protecting me. She's a hero."

This turned the attention back to me. "How did it feel to kill the animal?"

Sweat broke out along the planes of my body. "Um, I felt relief. We were thirsty and I knew we couldn't go another day without water. But it also was sad because I took the life of an amazing creature."

"A creature who was only trying to protect his territory. Miss Mathers, did you know the croc you murdered was on the endangered species list for years after being overhunted?"

"No. I—"

"Only in the last couple years has it come back from the brink of extinction."

"We ... we had to have water."

"My sources say there are fissures of fresh water throughout Sovereign Island. Isn't it true that you just wanted *that* water because it was easy to get to?"

My head was hot, burning. "No. The only other water was up a mountain."

"So there *was* another source for water. Just not as easy to get to."

Bray took a protective step in front of me and addressed the reporter. "Summer didn't want to kill the croc. In fact, she begged me not to, but I couldn't justify the danger of going up the mountain every day and trying to haul water back down."

The questions started again and he raised his hands; it was such a movement of authority, it hushed the room. He leaned forward, resting his elbows on the podium and trapping all of them. "Have you ever been starving?"

Silence in the crowd.

"Have you ever gone days without water? Slept on the sand where you might wake up with rats gnawing on your fingers? If you haven't, then please try to offer some compassion. We did what we had to do to survive. I'd do it again to stay alive." He reached down and slid his hand into mine, then raised our hands in triumph. He was winning them over. "We're both alive. We didn't make easy choices and, sure, we didn't do everything right, but we survived. And I won't apologize for that. Neither will Summer."

I didn't know it was possible for a crowd of reporters to stay quiet, but for a few long moments, they did, as if Bray had popped a giant pin into their massive wad of accusation. It was a beautiful thing.

Off to the left, a side door burst open and a tall blond girl came rushing in. All the attention went to her, reporters yelling the name *Katie* and pelting her with questions. She headed straight for us. I searched Bray's face, but he looked like a deer in the headlights, only moving when she stepped right past me and trapped him in an embrace, lacing her arms around his neck. I shuffled back, almost off balance.

Bray gave her a quick hug, and then pushed back. She turned her attention to the crowd. "How does it feel, Katie, to have Bray home?"

Her light blue eyes flashed. "Amazing. I knew he'd make it home to me."

The reporters laughed, and I realized a whole new energy had entered the room with her.

She tossed her hair over her shoulder. "I bet now he's wishing he'd come to the Hamptons with me and my family for the summer like I *wanted* him to."

My mind froze. She stood between Bray and me and commanded the entire room. If the world was full of pretty people, she was quite possibly their queen. Someone near the back spoke up. "What kind of wedding plans will be in the works now?"

Wedding plans? How had they known? Maybe Bray told people at the hospital while his blood was full of pain meds. I tried to swallow, but my saliva was thick, my throat closed. This wasn't the way I wanted to do this.

Katie held up her hands in a mock surrender. "Back off, guys," she teased. "Bray's barely home, and we have all the time in the world to make our plans."

What? *What?* She had to be kidding. Or wrong. She'd made a mistake. When her left hand shot into the air and she pointed at the small rope ring around her finger, my knees buckled. It was just like mine.

"Maybe now he can get me the real thing, instead of this one he made for me after a day of sailing."

The flash of heat and pain started in my head and shot down to my feet. Katie grasped his hand tightly. Bray's mouth hung open, a frown on his face. But even so, they looked so right together: tall, beautiful, tan. Both wealthy, both perfect. My eyes blurred, and I stumbled as I turned and ran out the side door. I heard Bray call after me and a shuffle at the podium. Then he yelled, "No." And I knew he'd broken free of her grasp and was coming for me. I ran into the hall, passing more people with their mouths hanging open. Off to the right was a supply closet. I tucked inside and tried to hold back the sobs. They came anyway, and I pressed a stack of clean linens to my mouth to muffle the sound wrenching from my gut. Who was I kidding? Summer Mathers was a practical girl. She didn't fit in Bray's world. And she never would.

CHAPTER 19

Summer

In the hallway, I could *feel* Bray searching for me. I positioned my body behind the door in case he knew where I'd gone. I'd have to deal with him, but I wasn't ready yet. I knew Bray; he'd tear the hospital apart until he found me so he could explain. But there was no excuse for this. I pulled my ring from my front pocket and held it to my heart. My ring. Mine. But hers was just the same. Fashioned, no doubt, by the same hands. I'd trusted him with everything from my past, but he hadn't told me he'd made another one of these? That he'd already proposed to someone else?

It was more than I could bear.

After a long time, I opened the door. Bray stood there, on the other side of it, leaning against the wall. It didn't surprise me he was there. He always found me. Always.

My feet shuffled back, and he stepped inside the closet with me.

I was all cried out, my body sore and tired from the sobs and my face a salty mess from the tears. "How'd you know I was in here?"

He didn't touch me, just stood there, giving me space but also blocking the exit. "I know you, Summer. Will you let me explain now?"

I shrugged. "I told you everything, *everything* about my past. About Michael, the accident, how I felt responsible. And you failed to mention that you'd already asked someone to marry you?"

"I'm not engaged to Katie, Summer. I never was. Until she showed the ring, I'd forgotten I'd even made it."

I shook my head. "It was meaningless?"

"Yes."

"So, you made one for me? A meaningless piece of jewelry."

Bray ran his hands through his hair. "It wasn't meaningless that time."

I rolled my eyes. "Did she really invite you to spend the summer with her in the Hamptons?" He knew what I was doing, establishing that Katie was more important to him than he let on.

"She did, and I told her no. We're not a couple. Never were."

"Never?" My arms crossed over my chest.

"No."

"Tell me about her ring." My heart felt like it was on fire, burning holes in my chest, but I had to know.

"I'd gone sailing with about ten friends from school." His gaze drifted to the shelving unit on the wall, and I knew he didn't want to talk about it. "A lot of people were couples. I didn't even know anyone had invited Katie. You know, it was just an overnight party thing. Around midnight, I was sitting on the front of the boat making the ring because an old guy on the docks had taught me how the day before. She came out and took it."

Blood whooshed through my system.

"She put it on and joked about getting married. *It was a joke*, Summer. Nothing more. I swear."

"Then what?" Because I knew where this was headed, and if he thought I'd let him off the hook, he was dead wrong.

"Then nothing." He was lying.

"You and Katie didn't end up together that night?"

Bray took a step back. He worked the muscle in his jaw. I knew the direct question would force the truth from him. "Yeah. We did."

My heart shattered into a thousand tiny pieces because Bray wasn't mine, not really. And he never would be. Never *could* be. Not in the way I wanted to be his. And I'd known that, I'd *always* known that. There was no fairy-tale ending for us. Because he had a past that would always be right there in my face. "My parents are going home to Florida tomorrow. I'm going with them."

He reached for me, but I withdrew. "Summer, please. Don't do this. Don't run."

My head shook, fierce resolve replacing my pain. "You want me to stay? Why? So I can be reminded that the guy I love has been with other girls who might show up with rope rings he doesn't even remember making? No, Bray. I deserve better than that."

He was pleading now, his eyes intense and misty. "Listen to me. What happened between me and Katie ... it didn't mean anything. It was just a stupid party. We were just trying to have some—" He stopped, realized he was about to utter the last words Michael said to me. The noise of people shuffling past the closet door quieted, and I watched the frown on his face deepen. He finally understood.

"You were just having some fun." I was dead inside. Tears all cried out, emotions twisted to the point of numbness. "I'm so tired of other people's fun ripping out my heart. This hurts too much, Bray. I don't blame you. I really don't. I blame myself. I knew what kind of guy you were when we first met."

"But I'm not that guy anymore, Summer." He blinked, and a tear caught the light as it trickled down his cheek.

"Your past leaves a wake. I'm sorry. I wish I was stronger, but I'm not, not now, maybe not ever. Those reporters shredded me. Do you think they'll stop? Not as long as we're together. Katie is their little darling, and she's convinced everyone you two are destined to be a couple. I just need this nightmare to be over, Bray. All of it." I pulled a deep breath. "You promised to protect me, right?"

He nodded, more tears spilling down his face. "Always."

"Then, protect me now. Let me go."

My words stabbed and he sucked a sharp breath. He started to reach out, but instead flexed his fingers at his sides, giving me the last thing he wanted to give and the one thing I had to have. With the back of his hand, he brushed the moisture off his cheeks. "I'll protect you. If this is really what you want. But I also promised you I'd never let go."

I started to step past him, reminded of the mountain where he'd held my weight and dragged me to safety. I wished I wasn't such a fragile thing. Life on the island was a snapshot in time, both of us rising above ourselves. But now we were in the world, the real world, which in some ways was as unforgiving as our island. But on the island we could forget. Here, we couldn't. And that was why I had to go. I took a step.

He caught my arm. "If you're set on returning with your parents, I won't try to stop you. But I will *never* let go, Summer. *Never*. And I'll be waiting when you're ready." His blue eyes swam, and I wished I was strong enough and brave enough to stay. But I wasn't. I gave him one last look, taking in every feature, and then I closed my eyes and moved past him and out the door.

· · · · ·

We flew into the Sarasota Bradenton International Airport. My parents had been supportive, quiet, and solid. They knew I was exhausted. Two days after we got home, my dad handed me a brochure. "What's this?"

"The reason we couldn't stay in Belize." He pointed at it. "Take a look."

Dad's hotel graced the cover with the words *Southwest Florida*

Writer's Conference. It was being held at the Sarasota Four Seasons resort my dad worked at as the Convention Coordinator. "It's in three months. I thought you might like to attend."

I stared down at the words, but didn't know what to say. I wasn't sure how I felt about it.

He placed his hand on my arm. "I know you haven't written recently, but—"

"No, I have."

He lifted a brow in question.

"On the island, Bray would tell me stories at night, but never finish them. He'd always fall asleep and be snoring before he got to the end."

My dad swallowed. This is how it always was when I mentioned being alone with Bray. I guess his mind had gone all kinds of places, but he'd yet to ask.

"Dad, Bray and I didn't *do* anything. I'm sure you and Mom have been worried about that. He was a perfect gentleman. Plus, I made a promise to God a long time ago."

My dad's kind eyes crinkled. He let out a long breath. My parents knew about my commitment to wait. They were—of course—in total support. An arm slid around my shoulders. "Do you want to tell us about the island now?"

I hadn't yet. It almost seemed cruel to make them live it while I relived it. I could see the apprehension in my dad's face. "No. Not yet."

"Well, when you're ready." He pointed to the brochure I'd lost interest in. "How about the conference? Would you like to go?"

"I don't know. Can I think about it?"

"Sure." I started to hand the page back to him, but he held his hands up. "Keep it. I have hundreds."

The following day, my best friend Becky and I went out for lunch. I bought. The Garrisons had insisted on paying me for the whole summer though I'd only been a nanny for Joshie for the first few weeks. Becky had a blackened salmon salad and I had a hamburger. Ordering it made me think of Bray. We never got to have our big celebration hamburger together. I wondered if he was okay and when his family would be returning to the States. Did they plan to stay in Belize for the rest of the summer? What I *did* know was Markus and Sandra were no longer getting a divorce. Bray's disappearance had caused them to realize how lucky they were. Sandra told me the night before I left in a tearful good-bye. She also said that in many ways, I'd become—and always would be—the daughter she never had. I already missed her.

"Hey there," Becky pointed at me with a forkful of salad. "You still on this planet?"

"Sorry." It was great seeing her. A smooth waterfall of shoulder-length auburn hair paired perfectly with her sassy personality. She'd gone on for the first half hour about how beautiful I looked, but she was my best friend and as such was required to make such sweeping statements.

"How's the burger?" She had ranch dressing in the corner of her mouth. I wiped it off with my napkin.

"Heaven. I can't even describe it."

Her hand closed on my wrist and drew my burger to her mouth. "Eh, it's okay."

Okay? Was she nuts?

"So, you're kind of a celebrity now. How's that feel?"

I could talk to Bec. Tell her what was really going on, so I pulled a breath and tried to figure out where to begin.

"It feels weird. Reporters sometimes call the house wanting to talk to me. I guess I understand. We were supposed to do damage control and instead, I ran out of that stupid press conference like a …"

"Like a what?"

I had to smile. "Like a wildcat trapped in a corner." My eyes rolled. "Probably made everything a thousand times worse."

Bec, ever loyal, pushed her salad away. "It made me so mad when those reporters hammered at you about that crocodile."

"Right?" It made me mad too.

"And asking you about Bray. How insolent. I mean, that's *your* business." She tilted her head back and forth, hair dusting her shoulders. "And my business — as your best friend."

"They were rough on me. But I survived."

"You know what I wish? I wish every single one of them could have been in your place." Fire sparked from her emerald eyes — just one of the many reasons I loved her. "I wish every one of them would be on a deserted island. Then they'd be singing a different tune."

"If only." But I didn't really wish that on anyone. The island was treacherous. If the reporters *knew*, if they *understood* what it was really like . . .

Bec had given me something to consider, and as we finished our meal, the possibilities ran tirelessly through my head. It was a crazy idea. But, honestly, crazy was a close companion these days.

I booked it home after lunch and went straight to my room. My PC whirred as it came to life. I opened a new document and started with the title.

Summer by Summer
An adventure novel by Summer Mathers
Based on the Real Events on Sovereign Island

I wouldn't try to defend myself in front of reporters. But what I would do was put them there. Let them live my story. And maybe, just maybe, when they reached the end they'd understand a little more.

Either way, I needed to share it. All of it. The boat, the croc, falling for Bray. I wouldn't hold anything back, except of course, the parts I had to keep hidden for the sake of an upcoming murder trial. But everything else I'd tell. Not just tell—I'd give them the ability to feel every emotion, sense every fear. From the hunger to the elation of finding food. The shark chasing Bray. The pitch-dark cave where I thought I'd die until a shaft of air kissed my fingertips.

A fresh wave of excitement washed over me. I had a purpose … to write. After another giant intake of air, I dove in.

Chapter 1
I went on a dive trip with a guy I hated and was rescued with the man I love.

For the next five weeks I wrote, edited, reviewed, and wrote more. Most of my time was spent in my room, but when I knew my mom was getting worried about me, I'd take a pen and paper and go to a downtown coffee shop or out to Siesta Key and sip a latte while filling up a notebook.

I loved downtown Sarasota, with its artsy vibe and relaxed atmosphere. I could walk around there for hours, but not right now. I was on a mission. Write my story. And it was coming together more quickly than I would have guessed possible.

During the sixth week, my dad came home with a gift; a lightweight laptop, much more portable than the PC in my room. It made me cry. My parents were really on board with this whole writing thing, and since I'd gotten paid for the entire summer by the Garrisons, I treated the writing like a job. Or maybe like an obsession. The story was no longer for the reporters. Writing it was therapeutic for me. Until Bray, I'd never known the importance of talking about things. Bottling up wasn't healthy. I thought about Bray often, but getting to relive our stormy relationship through writing about it helped in some ways. It made me lonely too. I missed Bray. Loved him. And maybe there was a part of me that hoped somehow things could eventually work out for us.

That is, of course, if Bray would have anything to do with me. Which he probably wouldn't, and I couldn't blame him. But I *could* show the world what an amazing hero he was while we were on the island together.

After week six and with my new laptop, the writing went even faster. I'd hit the halfway point and contacted a former English teacher, Mrs. Singer, to get a read-through and see if my grammar was okay.

She told me to drop it off at her house, so I printed the one hundred thirty pages, said a little prayer, and went by. Both her kids were playing in summer baseball leagues so it'd be a couple weeks before she could read it. That was fine. I was nervous about anyone besides my mom and dad seeing it anyway.

Mrs. Singer called me the next day. She'd already read the entire thing. Stunned, I listened to her go on and on about my story. Later that morning, I went to pick up the pages. She'd made a few grammatical changes — red ink, of course — and told me to keep working. So I did.

Becky stopped by that night. "You heard about what happened with that Katie Van Buren, right?"

No, I hadn't heard.

"Her dad found out she'd lied about Bray after his public announcement that they weren't *ever* engaged. Her father made her go on a talk show and give a public apology, said she'd ruined her credibility. It was awesome."

Oddly, I actually felt sorry for her. My thoughts turned to Bray. Poor guy. When he needed me most, I ran. Just like a wildcat. Right now, I wasn't proud of his nickname for me. I was ashamed of it. The idea of reaching out to Bray was nearly irresistible, but the timing wasn't right. Soon, but not yet.

The writer's conference was fast approaching, but it did little to motivate my writing progress. I just wanted to tell my story and that was fuel enough. A small part of me wanted to defend the actions Bray and I took against the croc. Another part wanted to encourage people to never give up. Another part just wanted to share the journey. And still another part—a tiny little voice—said maybe this could help others in a survival situation. Not just a deserted island, but surviving the death of Michael that had emotionally shipwrecked me long before the rocks of the island punched through our boat. Maybe my words would speak to others who had suffered a loss like that.

Maybe I could bring them hope. That's what Bray would want. To help bring hope to others. In it, they'd see what a hero he really was. He deserved that, for the world to know.

I chickened out of going to the writer's conference. It was Saturday morning and the conference ran through Tuesday. I'd dressed to go to town and stood at the kitchen sink eating Cheerios while dad chatted on the phone. "Worst time ever for four restaurant staff to get the flu." He winked at me as I held my spoon halfway to my mouth. Poor Dad.

He pinched the bridge of his nose. "Nah, we'll have to make do. Not much choice. We can pull a couple of the maintenance guys. And *please* remind the staff not to talk about a flu going around. Okay, thanks. Be there in about fifteen minutes."

"Sounds bad." I took the last bite and rinsed my bowl in the sink, then reached for the manuscript resting on the counter.

"Hospitality biz. Never gets boring." My dad was forty-five, and this morning he looked his years.

"I can help out."

"Aren't you writing today?"

"Not now. My daddy needs me." I crossed the kitchen and dropped a peck on his cheek. "I've worked the buffet line before, it'll be easy."

He considered me for a long minute. "You sure?"

"Yeah, let me grab my bag."

When I came back in the room, he had my book tucked under his arm.

I cocked my head and my hip.

One bright blue eye winked, sparks of mischief playing in his irises. "Just in case."

"Dad, writer's conferences don't work that way. You don't just go and dump armloads of manuscripts on literary agents' laps." What could I say? I loved him for what he was trying to do. But publishing was a business. I'd been doing my homework. Besides, I was a nineteen-year-old. What were the odds anyone would want my story? It wasn't about that anymore, I reminded myself. It was for me. Just for me.

Breakfast was simple, with groups of people flittering through the banquet area helping themselves to coffee in gleaming silver urns, trays of pastries, and fresh fruit cut into a myriad of whimsical shapes. The entire hotel buzzed with an excitement I thought only I felt for the written word. Editors were tagged with orange badges that announced where they were from—so cool to me because I *knew* those publishing houses and had read their books. The literary agents' badges were green.

"Are these real eggs?"

I glanced forward to find a sweaty little man staring at me. He pushed a pair of glasses up on his shiny nose. Through the glasses, his eyes looked too big for his head. "Uh, I . . . I think so."

A small, wet mouth pursed into a pucker. "I have to know for sure. I have allergies."

"Let me check." I turned from him and spotted my dad in the corner of the room, overseeing. A motion of my hand brought my dad toward us.

"Can I help—"

"Are these eggs real?" The little man cut my dad off and gestured with an open hand, his bottle-glass eyes unblinking.

My dad smiled, polite and professional. "They are actually from a mix. Very good, though."

Bottle-eyes released a long, labored breath and crossed his arms. "I have allergies." As if that explained the mysteries of the entire world.

"I'd be glad to have one of the chefs cook you a couple of folded eggs." Such composure in the face of the man's rudeness. Go, Dad. He really was great at his job. I wanted to punch the snotty guy in the nose. It wasn't our fault he had allergies.

"No, that's fine," he said in a breathy voice. "I'll just go across the street for breakfast."

As he turned, Dad and I gave each other an almost imperceptible shrug. The man spun back around and pointed at me. "I would suggest better training for your employees." The finger to the glasses again. "*She* should know what she's serving."

"Thank you," my dad said. I watched the muscle in his jaw flex. Nobody picked on his little girl. It was good the guy was leaving.

We both bit our tongues until the man was out of earshot.

It was a moment before we realized someone else had paused in front of us. "Is he gone?"

The woman was kind looking, albeit a little harried until I told her, "He's going across the street for breakfast."

"Whew. That's a relief." Her hair fell past her shoulders in long waves that were neither brown nor blond, but her own personal shade somewhere in between. A deep-red alligator briefcase dangled from her hand. I wondered if it felt like my crocodile, but decided it was probably not real skin. It looked expensive enough, but a lot of people were anti-exotic leather these days. I knew I was.

She helped herself to the scrambled eggs.

"Do you know him?"

She reached across the banquet table and placed a croissant on her plate. "Not officially. He wants me to read his one thousand and ten-page manuscript."

My eyes widened at the sheer volume. "One thousand and ten *pages?*"

She shot a glance behind her. "Says it's so brilliant, it will change the world." Her eyes sparkled with mischief, making me instantly like her.

When she stretched to get the butter, I grabbed the small dish and handed her the knife. My dad spoke up. "That's a very *long* book, isn't it, Summer? The one you wrote is only about three hundred pages, right?"

Heat crawled up my face. *You didn't just say that.* "We have homemade apple butter—it's a hotel specialty. Can I get you some? It's really good on the croissants."

Her eyes narrowed with an inquisitive stare, and then her effervescent smile returned. "That sounds like an odd combination, but yes."

I started breathing again after walking away from them. There were stations of jelly and apple butter on each end of the buffet, but I walked to the farthest, trying to release the mortification. It didn't go easily.

Her name badge said Kay Ballinger, and she wore the green name tag that labeled her as an agent. A *literary* agent, and my dad had just made the cardinal mistake. I wondered how many times she'd been approached by fathers saying things like, "My little girl wrote a book, and I just bet you want to read it. It's probably going to be a bestseller. Hey, we're doing *you* a *favor* by letting you have the first shot."

Nausea swirled in my stomach. I placed my hand there, but the contents didn't settle. I couldn't stay away forever. After all, she was waiting on apple butter, so I gathered my courage and returned.

"I'm very pleased to meet you, Summer." A smile. Her hand went out to shake mine. *Oh, Dad.*

"Thank you." We shook hands and I pointed to her plate. "You don't want that to get cold. Plus, your stalker will be back before too long."

"Right!" She turned and shook my dad's hand. "See you two tonight, then?"

My heart stopped.

"We'll be there. And like I said, feel free to use that service elevator anytime you need to duck out of the line of fire. No one will say anything. If they do, just tell them Jerry Mathers told you to use it."

She grinned. "I feel like I've been given the keys to the kingdom."

He nodded. "Anything you need. Don't hesitate to ask. The manuscript is at the front desk. I'll call over so they know to give it to you."

Black spots materialized in front of me as she walked away. Had I heard that right? Manuscript? *My* manuscript? Dad reached over with a steadying hand. "You gonna pass out, Baby Girl?"

I shook my head. My manuscript. She was picking up my manuscript.

"Close your mouth then. It looks like you're trying to catch flies."

Through the hazy swarm of people in front of me, I found his eyes. "I'm ... not ready."

"You've been polishing it for days. When *will* you be ready?"

"Never." It was an honest answer. My heartbeat finally began to slow as I watched Kay Ballinger take a seat across the room and toss all that pretty hair behind her chair. The alligator bag found a spot on the seat beside her.

"This is how it works, sugar. Don't worry. She knows it's your first attempt. But when I told her who you were, she was intrigued. She followed you in the news just like half the country."

"I'm really nervous."

Dad's arm came around and gave my shoulders a quick squeeze. "Nothing to be nervous about. She said she has a little down time before dinner. We're meeting her after the banquet tonight. Around nine by the pool. I'll reserve a back table at the tiki bar and let the staff know to deflect any interruptions."

My eyes turned misty. "Dad, you're the best."

He hugged me and I hugged him back. Then he cleared his throat and took his post back at the corner, a giant smile lighting his face.

• • • • •

Kay Ballinger sat at the wicker tiki table, a stack of papers on her lap. A pen hovered above the pages, and when I realized she might actually be reading my book I got queasy all over again. She pulled a set of reading glasses from her face as we approached and dropped the pages on the table.

"Thanks for letting me take a look at this." Her smile was genuine. Or practiced. Or genuinely practiced. I didn't know for sure, but expected the ball to drop any second. She stood and shook my dad's hand. "Your staff is fabulous, Jerry. They've been great. As far as your story, Summer . . ."

My heart geared for the worst as Dad interrupted her to excuse himself. Kay motioned for me to sit.

"I'm sorry my dad asked you to read this." It's all I could think and it popped right out of my mouth.

She flashed a frown. "He didn't."

I glanced over my shoulder where Dad disappeared into the small kitchen of the tiki hut.

"He told me who you were and that you'd written a book about the experience. I *asked* to see it."

"Oh."

"Honestly, Summer, I thought it might be possible to take the adventure and give it to a ghost writer. Often, when a celebrity wants to tell their story, a professional helps with the writing."

My heart started the long sink into my feet. "But this one isn't on that level?" It had to be worse than I thought. What was I thinking, writing a book without any formal training?

She chuckled. I failed to see what was so funny. "No. This one isn't on that level."

My nose tingled.

She leaned forward, trapping me in her gaze. "Summer! What I'm trying to tell you is I love it. There are a few technical things, of course, but the essence of the story, your voice, it's all great. I tore through it."

My eyeballs dried out, surprising because only a moment ago, I thought they'd be filled with tears.

"You should blink," she said. "Or your eyes are going to stick like that."

I obeyed and slumped into the chair. An agent. A real literary agent liked my book. "This is for real?"

"Real as it gets. I mean, it's not fighting a live crocodile with a handmade spear, but yes. It's real."

"Wha—what happens now?"

She leaned back in the wicker chair. "Now, I offer you representation. If you agree and sign the contract, I get to work on selling this little jewel to a publisher. I have a few in mind who I think would definitely be interested. You may have revisions to do for me or them. Are you comfortable with that? It won't be much for me though, as it's pretty clean."

"My English teacher said that too. She gave me a few suggestions."

"Great. You understand about the revision process then."

Stunned, I just kept staring at her.

"So, Summer, would you like to work with me?"

Beside me, I heard a small child squeal and jump into the pool. That's what I felt like, like a little kid being catapulted into a giant body of water. "Yes. Yes of course." Excitement burst inside my chest. "I have a literary agent."

She nodded. "You're the youngest client I've ever signed."

My face clouded.

"Don't worry. It's good that you're young. Gives the story even more punch. And my goodness, Summer … all you've been through."

The tabletop rested beneath my fingertips. I moved my hand back and forth, feeling the grooves. "Do you think it could help people?"

She pressed a hand to my arm. "It's very inspirational. Yes. I definitely think it could. I'll be back in my office on Wednesday and will send over the contract."

Dad stopped by the table. "Everything okay?"

I tried to look up at him with a sad face, but couldn't do it. "I have an agent!"

He pulled me up and hugged me so hard it hurt my ribs.

We said our good-byes and drove home in silence. I was on top of the world. Or should have been. Something was missing, and I knew exactly what it was. Bray. Even though the agent loved my book, it still didn't fill the void left by Bray's absence.

I thought about him all the time when I wasn't writing, and when I was, I was writing about him. I should never have left. I should never have let that stupid Katie win. Summer Mathers had faced an island and won the war only to be run off by a scrawny bleach blonde wearing too much makeup.

As soon as I got home, I'd call Bray. I had to tell him about the book anyway. He needed to be okay with our story being out there, and if he wasn't, it wouldn't happen. I wouldn't put him through that. I'd have to tell my agent, thanks, but no thanks. After all I'd put Bray through, I owed him that much.

It was late when we got home, but I couldn't wait to talk to him. I dialed Bray's cell phone number, but he didn't answer so I tried the house phone. A sleepy-sounding Sandra answered.

"Hi, Sandra. Sorry to call so late." It was only ten thirty. But maybe she'd gone to bed early. "Can I talk to Bray?"

"He's not here, Summer."

Something in her voice. Something wasn't right. "Is everything okay?"

"No, Summer. It's not."

My hands grew sweaty, palms gripping the phone tighter. I knew that tone. "What's wrong?"

There was a long pause before she answered, and I could feel every bone of my body coming unhinged. Giant invisible hooks tearing into my flesh and pulling it apart. "Sandra, what's going on?" Panic in my voice, closing off my throat.

"Bray is in the hospital. He's in a coma."

CHAPTER 20

Summer

I dropped to the floor, legs giving way beneath me, and landed with a thud. The accident, Michael's accident roared through my system. I tried to form words, but my throat had tightened, making it almost impossible. "He ... was in an accident?" I finally uttered.

"No. He had meningitis. Despite being vaccinated, they think he contracted it in Belize somehow."

"Is he going to be okay?"

Another pause. "We don't know."

"Sandra, why didn't you call me? I should be there."

"We didn't know what was happening at first. Then they had to determine if it was bacterial or viral, so they put him in isolation."

My mind tried so hard to form around the idea of Bray in the hospital. "How?"

After a long exhale, she answered. "We'd been at home, and he'd just finished filling out his paperwork for school. He's decided he wants to work for the US Forest Service. Bray loves to be outside. Anyway, he finished the paperwork and started complaining that he was nauseous. By the next day, he had a headache. His eyes were so sensitive to the light that I had to keep the shades closed. I thought maybe it was a migraine. He'd never had one, but I didn't know what else would make him so light sensitive. When he started complaining his neck was sore, we took him to the ER. Luckily, the doctor on staff knew what it was. He took a sample of spinal fluid. Summer, can you come? I think he'd like to know you're here."

"Of course, I'll leave tonight."

"Wait until morning. We're all beat, and I'm going to try to get some sleep. I'll meet you at the hospital early tomorrow."

"He'll be okay tonight?"

"Yes. There's been no change in four days."

Four days. My lungs squeezed tighter and tighter. I didn't want to wait until tomorrow. I wanted to leave now. I wasn't going to sleep anyway. I hung up with Sandra and she sent me a text with the address to the hospital.

I flew through my room, packing a bag in record time, then told my parents. It was eleven thirty by the time I was ready to go. My dad argued about driving me there, but he was still in the middle of the conference. Mom had already promised to watch the neighbor's kids tomorrow. She wanted to go with me but I told her I'd be fine. I wasn't tired. My mom didn't like to drive at night, so I would have been the one behind the wheel anyway. Finally, and knowing they were still warring with the whole our-daughter's-an-adult-but-she's-still-our-baby-girl thing, I convinced them to let me go alone.

I cried as I drove. It was ninety-nine miles from my house in Sarasota to the hospital in Naples. Tears kept me company most of the way. If anything happened to Bray . . .

Something already had happened to him, and I realized how stupid I was—how utterly stupid I was to let him go. I promised myself to never be stupid again. And if Bray would forgive me, if he *could* forgive me, I'd never let him go again.

I sneaked past the nurse's station when I arrived.

Bray's room was at the far end of the hall, so I entered silently and waited for my eyes to adjust to the darkness. I clutched a copy of my manuscript beneath my arm and felt myself squeezing it closer to my side as my eyes focused on him.

The room was private and filled with enough plants and flowers to make it less like a hospital room and more like a funeral home. And there he lay. Quiet. Flat on his back.

My throat closed.

What were they *thinking*? He wasn't dead. Just sleeping. I scurried to the wall and flipped on the light, bathing the room in fluorescent hope. Bray didn't flinch, didn't move. Just stayed motionless, his body stretched out on the bed.

"Looks like I got here just in time," I said, forcing the words through my cried-out throat. "Another day or two more and they'd confuse you with the garden." My voice was hollow. Trembling words bounced off the walls and returned to me. Terror filled them, my attempts at cheer failing miserably.

I stopped at the head of Bray's bed. A chair had already been pulled along the bedside, but I stood and stroked the hair from his brow.

"Time to wake up, sleepyhead." Nothing. Eyelids covered the most beautiful part of him. I wished I could see his eyes in that moment. But really, what had I expected? I'd say hello and he'd come out of the coma? Guess I really was gullible.

But this wasn't right. This wasn't Bray. He was all life and energy and movement, like a perpetual ball that never stopped rolling down a hill. "Bray," I whispered.

When waiting for him to answer became too much, I sat down and dropped the book on my lap. "Fine, if you won't wake up, I'm going to tell you a story. It's about us. I think you're gonna love it."

Before I began, I closed my eyes and prayed. How many times had I prayed on the island? Bray always knew when I did, though I never told him. He knew because he knew me. He was part of me. And I was part of him. I read for the next three hours without taking a break. My back hurt and my butt was numb from the uncomfortable hospital chair, but I forged on. When I got to the part about Michael, the night I'd huddled in the tarp to tell Bray about the worst night of my life, I heard a noise behind me. I spun toward the door to find a tall, slender nurse in the doorway. I jumped up, clutching the papers.

A Styrofoam cup rested in her hand. "I thought you might need a cup of hot tea."

"You're not going to make me leave?"

She smiled, her gray eyes full of compassion. "No. I don't think you're doing him any harm. You're her, aren't you?"

I took the cup, played with the rim. "Summer."

"He said your name sometimes before the coma. When he was sleeping, he'd call out for you."

The cup became a blur as tears puddled in my eyes. "Why doesn't he wake up?"

She shrugged and took the large lidded cup from beside Bray's bed. "There's no physical reason. Doctor Valens says he should be awake, but it's like he has no will to live."

"Is that from the meningitis?"

She'd been pouring him fresh water at the sink when she stopped. "I don't think so." Her gray eyes cut like lasers into me.

I stepped back. "Why, then?"

The nurse filled her lungs and paused at the foot of Bray's bed. "I heard of a man in Oregon who died of a broken heart."

My fingers tightened on the small cup in my hands, nearly collapsing it.

The nurse moved to the side of the bed and sat the water within Bray's reach. As if he needed it. As if he could just get a drink. She hovered over him, looking down at his closed eyes and smoothed the hair from his forehead, just as I'd done. "But I'm sure that won't happen here."

I watched as she left the room. Goose bumps spread across my arms. I hugged myself. But there was no comfort in it. Just the reminder of how alone I was. All because I was too shallow to give Bray what he needed. Forgiveness. I held his past against him, and that was a horrible thing to do when he'd allowed me to dump all my burdens on his shoulders.

Picking up where I left off, I read about the night I shared the story of Michael with him. I'd expected all the pain to return, hearing the words out loud, but it didn't. Bray hadn't kissed me that night, even though he'd wanted to.

In a tremendous rush of emotion, I realized Bray was everything to me. I tossed the papers on the floor and laid my head on his chest. "I'm sorry, Bray. I'm so sorry. You deserve better than this."

As I cried, more tears came, traveling from so deep within me, it felt like my soul was pouring out. "I was scared. I shut you out, but you never let me go. Bray, I love you so much it killed me to think of you with someone else. I'm so sorry. I should have been brave for you. I wish I was brave."

I choked on the last words. My hands fisted into the blanket. The scent of bleach was heavy as my tears soaked a spot on his chest. I tried to pull a breath, but each one caused a little more of me to die inside, so I held my breath for long stretches. Even that didn't ease the pain. I didn't know what else to do. Bray might not wake up. Not *ever* wake up. Panic filled my heart, causing my head to pound. Then, a tiny thought occurred to me. "I think . . . I think I see a ship on the horizon. I need you, Bray. I can't get to it alone." Those were the last words I had. It was my last shot of getting him to move.

But Bray remained still. And with his lack of movement, the last of my energy waned. So, I stayed right there, head on his chest, eyes closed and empty of life. I'd failed him. I'd so completely failed him.

I don't know how long I'd been there, but my hair was stuck to my face where dried tears had turned to glue. I started to move, but felt pressure against my head. Someone was holding me there. My eyes shot opened and I pivoted. Bray's arm was folded across his stomach and disappeared from my view. His hand was on my head. I reached up and grabbed it, excitement and joy causing me to grip it too tightly. I kissed his fingers, pressed them to my face, kissed them again. His hand wasn't moving on its own. I pressed it to my heart and took a deep breath before I turned to look at Bray's face. He looked the same. Eyes closed. Just sleeping.

"Bray?" I whispered.

His lids opened slowly, dusky blue eyes having trouble focusing. Then he found me.

"Summer." It was barely a rasp. "I heard you calling out for me."

My heart erupted. "I love you, Bray." I kissed his hand again, then his cheek, then the top of his head.

He blinked, frowned as if trying to track my every movement and unable to. "Slow ... down."

"I'm sorry. And you might hate me, but I love you. I love you so much and nothing will ever, *ever* cause me to doubt you again. I'll be brave, Bray. I swear I will if you'll just give me one chance." I knew he was still groggy and probably only catching half of what I said, but half was enough to hear *I love you.*

"Told you ..." He licked his lips—they looked so dry—his tongue a pale shade of pink. "I'd never give up on you. I never did."

I clasped his shoulders. "You gave up on *yourself*, Bray. That's just as bad." I shouldn't be scolding him, but couldn't stop.

His face creaked into a smile. "Am I in trouble?"

"No, not if you marry me."

For a man who'd been comatose for several days, his strength surprised me. Before I could protest, he dragged me into his arms.

There was nowhere else I'd rather be. And no one else I'd rather be with. Bray belonged to me and I to him.

After a long time, he took my face in his hands. "Can we plan that wedding now?"

"Yes," I said, through happy tears.

He coughed, and I reached for the big lidded cup beside his bed. He took a few sips.

"I love you, Summer."

I curled onto the bed beside him. "I think we finally reached the ship on the horizon."

EPILOGUE

My fairy-tale wedding was everything I'd dreamed. I hadn't wanted a huge, flashy wedding, just a small one that was a reflection of Bray and me and the love we shared. The honeymoon I left to Bray. My only request: no tropics. I did love the ocean though, and Bray took that into consideration as he drove me to the beach house he'd rented for us on the South Carolina shore. Salty air, sand beneath our feet, but this time all the comforts of home.

My book sold after three New York publishers fought over it at auction. The publishing house that won the bidding war expedited the process so the book would be on the shelves in the next few months.

It was crazy, and the only person more excited about it than me was Bray. We shared it all. He completed me. I completed him. Together, nothing could stop us.

We dropped our bags on the floor of the living room, and he took me by the hand. At the top of a wide staircase, a door opened into a beautiful loft bedroom. I stepped inside and tried to look in every direction at once, but it was impossible. A thick rug covered the floor, white flowers dotted with greenery sat on every surface, and a set of French doors that led to a balcony overlooking the Atlantic Ocean took up one entire wall.

"It's beautiful."

He smiled and headed for the doors. "Open?"

I nodded. "Yes." Instantly I was hit by the gusting wind. It wove into my hair and pressed my dress to my body. The breeze was chilly, but wonderful. Bray stepped behind me, his hands roaming over my arms. We knew each other so well. Knew the curves of the other's body though we'd never broken our vow to wait. But the island had caused an intimacy between us. I wasn't nervous. I belonged to Bray, and this was just one more step to joining ourselves forever.

When I angled to look up at him, he captured my mouth with his, and I was swept away in the sea that was Bray. My protector, my friend, my husband. Eyes dark with desire drew away to look at me. "Are you scared?"

"No." Every part of me was at perfect peace. A hand slipped behind my knees and he scooped me into his arms. He'd be my first and only. I didn't give myself away easily. And Bray was worth the wait.

Later that night, we lay side by side, listening to the ocean crash against the shore. Bray wound his hands into my hair. "Any regrets?"

What could I regret? I was with the man I loved and we'd proven our commitment by honoring a promise I'd made to myself long before I ever knew him. Bray had saved my life, pulled me from the grave of depression, even took a bullet to protect me, but I'd never, ever felt more safe than at this very moment. "None. You?"

"Only that I've got just one lifetime to spend with you."

"Well then, let's make it count." I leaned up, letting the silk sheet slide from my shoulders, and took his face in my hands to kiss him. I didn't hold back, I didn't draw away. I was fully and completely his. And every ounce of difficulty it had taken to not give in to him on the island was worth the suffering. It was worth the waiting. This, this was perfection.

And even if we loved each other from this lifetime right into the next, it still wouldn't be enough.

Replication

The Jason Experiment

Jill Williamson

What if everything you knew was a lie?

Martyr—otherwise known as Jason 3:3—is one of hundreds of clones kept in a remote facility called Jason Farms. Told that he has been created to save humanity, Martyr has just one wish before he is scheduled to "expire" in less than a month. To see the sky.

Abby Goyer may have just moved to Alaska, but she has a feeling something strange is going on at the farm where her father works. But even this smart, confident girl could never have imagined what lies beneath a simple barn. Or what would happen when a mysterious boy shows up at her door, asking about the stars.

As the reality of the Jason Experiment comes to light, Martyr is caught between two futures—the one for which he was produced and the one Abby believes he was created to have. Time is running out, and Martyr must decide if a life with Abby is worth leaving everything he's ever known.

Available in stores and online!

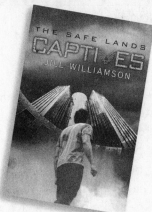